D0210178

The Bestselling Novels of
TOM CLANCY

RED RABBIT

Tom Clancy returns to Jack Ryan's early days—in an extraordinary novel of global political drama.

"AN OLD-FASHIONED COLD WAR THRILLER."

—*Chicago Sun-Times*

THE BEAR AND THE DRAGON

A clash of world powers. President Jack Ryan's trial by fire.

"HEART-STOPPING ACTION . . . CLANCY STILL REIGNS."

—*The Washington Post*

RAINBOW SIX

John Clark is used to doing the CIA's dirty work. Now he's taking on the world.

"ACTION-PACKED."

—*The New York Times Book Review*

EXECUTIVE ORDERS

A devastating terrorist act leaves Jack Ryan as President of the United States.

"UNDOUBTEDLY CLANCY'S BEST YET."

—*The Atlanta Journal-Constitution*

continued . . .

DEBT OF HONOR

It begins with the murder of an American woman in the back streets of Tokyo. It ends in war.

"A SHOCKER."

—*Entertainment Weekly*

THE HUNT FOR RED OCTOBER

The smash bestseller that launched Clancy's career—the incredible search for a Soviet defector and the nuclear submarine he commands.

"BREATHLESSLY EXCITING."

—*The Washington Post*

RED STORM RISING

The ultimate scenario for World War III—the final battle for global control.

"THE ULTIMATE WAR GAME . . . BRILLIANT."

—*Newsweek*

PATRIOT GAMES

CIA analyst Jack Ryan stops an assassination—and incurs the wrath of Irish terrorists.

"A HIGH PITCH OF EXCITEMENT."

—*The Wall Street Journal*

THE CARDINAL OF THE KREMLIN

The superpowers race for the ultimate Star Wars missile defense system.

"*CARDINAL* EXCITES, ILLUMINATES . . . A REAL PAGE-TURNER."

—*Los Angeles Daily News*

CLEAR AND PRESENT DANGER

The killing of three U.S. officials in Colombia ignites the American government's explosive, and top secret, response.

"A CRACKLING GOOD YARN."

—*The Washington Post*

THE SUM OF ALL FEARS

The disappearance of an Israeli nuclear weapon threatens the balance of power in the Middle East— and around the world.

"CLANCY AT HIS BEST . . . NOT TO BE MISSED."

—*The Dallas Morning News*

WITHOUT REMORSE

The Clancy epic fans have been waiting for. His code name is Mr. Clark. And his work for the CIA is brilliant, cold-blooded, and efficient . . . but who is he really?

"HIGHLY ENTERTAINING."

—*The Wall Street Journal*

Tom Clancy's
NET FORCE®
CHANGING OF THE GUARD

Created by
Tom Clancy and Steve Pieczenik

written by Steve Perry
and Larry Segriff

BERKLEY BOOKS, NEW YORK

TOM CLANCY'S NET FORCE®: CHANGING OF THE GUARD

A Berkley Book / published by arrangement with
Netco Partners

PRINTING HISTORY
Berkley edition / December 2003

Copyright © 2003 by Netco Partners.
NET FORCE® is a registered trademark of Netco Partners.
Cover art: Binary code—Jason Reed/Photodisc/PictureQuest.
CD—Stockbyte/PictureQuest.

For information address: The Berkley Publishing Group,
a division of Penguin Group (USA) Inc.,
375 Hudson Street, New York, New York 10014.

ISBN: 0-425-19376-4

BERKLEY®
Berkley Books are published by The Berkley Publishing Group,
a division of Penguin Group (USA) Inc.,
375 Hudson Street, New York, New York 10014.
BERKLEY and the "B" design
are trademarks belonging to Penguin Group (USA) Inc.

PRINTED IN THE UNITED STATES OF AMERICA

10 9 8 7 6 5 4 3 2 1

Acknowledgments

We would like to acknowledge the assistance of Martin H. Greenberg, Denise Little, John Helfers, Brittiany Koren, Lowell Bowen, Esq., Robert Youdelman, Esq., Danielle Forte, Esq., Dianne Jude, and Tom Colgan, our editor. But most important, it is for you, our readers, to determine how successful our collective endeavor has been.

—Tom Clancy and Steve Pieczenik

PROLOGUE

October 2013 C.E.
Khvoy, Iran

Celik the Turk took a sip of coffee. It was bitter, full of grounds, and it had gone cold, but it gave him something to do with his hands. He was a little nervous. At fifty, even after twenty-six years in the game, he was always a little nervous at this stage. Death was a spy's constant companion, but Celik had outrun Him every time before, and even though he was slower now than he had been as a young man, he had no reason to believe he couldn't outrun the grave diggers one more time.

He took a deep drag from his hand-rolled, unfiltered cigarette. The cheap tobacco was harsh; the greasy blue smoke bit his throat and lungs when he inhaled. He would have better when he was home in Ankara.

The cafe was small—tiny, really—only four tables, a family operation that catered to locals. The building was concrete block, the floor packed dirt, tamped hard over the years, and the furniture was clean but very old. The people who owned the cafe were Turks, though they didn't wave that in anybody's face. Even though the border was only a few kilometers away, this was still Iran, and the Irani and the Turk had not been the best of friends in anybody's memory. The food might or might not have been good. For Celik, when he was on a mission, breakfast was always the same—coffee and a cigarette. A full man did not move as fast as one with an empty stomach.

Kokmak was late. This might be a bad sign. Or it might mean nothing at all, save that Kokmak had overslept.

Except for the old man serving him coffee and a younger version of the old man sometimes visible through a beaded curtain hung over the door to the kitchen, Celik was alone.

He smoked the cigarette down to a nub, until it was too hot to hold. He stubbed it out on a chipped, clouded glass ashtray somebody had stolen from a Hyatt Hotel. He stripped the paper and carefully put the last bit of tobacco back into the tin he carried in his left vest pocket, shook the tin to mix it in, then rolled another cigarette, using a strawberry-flavored Zig-Zag paper. The paper was pink and, he supposed, had some distant relation to the taste of strawberries. He did not care. It amused him to smoke pink cigarettes, and he knew that no one would mark him as a secret operative of a foreign service from the colorful paper; in fact, they would notice a man who smoked pink fags, and in so doing, assume that he wasn't a spy—a spy would not do anything as stupid as that to draw attention to himself. A bit of reverse psychology, and one that Celik was proud of.

The color of his smokes notwithstanding, he looked like most men he had passed in this town. Swart, a thick black moustache, black hair going gray under a cap, clothes that were old, patched, dusty, but not too raggedy. Just another poor Turk on his way back to his dust farm or small shop, stopping in for coffee before he got back on the road. Nothing unusual about him.

Outside, a twelve-year-old flatbed truck, a German machine with a hundred and fifty thousand kilometers on it, sat parked on the side of the building that would grow shady when the sun began its morning climb. Not that he would be there when it did, but it was an old habit to prepare for the sun when it came.

He lit the cigarette with a throw-away yellow plastic Bic and inhaled deeply. He did not wear a good watch openly, though he had one in his pocket—no point in pushing his luck when it came to drawing attention—but there was a clock on the counter, he had checked it against his watch when he had come in, and it was accurate. According to the clock, it was just past seven A.M. Kokmak was five minutes past the appointed meeting time, and Celik was ready to head for his truck. The rules were simple: If a meeting did not take place at the appointed time, it was not going to take place. All operatives knew this. You were on time or you missed it.

When he had been a young man, training under the old agent they called "Hard Ass," the need for punctuality had been indelibly impressed upon him. "You will be on time," Hard Ass had said to the class of green trainees. "This is not open for question. If you are to meet another operative near the new fountain in Ankara at noon, you will *be* there at noon. If your automobile has a flat tire on the way, you will have allowed time to repair it and arrive on time. If you fall and break your leg, you will splint it and hop if necessary. Anything short of a nuclear bomb is not an acceptable excuse for tardiness. And the bomb better have killed you."

They all had code names in those days, and the names stayed with them. Celik meant "steel." One of the trainees, Hasare—"Insect"—had started to ask a question: "But what if—?"

Before Hasare could finish his query, Hard Ass had stepped over to him and driven a fist into Hasare's belly. When the trainee doubled over, trying to catch his breath, Hard Ass clubbed the man behind the ear with his elbow, knocking him to the floor, unconscious. Hard Ass turned and looked at the class. "Was there anybody else who did not understand me when I said this was not open for question?"

Well, certainly there was nobody who would admit to it—

"Steel," Kokmak said, interrupting his memory. "Sorry I am late. A fire in the street, a vendor's stall. The road was blocked."

Celik shrugged. The old man came over bearing another coffee cup and a fresh pot. He put the cup down in front of Kokmak, poured it full, added more to Celik's cup, then shuffled away.

"You have it?"

Kokmak nodded. His personal fragrance drifted across the table, a mix of dirt, sweat, and fear, sour and pungent. He held a folded newspaper in one hand.

"I have a long drive ahead of me." Celik's voice was barbed.

"Of course." He laid the newspaper on the table, sipped at the coffee, then blew on it to cool it. "Vile," he said. "You'd think that a Turk would know how to make good coffee, no?"

Celik wasn't interested in the culinary opinions of a man who showed up late for a meeting. He picked up the newspaper, tucked it into his jacket pocket, and stood.

Before he could move, however, he saw Kokmak glance toward the cafe's door. It was quick, just a flicker of the eyes, but it was enough to send a chill through Celik's bones.

There was no one there. So why would Kokmak be looking at the door?

Celik's years as an operative for the Turkish MIT had put him into some dangerous situations; more than once, he had barely escaped critical danger, and not always unscathed. One of the reasons he was still alive was that he always trusted his instincts when they told him trouble was near.

Death waited just outside the front door. He was certain of it.

Celik reached for his cup of fresh coffee, as if to take a final sip. "Peace be upon you," he said.

Kokmak started to come to his feet, "And upon you—" he began.

Celik tossed the coffee into the man's face. Kokmak screamed.

Celik ran for the kitchen, shouldered the old man aside, and sprinted past the grandson, who looked up from a pot on the stove in surprise. They'd be watching the truck, they might already be outside, and he did not have a weapon. He looked around, saw the wooden block of kitchen knives on the counter, pulled out a short and stubby carving blade and hefted it. It would have to do—

"Hey!" the young man said. "What are you doing?"

"Men with guns are about to come through your front door," Celik said. "Men with no love for Turks. Best you and your grandfather leave, if you don't want trouble."

The old man came through the beaded curtain and glared at Celik. In the background, Kokmak continued to scream through his burned lips.

Celik grabbed the door handle. As he did, he felt it start to turn. He jerked the door open, surprising the Irani soldier holding on to the handle outside, pulling him off balance. As the startled man tried to regain his footing, Celik stabbed him with the short knife, twice in the throat. The soldier's eyes went wide and he clutched at his neck with both hands, dropping the assault rifle he held.

Celik grabbed the fallen weapon and leaped through the door.

He was alone. A trio of rusty, battered oil drums, used for rubbish and trash, stood next to the door. He ran for the south end of the alley, assault rifle held ready to fire. There should have been more men at the back. Why weren't there? Sloppy, but he would thank Allah for the favor of it later.

He rounded the corner, cut away from the front of the cafe, and ran along a narrow street, looking for a vehicle. They hadn't spotted him yet. If he could get a car or a truck, if he could get out of town, if he could make it to the border, he'd be safe.

He had a gun, that would get him a vehicle.

His lungs were on fire after a block. All those cigarettes coming back to choke him. Fine, he could cough later.

He rounded a corner and saw a young man about to climb onto a big motorcycle, an old BMW. Perfect!

"Hey!" Celik called. "You on the bike!"

There was no time for finesse. The young man turned to look, and Celik slammed the assault rifle's butt into the man's nose.

He straddled the motorcycle, pressed the starter button. The motor came to life quickly—good, good! Holding the weapon pointed over the handle bars, he clicked the foot shifter into gear and turned the throttle, rocked the bike off the stand, and started up the street.

He was beginning to feel better. He had a weapon, he had transportation, he was headed for home!

A pickup truck full of soldiers was parked ahead of him and he went past at full speed. An unwise move. They screamed something at him, but he kept going. He was a hundred meters away and gathering speed, thinking he could certainly outrun that loaded truck on the motorcycle, when they started shooting.

No matter. They wouldn't hit him at this distance!

He was wrong. The bullet punched through his back, low, at the right kidney, went right on through him—he looked down and saw the exit wound, a welling red crater the size of his thumb. It felt as if he had been hit by a hammer, but he didn't fall, didn't put the bike down.

Maybe it wasn't a fatal wound. It didn't hurt that bad.

If he could just get across the border, he'd be okay. They'd find him a doctor. If he could just get back to Turkey, he'd be all right.

1

Alex Michaels put the gold ink pen given to him by the late Steve Day into the box, next to a laser pointer and a couple of mechanical pencils. Amazing how much crap you picked up when you sat behind a desk in the same spot for a few years: rubber bands, paper clips, batteries, flashmem cards . . . It was not as if he hadn't cleared out a desk before, but this time was different. He was leaving government service for the private sector, moving far away in time and space, into a new life with his wife and son.

It felt strange. Unreal, somehow.

Would he miss running Net Force? Sure, no question. There was a great satisfaction in being part of the solution to America's problems. Under his direction, the organization had nailed some very bad people, and, however briefly, made the world a safer place. Given the times, that was not a bad thing. But it was time to move on. There were some things more important than a job—any job—and his family was one of those things.

His work had put them at risk, and that simply wasn't acceptable. He didn't mind dying for his country, if it came to that, but he was not going to let his wife and child die—not for any reason. If a man didn't take care of his family, he wasn't much of a man, no matter how well the rest of the world might think of him.

He opened the drawer on the right side, saw the *kerambit* case nestled there. That pair of short, hooked knives had saved his life and that of his family, when Toni had been pregnant. Coupled with his knowledge of the esoteric Indonesian fighting art called *pentjak silat*, he had been able to stop a madman bent on rape and murder. But such occasions should not arise, should not *have* to be dealt with, and removing his family from harm's way was much smarter than contending with such adversaries.

He had done his part. Now let somebody else stand in the line of fire. He would not miss that aspect of it.

"Commander?" came his secretary's voice over the intercom.

"Yes?"

"Thomas Thorn is here."

"Ah. Send him in."

Michaels looked around. Being here had been good. Leaving was good, too. . . .

The secretary showed Thorn into the office. Michaels, on his feet and apparently packing personal belongings into boxes, came from around his desk and extended his hand. When they shook, Michaels used his left as well, clasping Thorn's hand in a firm grip, but not a crusher.

"Commander Michaels," Thorn said. "I'm Tom Thorn. A pleasure to finally meet you, sir."

Michaels smiled, showing a lot of laugh lines at the corners of his eyes. "Just 'Alex'," he said. "You're the Commander now. I've heard a lot about you. Have a seat."

Thorn started for the couch. "No," Michaels said. "Behind the desk. It's yours."

Thorn paused.

"I'm serious," Michaels said. "When I walk out the door, I might look back, but I'm essentially gone. I've got all my stuff almost cleaned out." He waved at a box on the desk. "It's your house now."

Thorn nodded. "Okay." He moved around the desk. Michaels sat on the couch.

"I'm not sure I'm ready for this," Thorn admitted.

Michaels laughed again. "You came up with the basic VR interface most people still use. Half of our high-end software packages here are systems you wrote, or based on those you did. You'll feel right at home."

Thorn smiled. Well, yes, that was true. And it was also true he wasn't *that* worried—he had run his own company until he sold it, and had been on the boards of several major corporations since. How different was managing a government computer agency from running a private one? People were the same.

"Any questions I can answer, just ask. For computer stuff, you have Jay Gridley; he is the best there is. General John Howard will still be on board at military operations for another week or so, and his replacement, Colonel Abe Kent, is, by all accounts, a first-class military man. I don't have an assistant at the moment, but there's a pretty good pool of qualified folks who know the systems, either here or over at the regular FBI shop."

Thorn thought about it. He did have one question, but asking it would no doubt make Commander Michaels uncomfortable at the very least. After a moment, he decided to ask it anyway. He needed to know.

"I understand that you are leaving for personal reasons, Commander," he said, "and that John Howard's departure is also by his choice for the same rationale. And your assistant—your wife—gives the same justification. Do you mind if I ask what those are? I don't want to step into a hornet's nest of politics here—if you're being dumped because you screwed up or peed in somebody's Frosted Flakes, I'd rather know it coming in. It seems awfully coincidental that the Commander of an agency and his top lieutenants all decide to bail at the same time."

That got him a big grin.

"Good question," Alex said. "But there's no conspiracy to worry about. I was a little more hands-on as Commander than I should have been. Got into the field a few times when it would have been smarter to stay in the office. Mostly, computer criminals are chair-warmers, not known for their exploits in RW. A few of them are more . . . active. A couple of times, I found myself in situations that were physically dangerous. When I was single, that wasn't a problem. Once I got married and had a child at home, going into harm's way wasn't just about me."

Thorn waited. He had heard that Michaels was a cowboy who liked to go into the field, and that he had some kind of martial arts training he had used a few times. Not a good idea for the head of the agency to be doing that. Not smart. Not something he was going to be guilty of, for certain. Leave the field work to those who got paid to do it.

Michaels paused. A cloud seemed to pass over his face as he obviously remembered something unpleasant. "We had a couple of incidents involving deranged criminals, and the last one put my wife and son in some danger. Toni and I decided that was not going to happen again."

"You could have stayed in the office from then on," Thorn offered.

Michaels shook his head. "Too late. The criminals involved didn't really know me, only that I was Net Force's Commander. They found out where I lived and went to my home because they had seen or heard who I was from my public appearances."

"You surely rated bodyguards?"

"Yes. Had some, for a time."

There was another pause. Thorn waited, not speaking.

"You aren't married, are you? No children?"

"No," Thorn said. "But I understand your point."

"With all due respect, Commander, no, you don't. Having your two-year-old need an armed guard to go to the park? No job is worth that if you have a choice. I was a target just by being the man in charge, and that put my family at risk. Life is too short."

Thorn nodded.

"I can't speak for General Howard," Alex went on, "but he also has a wife and son he wants to see grow up, and he's been into the field enough times to prove to himself and anybody else that he's a brave man. Not to mention he can get twice the money he makes now as a consultant in private industry. So can I, for that matter."

Thorn smiled again. Was that a dig? Was he saying that it was easy for Thorn to take this job because he was already a wealthy man?

Michaels said, "We did our job, did a little good now and then, and now it's our time to move on. Nothing sinister—although the politics of the job *are* a bitch. Some of the hearings up on the Hill you'll have to attend, you'll need an iron bladder."

Thorn chuckled politely.

"My advice is for you to do what you do best and leave the heavy lifting in the field to the regular feebs or the military arm. Stay in front of the computer, work Congress to keep the wheels oiled, and you'll do fine."

Thorn nodded. "Thank you, Alex. I appreciate the advice." Not that he needed it. He had his fencing, but you didn't get to carry an épée or saber around in polite society these days, and facing off with thugs was not his forte. His mind was his most valuable tool, not his fists. Muscle was easy to hire.

"Well, I'm about ready," Alex said. "You'll want your own people, of course, but you have a pretty good team here already. I would stay and help you in the transition, but I have only a couple of weeks before I have to be at my new job, and we need to get moved and settled. Jay Gridley can answer any questions you might have."

"I know Gridley's work," he said. "Thank you, Alex."

"You're welcome. I hope the job is what you want, Commander."

Me, too, Thorn thought.

Jay Gridley sat in his office and stared at the zip disk. Another day, another top-secret code to unravel. Ho, hum.

Change was in the air: Alex and Toni were leaving; John Howard, too, and new faces were coming in. Soon just about the only familiar face around here would be Jay's own. Which was odd—he had never thought of himself as the survivor type.

He supposed he could be worried about that. New bosses sometimes cleaned out the cupboards when they came on board, re-shuffling the deck and dealing in their people. But Jay wasn't too concerned about that. He was Jay *Gridley* after all—there weren't *any* people who could replace him—well, at least not on this side of the law. Besides, if he had to, he could always do what Alex and Colonel Howard were doing: get another job somewhere else. He could find another one, and for a lot more money, at the drop of a hat. It would be their loss. . . .

Either way, though, he was going to miss the old crew. They were his friends. Oh, they'd probably stay in contact, but it wouldn't be the same. It might be better. It might be worse. But it was for sure that it wouldn't be the same.

He glanced at the zip disk. It wasn't often he got to play with old-style media these days, what with flash memory and cardware being so cheap, and data disks so wonderfully dense.

Shoot, the thing held less than a half gig. Hardly worth going into VR for. It would barely touch his desktop's CPU for sifting, much less require the mainframe.

But that was the way it was in third-world countries—most of the toys they got to play with were outdated cast-offs. Which did make his job easier when he was trying to pry information from its hiding place.

A cheap, rough-looking, dot-matrix-printed label covered the hard plastic protecting the disk. It was really *ugly*, too—blocky black-and-white dots portrayed a cartoonlike lion's head, with an even uglier-looking border surrounding it. Arabic numerals and script proclaimed "Mosque-by-the-sea Tourist Photos disk 11." At least that was what the neat hand-written print in English underneath the script said.

A Turkish spy in Iran had died just after delivering the disk. Jay didn't think that the Turkish ambassador himself would be asking Net Force to dig around in it if all it held was tourist photos.

Jay slid the disk into the drive he had dug up from a storage closet and jacked into VR. . . .

He stood next to a cold and muddy stream, dressed in period Levi's, the pants held up by suspenders over a faded red-flannel shirt, a battered leather cap jammed tight onto his head. Next to him was a gold sluice, water tricking over its riffled surface. Behind this was a large pile of ore.

Of course that wasn't what it *really* was—but visual metaphors took on some serious substance in VR.

In this case, the data on the disk was the ore, and the sluice was a complicated search engine he'd put together with code lifted from the NSA, with some of his own special touches. Running the ore through the sluice would wash away the dirt, uncovering objects on the disk. Regular files would show up as rocks, and encoded ones—the kind he wanted to find—would appear to be gold nuggets.

Far more fun than a command-line process.

He smiled—a gap-toothed smile in this VR scenario,

unkempt whiskers brushing his lips. Kids these days thought a command-line was some kind of military authority.

He shoveled ore sand into the sluice, enjoying the sensation. The new stim units he'd put in would actually stress his muscles in RW as he worked in VR. If he worked out here, he'd get the benefit there. He hummed the tune for "My Darling Clementine."

The sun shone brightly in the pre-pollution California of the 1850s, birds tweeted, and the creek burbled. He let himself flow into the "is" state he and Saji had been practicing, allowing himself a brief stab of pride at the craftsmanship of his scenario. Not everyone would bother with such touches.

In very little time he'd sluiced all the ore. He dropped the shovel he'd been using, enjoying the *thunk* it made in the damp sand of the riverbed, and went to see what he'd found, walking alongside the sluice.

Rocks . . . more rocks . . . yet *more* rocks . . .

Huh.

Which shouldn't *be*. The disk had been recovered from a dead man, just seconds before a couple of his killers had died trying to collect it. If it was worth that many people dying for, it must have *some*thing on it. . . .

Jay snapped his fingers and was suddenly in a brightly lit kitchen, wearing a huge chef's hat and the associated double-breasted white top.

A bag of flour sat on the countertop. Next to it was a bowl and a sifter.

Carefully he scooped flour from the bag and dumped it into the sifter. A crank turned a wire whisk in the device, brushing only the tiniest particles through a wire mesh set in the bottom and into the bowl, keeping anything else.

The dry, yeasty smell of flour filled the air as he worked.

Nice touch, he thought. *I'd forgotten that one.*

Straining the stuff through the sifter would give him the closest inspection possible of the data on the disk. This program, unlike the prospector, used more CPU power, tapping into the mainframe and taking up a large portion of Net Force's available processing power. Word processors on Net Force's network wouldn't feel it, but anyone doing anything complicated right now would probably be cursing him.

Sorry, guys.

He paid close attention, inspecting everything that stuck to the bottom of the mesh.

Which was nothing: If it was hiding here, it was microscopic.

Damn! Apparently the third world was stumping him. Had they given him something he couldn't crack?

Not bloody likely.

He remembered a line he'd read in a newspaper article once, a quote from Jonas Salk, inventor of the polio vaccine. "You can only fail if you give up too soon."

He killed the chef scenario.

Back in his office, Jay blinked. What was he missing here? Could there be something hidden within the pictures on the disk?

He jacked back into VR. . . .

Jay slipped into a viewer program modeled after a movie theater he'd liked as a kid. His shoes stuck and released as he walked on the gummy concrete floor. When he sat, he felt the rough fabric of the old cloth seat against his back.

The disk was full of pictures exactly as advertised—a beautiful old mosque near the sea. A few video clips showed worshippers bowing toward Mecca, kneeling and bowing on beautifully woven prayer rugs, and others showed old-style stitched-photo VR views of various points around the temple.

The program he'd used would have detected any hidden steg-artifacts in the compressed images, and he didn't see any obvious *here-it-is!* clues. All of the images had been shot within a single day—a filter he ran on the backgrounds checked visual cues, sun angle, clouds, repeated tourists and the like, so no new images were hidden with the rest that might be worthy of further study.

Double damn.

Hmm. Maybe that was it. Could there be a slim datafiche built into the surface of the disk?

Jay killed the scenario—

Back in RW, Jay ejected the disk. He scrutinized the surface, looking for any pits or depressions that could be a disguised interface for a film of nanotransistor RAM. Maybe he'd underestimated the resources of the third world.

It looked as smooth as the proverbial baby's butt. Not a dimple, a scratch, nothing.

He scanned the disk for the third time. *Come on, Gridley, think outside the box!*

And finally, it came to him. So simple. So . . . obvious. *No way!*

He pulled his hi-res cam from its holster on the side of his ancient flat panel and captured a scan of the ugly dot-matrix label.

He yanked his VR goggles down—

Jay strode into his electronics-lab scenario. Once there, he tapped a console, and the scan of the label appeared as a holoproj in midair.

Look at that. Two-dimensional code. Son of a bitch!

It was like Poe's purloined letter, right there in plain sight. The dots making up the border and the lion made an ugly picture, but they served a hidden purpose as well—they filled a two-dimensional data matrix with information.

He smiled, feeling a thrill of pleasure, admiring whoever had come up with the code scheme. *Gotcha, sucker!*

In the late eighties and nineties, programmers had devised ways of storing data by printing it. Primitive UPC barcodes evolved into data structures that were read up-and-down as well as left-and-right. The result was that several pages of data could be stored in a tiny space, looking like nothing so much as a series of dots.

The technology had advanced as printer technology and CCDs had gotten more powerful, and had included basic error corrections that allowed part of the matrix to be lost without loss of information.

As a boy, Jay had had a battered and much-loved Nintendo Gameboy that had featured a card reader. Games were "printed" on the back of the card in 2-D formats and "read" by the handheld. Run the card through the reader, and *pow!*—you got game.

Of course no one did that anymore, it was more trouble than it was worth given flashmem and cardware.

Well. Almost no one did it, apparently. So old and hoary, it was like shaving the head of a slave and tattooing a message there, waiting for the hair to grow back, then sending him on his way.

He zoomed the scan and took a closer look. A lot of 2-D codes had been developed, each with different characteristics and different baseline reference points—bullseyes or L-shaped lines used to orient the camera reader. The programmer of this one had been smart. There were no reference points at all. Which made things more difficult—unless he read the code from the exact direction it had been intended to be read from, he'd get nothing.

And that was *before* any decoding of whatever he found.

Well, well. It looked like this was going to be more interesting than he'd figured. He might even have to *think* about it.

He laughed aloud at that. It was so much more fun if you had to stretch a little now and then.

2

Samuel Walker Cox spared a glance at the timer on the stair-stepper, even though he was sure he had four minutes and a few seconds left before he was done.

The timer, flashing down from twenty-six minutes to zero, read 04:06.

He smiled. The internal clock he carried was still working pretty well for a man in his mid-sixties. Well, all right, to be technically accurate, sixty-six. Even better.

The stair-stepper, which was the top-of-the-line DAL Industries model, was a marvel of hydraulic and electrical engineering. It was essentially a set of endless risers, and worked like a treadmill: You climbed stairs, but you never went anywhere.

He had no idea what it cost—probably a couple of thousand dollars. His assistant had bought it and had it installed in his office on the fortieth floor of the TPC building. Every workday, for twenty-six minutes, he used the device. Coupled with a quick shower and fresh

clothes, it worked out to thirty-five minutes exactly that
he spent on his conditioning, which was sufficient. He was
not a threat to any Olympic athlete, but neither was he
going to run out of steam if he needed to take the stairs
to the lobby in the event of a fire or terrorist attack on
his building. He had talked to personal trainers and sports
doctors and determined that twenty-six minutes was the
amount of time he needed to maintain optimum health at
his age, and that was what he gave it, no more, no less.

During his workout, no phones rang, no computer
voices announced incoming mail, and nobody came
through the Chinese carved-cherry double doors into his
office. He did go so far as to opaque the de-stressed triple-
layered Lexan windows, which formed an L-shaped floor-
to-ceiling panorama looking out over Manhattan. The
windows were three inches thick and bulletproof, and
would stop anything short of an armor-piercing rocket. A
special service came and cleaned the windows' exterior
once a week, and once every three months they polished
the surfaces to remove any scratches from dust or nearsighted birds.

Cox didn't know how much that cost, either, nor did
he care. When your worth was measured in the billions,
you didn't worry about the small stuff.

Two minutes remaining. He kept his pace even. There
were all kinds of monitors he could have hooked to himself—pulse rate, blood pressure, temperature, and the
like—but he didn't bother. He was sweating, his muscles
were working hard and he knew it, and he wasn't going
to cheat himself out of a full effort. A man who wasn't
disciplined enough to exercise without somebody standing
over him counting cadence didn't have any fire in his
belly.

Usually, he managed to avoid going off on mental voy-
ages while he trod upon the never-ending stairway—con-
centration was supposed to help the body benefit fully—
but now and then, something would be pressing enough

so that he could not help but think about it.

Now was one of those times. He had gotten a coded message from Vrach—"the Doctor"—and as usual, the Russian wanted something from him: a small matter of some pressure against a reluctant oil executive in one of the Middle Eastern countries. It was nothing Cox couldn't do with a come-hither of one finger and a few words in the right ear. Still, it was annoying, even after all these years. *Especially* after all these years.

He shook his head. Of all his regrets, this one was the biggie. While still in college, he had made the dumbest mistake of his life. He had been young, idealistic—another word for stupid—and full of himself. He had drifted into a crowd of socialistic types, and the next thing he knew, he was a spy. For the Soviets.

It was the sixties, times were turbulent, nobody trusted the government, and maybe he could be excused. At least he hadn't been out in some hippie commune smoking dope and talking to the trees. He had, however briefly, believed that what he was doing might be part of the solution instead of the problem. After the Cuban Missile Crisis, the idea of a nuclear war felt way too real, and the U.S. was way too aggressive. Or so he had believed at the time.

Young, ignorant, and stupid—that had been him.

Of course, he had never really done much spying. His control had explained he would be more useful as a mole, and they would wait to activate him. They gave him a little money. It had seemed like a fortune at the time. Now, if that much fell out of his pocket, it wouldn't be worth the time and energy to stoop and pick it up. But still, he had been on the payroll.

As the years passed, the Soviet Union eventually went belly-up, as did his idealistic and foolish notions, and eventually he found himself running a major corporation and richer than a small country. Unfortunately, he didn't get lost in the shuffle when the Soviet Union fell apart.

The Russians had long memories, and one day, after he hadn't thought about them in a decade, they gave him a little heads-up: *Ho, Comrade! How are you? Ready to serve the cause?*

At first, Cox had been amused. Cause? What cause? Communism is dead, pal. The war is over. You lost. Get over it.

Perhaps that is so. We have moved on. But we have new objectives.

I'm happy for you, he had said. Go away.

But of course, they had not. They were capitalists now, and they laid it out flat and straight: *Help us—or we'll tell everybody how you betrayed your country. . . .*

Blackmail! Son of a bitch, he couldn't believe it—!

The timer chimed, interrupting his bad memory. He stopped climbing the stairs, grabbed a towel, and headed for the shower. The phones would start ringing again in nine minutes, and he needed to clean up and put on fresh clothes.

Done was done. Maybe someday he could figure out a way to get clear of them. Isolate the few who knew about him, have Eduard pay them a visit and shut down their memories, permanently.

Yes, he was rich, he was powerful, but the scandal would ruin his name, wreck his family, and he couldn't live with the looks he'd see in all those faces. Sam Cox, a commie spy?

No. He couldn't have that. No matter what it cost. He didn't like having to dance to their tune, but it was better than the alternative. For now, at least.

Net Force Shooting Range
Quantico, Virginia

John Howard stood in the underground firing range looking down the lane as Julio Fernandez approached. The

smell of burned gunpowder was an old and familiar one.
He was going to miss it. Not that he'd have to stop coming, but, working in the city, he knew he wouldn't get out
here nearly as often.

"Lieutenant," Howard said. "You're running late."

"Sorry, General. I had to have Gunny update my ring."
He held his hand up and waggled his fingers. What looked
like an ordinary gold band gleamed on his right middle
finger. All Net Force personnel who carried weapons had
them, and each gun coded to a broadcast ring that had to
be reset every thirty days. If somebody picked up a Net
Force weapon without the correct ring on his hand, the
gun simply wouldn't fire.

"How are Joanna and little Hoo?"

"Pretty good, both of them. He's completely potty-
trained now, goes all night without an accident." He
paused. "Lord, I can't believe I'm talking about such
things!"

Howard chuckled. "I understand."

"How about yours? Tyrone coming back to the pistol
team?"

"I think so. I think he's finally accepted he didn't have
any choice in what he had to do."

"He's a good man."

"Yes, he is." Still a teenager, Tyrone was not really old
enough to be a man, but he had gotten a big push in that
direction when he'd had to step up to do something a boy
ought not have to do.

Howard pushed the unpleasant thought out of his mind.

"You want to warm up before we get serious?" he said.

Fernandez laughed. "Get serious? I do believe I outshot
you the last three times we were here. How serious do I
need to be to beat one old armchair soldier and his ancient
wheelgun?"

Howard smiled. The sidearm he carried, a P&R Medusa, was about as high-tech as revolvers got—it could
fire twenty different calibers—but the basic technology

was a hundred and fifty years old. Indeed, his "modern" weapon was not so far from Sam Colt's original design that, were the old boy still alive, he would have any trouble recognizing it. Still, the K-frame black-Teflon-coated Medusa was smooth, accurate, made of hardened steel, and when loaded with RBCD .357 Magnum rounds as it usually was, would knock ninety-six of a hundred men down and out of the fight with a single shot, as good as you could do with a handgun. Howard felt very comfortable with it in his holster.

"So, in that case, you want to up the usual wager?"

Fernandez raised an eyebrow. "What'd you have in mind?"

"You win, you activate your retirement status now and come to work for me at the think tank next month—but with a week of paid vacation before you have to show up and put on a suit. You lose, you stay here for eight weeks and make sure Colonel Kent has a smooth transition before you bail."

"Good Lord, John, you want me to stay and work two whole *months* for a *jarhead*? I'll be lucky if I don't deck him after two days."

"When he takes over, he'll be reactivated as National Guard, just like us."

"Sure, technically he will. But once a jarhead, *always* a jarhead, you know that. Never met a Marine officer who wasn't Semper Fi to the core. The right way, the wrong way, and the Marine way . . ."

Howard smiled. "Yes. But if you think you are such a hot hand with that old Beretta of yours, with those cheating laser-beam handgrips and all, why would you have anything to worry about?"

"Well, that's true. A week off with pay, huh?"

"Versus two months more here. Your new job'll wait— I can stumble along on my own that long."

"I doubt it." There was a pause. "You owe Abe Kent something, General?"

"In a manner of speaking. I don't want him to start out in a hole."

"They shoulda thought of that before they picked a Marine to run the show. Them people dig their own holes wherever they go."

"You gonna fish, or you gonna cut bait, Lieutenant?"

"Rack 'em up, General. I'll try not to embarrass you too bad."

Howard grinned again. He touched a control on the lane's computer. The first scenario was a pair of single attackers who would holographically appear thirty feet away in the double lane. Each man would fire at his own target, and the computer would mark the elapsed time and zones where the bullets hit.

This was a simple Stonewall Jackson dueling set: Whoever got there firstest with the mostest won the round. You could be a hair quicker, but if you drifted your point of aim out of the A-zone into the B- or C-zone, you would lose. If you shot too soon, trying to anticipate the target's appearance, you got a clean miss. The computer was state-of-the-art and it wouldn't let you cheat. Fast was good; fast and accurate were better.

Howard relaxed, dropped his hand by his side—

His attacker, a big bald man in a jumpsuit waving a tire iron, blinked on like a light, and started to run toward Howard. Howard pulled his revolver and thrust it at the attacker with one hand, point shooting, indexing with the entire gun rather than using the sights, squeezing the trigger double-action twice as he did—

Bam! Bam!

The sound was muted by the earplugs he wore, and it was already much quieter than normal—instead of .357 Magnums, which went off like bombs, he was loading .38 Special wadcutters, an accurate, mild target round with considerably less power, and thus much less recoil, making recovery for the second shot faster. Point shooting was a hair quicker than searching for the front sight, and he didn't need to look to know he had beaten Fernandez by at least a quarter-second.

Fernandez knew jt, too, and he knew he'd been suckered. "Talk to *me* about cheating!" Fernandez said. "You're shooting mouse-load paper-punchers over there!"

Howard smiled. "Not my fault your old issue piece only likes one caliber. You could shoot flatnose target rounds, too; I wouldn't mind."

"Start it up, General Backstabber, sir. We got nine more runs. I'll whip your perfidious old ass anyhow!"

" 'Perfidious'? Is that any way for a lieutenant to talk to a general?"

"When the general is a hustler, yes, sir, it is."

Howard smiled again. "Did I mention as how I might have been letting you win the last couple times we shot? Just so you'd think you could do it again?"

"You lie!"

Howard chuckled. The seed of doubt was planted. He had the edge and he knew it. All he had to do was stay one round ahead, and he and Julio usually were pretty close. Six out of ten would be good enough.

Of course, he could have just asked Julio to stay for two months and his old friend would have done it, no questions. They went way back together. Either one of them would take a bullet for the other, and had. But it was much more fun this way. . . .

Temple del Sol
Somewhere deep in the Amazon Jungle

The pyramid before him held the ruined throne room he needed. Jay stood at the entrance, planning his attack.

At its peak, the room must have been stunning, but hundreds of years in the warm jungle climate had taken its toll. There were still beautiful stone carvings on the less exposed sections of the walls, and the huge pillars holding up the sagging roof maintained a sense of grandeur despite the clinging vines and cracks that marred them. But mold and decay permeated the ancient stones, from which an almost visceral miasma seemed to whisper the demise of all things man-made.

He grinned at himself. *Not bad, Gridley, not bad at all.*

Whatever force had caused the end of the ancient kingdom had motivated the fleeing king to install traps in the room—it was a maze of death. To encourage his ancient foes to enter this trap, the king had left his jeweled scepter on the throne.

All Jay had to do was cross the floor to get it.

The problem was that the large blocks of stone that made up the floor of the room weren't all solid. If he stepped on the wrong block, he'd fall into a pit filled with who knew what.

Well, actually, he did know what—snakes. Lots and lots of snakes.

Of course he wasn't *really* traversing an ancient throne room. He was trying to crack the data he'd found. Unfortunately, the printed label had vastly increased the difficulty of the decoding process.

In most code-breaking scenarios, the encoded data was run through a sifter that would find patterns, which revealed letters. But there were several factors complicating this particular code.

First, Iran had over seventy living languages—picking the right one to sift was a critical part of the process, and not the most difficult. The majority of the languages in the country used Arabic script as an alphabet, which had twenty-eight letters instead of English's twenty-six. Western Farsi, the most commonly used language, added an extra five characters to that, taking it to thirty-three—and making the code-breaking several orders of magnitude more difficult.

On top of that, the Arabic/Farsi alphabet had been represented by three different encoding systems since it had migrated to the computer. In the late twentieth century, back in the days when computer standards were still up for grabs, there had been no less than two different character sets for Arabic—one for Unix and Macintosh systems, and another for the Windows world. Then unicode had come along—a larger character set that made it easier to standardize. And the letters could be in any of the three, depending on the hardware used to generate them.

But all of that was relatively easy compared to the way the data had been encoded.

None of the 2-D codes he'd examined so far matched the ones on the zip disk label. Treating the border as four long strips of data had proven fruitless, which meant it had to be in blocks. Before he could sift it, he had to get it into the computer.

Without orientation markers, he couldn't tell which way the blocks ran—and to get enough data to make up an encoded sequence, he'd have to get several blocks in a row, so that he could see if it was encoded sequentially.

To make matters worse, he wasn't even sure that the blocks were on an axis that was parallel or perpendicular to the borders of the label. Many 2-D encoding schemes had enough error correction that they could lose up to 25 percent of their visual area and still be decoded at 100 percent accuracy. This code could have been rotated off-axis to make things really tough.

He grinned, his tanned-and-grizzled face wrinkling. His old brown leather bomber jacket creaked as he leaned forward to stare at the gray stones. He had an urge to hum the theme from *Raiders of the Lost Ark,* but he refrained.

Which way, which way . . . ?

He stared at the mortar between the stones. Did it look newer on the right or left?

Left.

Carefully, he began to put his weight on the stone to the left of the entry. Slowly he increased the pressure until nearly all of it rested on the stone he'd selected.

He enjoyed a moment's satisfaction before the block abruptly fell out from underneath him. Jay toppled, started to fall, and lashed out with the twelve-foot bullwhip he was carrying, wrapping it around a stone outcropping on the wall nearby and yanking. The effort pulled him back to where he'd started.

I guess it's not to the left.

The trap was clever—it wouldn't trigger until a heavy weight rested upon it. If he'd been standing there with both feet, it would have been "So long, Gridley."

He peered over the edge of the broken-off stones— more than one had fallen, to widen the danger area—and saw nothing but blackness. But there was a hint of sound—was it hissing? Slithering? Yes, definitely, both. He couldn't hope that the falling block had killed all the nasty wigglers down there.

He could brute-force it—drop weights on all the stones in the room and see which ones were left, but the idea offended his sense of style.

Someone clever had put the code together, and Jay wanted to figure out the key to the puzzle. There *was* a key, of course, there had to be. Any programmer who played the game this well always left a way in.

After all, *he* would.

So while he could easily run the numbers through the machine, he wanted to beat it himself.

He took a closer look around the room. As he usually did when he created VR based on a puzzle, he'd let a freeform algorithm give substance to the puzzle pieces after supplying base parameters. This was, as he saw it, the real advantage of a VR structure—a place that could have clues, things that hadn't been programmed consciously, to give his other senses a chance to help crack it. If he could cross the room, he'd have gotten enough blocks in a row to identify at least a part of the code.

Think, Jay, think!

He could go right, or angle off diagonally. . . .

He stopped and thought for a moment about the programmer. The man was clever—he'd hidden the code in plain sight.

But he'd hidden it on a disk about a Muslim mosque. What kind of man would have such a disk in his possession to use as camouflage?

A devout one.

Jay stepped to the east, the direction of Mecca, the way Muslims face during their prayers every day. He kept his whip ready to sling out and grab onto something if necessary.

The stone was safe. No trap, no danger.

Aha!

There was still room to continue in the direction he'd started, so he took another step, glancing down at the floor as he did so.

The stone gave way, and he just managed to lurch backward to safety.

Damn!

Now he could go forward, angle left, or angle right.

The direction of Mecca.

A thought came unbidden into his mind as he was looking at the scepter.

Maybe the scepter is Mecca.

A burst of excitement came with that idea. If he was right, there was only one way to traverse the puzzle—by looking toward the scepter the entire time. *On any of the blocks.*

A thrill ran through him.

Now *that* would be a cool paradigm shift. It would probably map in RW to having a central point on the label as a focal point to focus the direction of each data block. He'd been staring at the scepter when he took his first step, so that matched as well.

It felt right. It fit with the way the label instead of the disk had been used to hold data. It was his sense of intuition that made him more than just a good programmer, after all—he didn't just code from pure logic—he could *feel* solutions sometimes, take jumps that leapfrogged him to the same place he would eventually get by working it out.

But there was only one way to find out.

I've got you now, sucker, he thought, thinking of the programmer.

I won't need this anymore. Jay threw the bullwhip to his right and heard it hit—eventually. Faint hissing sounds came up from the pit below the throne room.

Jay fixed his gaze on the scepter, grinned, and ran all the way across the throne room.

No stones fell, and no other traps were triggered.

"Hah!"

As he laid his hand on the scepter and picked it up, a rumbling came from the back wall of the throne room, and he looked up, startled.

The wall had opened up onto another room, this one crisscrossed by a wicked-looking maze of spikes.

Across that room lay something else glinting gold.

"Oh, no," he said. "I've only cracked *part* of it."

Well. Half a loaf, and all that. This was what it was all about, matching wits in a virtual world.

And winning.

He grinned. "Bring it on," he said. "Let's see what you've got."

3

Eduard Natadze sat in the rental car outside the 7-Eleven, just inside the line from Virginia, waiting. He was dressed in a pair of thin wool slacks and a dark gray Harris Tweed sport coat—decent clothes, but not expensive and nothing to draw attention. He wore a pale blue cotton-blend Arrow shirt and a ten-dollar blue silk tie. His shoes were black leather Nunn Bush, with rubber soles, dressy enough so they didn't look like running shoes, but functional if he needed to move in a hurry. His watch was a basic Seiko, nothing special. His hair was cut to medium length, he was in decent physical shape, but not bulky, and just an inch or two over average height. Nothing about him screamed for a second look. He was, to a casual gaze, just another thirty-something businessman with a serviceable leather briefcase, on his way to or from work; nobody to notice at all.

Which, of course, was exactly as he wanted it.

His only real extravagance was in the satchel-type case, which was closed with a rip-strip of velcro and accessible in a hurry: A Korth Combat Magnum revolver, a German gun, and worth more than his clothes, watch, shoes, and briefcase put together, by a wide margin. It was the most expensive production handgun made—though "production" was perhaps something of a misnomer. There was a lot of hand-polishing and fitting on the weapon, which cost four times as much as a decent L-frame revolver from Smith & Wesson.

More than five thousand dollars for a double-action six-shot might seem excessive to some, but the one thing he never stinted on was his equipment. When your life was on the line, you did not want to lose it because you went cheap on your gear. Any revolver or pistol that would group three inches or less at twenty meters was sufficient for most combat situations. The Korth could, if you were adept enough, keep a grouping less than half that, using Federal Premium 130-grain Personal Defense loads, his personal choice.

When you could cover five shots with a quarter coin at that range, you had a precision instrument. When the instrument was what stood between you and the Reaper, you wanted the best you could afford. And when you worked on special projects for a billionaire who cared only for results and not the manner in which they were achieved, you could afford the best.

Natadze had two of the Korths. If he had to shoot somebody with one—and he had not had to do so yet—that gun would have to be destroyed, to avoid any possible ballistic connection to him. It was unlikely that investigators would think of the Korth as a possible weapon. They would examine any spent rounds they might find in a body, but the rifling was standard and not the European hexagonal often used in German guns. If he did have to shoot it, there would be no expended shells to worry about, since revolvers did not eject those. And if the authorities did by some chance suspect a Korth, they would hardly expect the shooter to destroy such an expensive machine. It would break his heart to do so, but in the end, it was a tool, and tools could be replaced. Dead was dead forever.

Not that he would need the gun for this mission. His preferred weapon at close range was a roll of quarters in his left hand—his left hand, never his right. He had to be too careful about the fingernails on his right hand, and so, over the years, had learned to punch left-handed. He also liked to wrap his hard fist in a leather glove. A roll of coins gripped to add heft and mass to his fist was a formidable weapon, especially against someone not expecting it. And burning a pair of twenty-dollar gloves was much cheaper and easier than getting rid of a revolver or pistol. But if he needed it, he had the gun, and he could get to it in a matter of a second if things did not look as he thought they should look.

He should not need his fists for this, either, though. Only his wits.

He smiled at the thought of what they would think back home if they knew that he was willing to smash and grind to bits a five-thousand-dollar handgun. A family in rural Sakartvelo—formerly Soviet Georgia—could live on half that for a year. Then again, the authorities in his homeland did not have the resources that the United States had at its beck. There, if you weren't noticed in the act of shooting somebody by a dozen witnesses, you might stay free forever. Of course, you also might be unjustly accused of some other crime, tried, convicted, and executed for it. That happened all the time. If they needed a criminal and could not find the right man, anyone nearby would serve. There was a kind of balance, if not one that was fair.

As he waited for the target, he checked to make certain there was nobody watching him. This was a public parking lot and he had been parked here for less than a minute, so it was unlikely anybody would have paid him any mind. Part of the reason he had been able to operate outside the law for as long as he had without being caught

was adherence to the Six-P Principle he had learned from
an American movie: Proper planning prevents piss-poor
performance. The less you left to chance, the less that bad
luck had to work with. Think of everything that could go
wrong, then have a way to deal with that; and a way to
deal with the back-up going wrong, as well.

In this case, the job was simple, and chances of failure
small; still, it paid to be as certain of every detail as possible.

The target arrived and alighted from his automobile—
an expensive late-model whatever—and walked the few
meters to the 7-Eleven's entrance. He did this every morning—or at least he had every morning for the week that
Natadze had observed him. Inside, the target would buy
a cup of bad coffee, a sugary confection—usually a
doughnut, sometimes a cinnamon twist or a danish—and
a morning newspaper. He would then return to his car and
drive to work, sipping coffee and eating the empty calo-
ries of his breakfast, and often trying to read the newspaper as he drove. Dangerous and stupid, this process, but
one he had apparently been managing for some time.

The man entered the store.

Natadze exited his own car and headed for the market,
walking behind the target's auto. He had untied his shoe
lace before he left his car, and now he stopped, squatted,
and began to re-tie the lace. His briefcase covered the
right rear tire from view, and it was the work of only a
couple of seconds to pull the cut-down ice pick from
where it was tucked away in his sock. Only three inches
of the shaft remained on the handle, filed to a needle
point, plenty long enough. He thrust the point into the
tire—once, twice, thrice—between the treads, and heard
the hiss of escaping air. Self-sealing tires would have
likely stopped the leaks, but the target did not have those
on his car, Natadze had checked the brand and model the
day before to be certain.

He put the pick back into his sock, re-covered it with

his trouser cuff, and stood. Nobody was near. He went into the market and to the rear of the place, selecting a bottle of water from the cooler. Part one was complete.

After the target checked out his purchase, Natadze paid for the water and returned to his car. The tire was flat, and the target stood next to it, glaring at it as if that might matter.

Natadze moved toward his car slowly, opening the cap of the bottled water.

The target pulled a small cell phone from his jacket pocket.

As he did, Natadze reached into his own jacket pocket and triggered a cell-phone jammer. This was of Japanese manufacture, not legal to use in the U.S., but with quite a following in more civilized countries. Larger models were utilized in restaurants, theaters, and anywhere else people were unwilling to listen to their fellows yammering on a mobile phone, especially in Japan. The devices produced a signal that made wireless phones useless. This small one would work for a short range, enough for this.

The target grumbled something and slapped his phone closed.

"I beg your pardon?" Natadze said. His intonation was a studied and much-practiced British. Maybe not enough to fool somebody with a genuine posh accent, but it had gulled plenty of Americans.

"Oh, sorry. My tire is flat, I need to call Triple-A, and my cell phone isn't working!"

"Oh, dear," Natadze said, frowing. "You can use my phone if you would like." Natadze retrieved the little Motorola phone inside its leather case from his shirt pocket, took it from the case, and offered it to the target.

"Thank you," the target said, as he took the phone. Natadze reached into his pocket and shut the jammer off.

The target made his call, and handed the phone back. Natadze carefully replaced the phone in its case, then put it back in this shirt pocket.

"Thanks, friend."

"No trouble at all."

Natadze went to his car, entered it, and carefully drove away. He waved at the target as he left.

He smiled as he departed. He could have done it one of several other ways—could have slipped into the man's condo when he was gone, or to his office, but this was easy, involved no real risk, and it amused him to have the man hand him his fingerprints.

The phone had been treated with a special surfactant that would promote a good impression. A little super-glue vapor and he would have the print he needed. Some adapto-gel and a mold, some silicone, and he would have a fake thumb that would fool most of the print readers made—including the one that admitted the target to places where computers would record his coming and going. That would be the really easy part.

Mr. Cox, he knew, would be pleased.

Net Force HQ
Quantico, Virginia

Colonel Abraham Kent arrived at General Howard's outer office thirty seconds early. He paused outside the door for almost that long, took a deep breath, squared his shoulders, and went in.

Through the open door to Howard's inner office, he saw Howard glance up, then down at his watch, then smile.

There wasn't a secretary in evidence. Howard stood and waved him in.

"Abe. Come on in."

Kent tried to keep it from being a march, but it certainly wasn't a stroll. Thirty years in the Corps gave you a posture that was hard to abandon.

"And don't salute, you old jarhead."

Kent grinned. He and Howard had known each other for twenty years, and they had a mutual respect. Howard hadn't gotten into combat when he'd been Regular Army, but he'd had a few dustups since joining this organization and had, by all accounts, acquitted himself well. One could never be sure—once the bullets began to fly, many a paper tiger turned pale and hugged the ground. He was glad that his old friend had been made of sterner stuff. And that there was still action to be had somewhere.

Howard gestured at the chair next to his desk. Kent nodded and sat in the hard-backed chair, his own back straight enough so he didn't need the support.

"You ready to do this, Abe?"

"Yes, sir, I believe I am."

"It won't be like the Marines."

"I don't see how it could be, John."

"But you could make General here. They reward results."

Kent nodded. Howard didn't need to mention what that meant. Kent had been a Colonel for years. Unless a shooting war broke out, he was never going to get his star in the Corps. There were too many other birds roosting and waiting for the same thing.

"I'll give you the fifty-cent tour," Howard said, "as soon as my secretary gets back. You know Julio Fernandez?"

"That scrounger?" Kent said with a grin. "You bust him from sergeant lately?"

Howard didn't smile back. "Actually," he said, "I promoted him. Lieutenant, now. He got married, has a son, and has settled down considerably. I know you'll want your own team, but he'll be sticking around a few weeks to make sure you get settled in."

"I appreciate that."

Howard nodded. "The new boss should be in his office," he said. "Have you two met yet?"

Kent shook his head. "Not formally. I saw him at some political thing once."

"He seems okay, for a civilian. Michaels was a good man—backed me up every turn, and was willing to get his own hands dirty. I hope you do as well with Thorn."

"Me, too."

"Ah, there's Betty. Come on, I'll show you your new toy."

"Sir," Tom Thorn's secretary said, "Marissa Lowe is here."

"Send her in."

Lowe was an attractive black woman, a few years older than he was, and tall, maybe five-ten. Her curly hair was cut short, and her gray suit was businesslike enough, the skirt reaching nearly to her knees. She wore a red silk blouse, and what looked like gold and ruby earrings that dangled an inch below her lobes. Dark brown eyes and lots of smile wrinkles at the corners. A fine-looking, very . . . *earthy* woman.

Thorn shook the woman's hand. She had a firm grip.

"Please, have a seat," he said with a smile.

She flashed him a smile in return, her teeth very white against her milk-chocolate skin. She walked to the couch and sat. She moved very well, he saw, smooth and controlled.

"What can I do for the CIA, Ms. Lowe?"

"Marissa, please, Commander."

He smiled again. "Call me Tom, then."

She nodded. "Shortly before you took over Net Force, our embassy in Ankara had a little visit from the Turkish ambassador, Mustafa Suleyman Agar. The Ambassador's people had come across some intel he figured might be important to the Turks' national security." She had a silky, deep voice.

Thorn nodded. "Okay."

"Well, calls were made, people talked to, and someone somewhere decided that Net Force ought to be asked to help out the ambassador by having a look at the information—which was hidden somehow on a disk of tourist photographs that came from Iran. The Turks were fairly certain something was there because their agent got himself killed in the process of collecting and bringing it home."

"I see. Go on."

"Your Jay Gridley has been digging into it and found a code. He managed to crack part of it. It turned out to be a list of secret agents from the former USSR stationed in Africa and the Middle East, going as far back as the nineteen sixties."

Thorn seemed to remember a report he'd barely had time to glance at from Gridley, who he had just met. "Ah, yes. I recall Jay said something about Russian spies."

"Well, it has been a while since the evil empire collapsed, but the Russians never throw anything away, you know, so some of the agents were still in place, if a bit long in the tooth. Real names, code names, dates, places, everything."

He nodded. "I can see where that would be very valuable."

She echoed his nod. "The Turks scooped up the ones in their territory, and passed out names of the others to their friends in the region."

"So we get points for helping the Turks?"

"Oh, yeah, big time."

Thorn searched his memory, which was usually pretty good about such stuff. There was something else . . . ? Ah, he had it.

"I've been swamped with e- and paperwork and I'm not up to date," he said, "but if I recall correctly, Gridley said he thought there was more material to be decoded."

"Yes, sir, that's what we understood. And we are hoping that it is a continuation of the list into our geography."

"Any reason to believe that?"

"Your man seems to think so, from the report he sent. The way the countries and spies are listed shows a progression in this general direction, going from east to west. We're hoping it will jump the ocean."

"You're thinking maybe there are some Russian spies still knocking around in the U.S.?"

"Oh, we *know* that. We even know who some of them are. The regular FBI keeps account of them, devil-you-know-versus-the-devil-you-don't and all. Everybody has secret ops over here—our enemies, our friends, probably even the Swiss—just like we do in their houses. Today's best friend might be tomorrow's worst enemy and vice-versa, so we need to stay on our toes. Look at how many times in history we fought knock-down-drag-out wars against folks who are now our best allies: British, Spanish, Mexican, Germans, Japanese, Italians, that wheel just keeps on spinning." She gave him another little smile. "Anyway," she went on, "the question is, would this Iranian-Turkish list tell us about a bunch of others we don't know about? That would be very useful to us."

"Indeed. So, what is it you want me to do, Marissa?"

"Nothing, really. We'd just like to make sure you keep this one on the front burner. We would appreciate it."

"I believe we can do that."

She gave him her brilliant smile yet again. He liked it, and he liked her. She seemed grounded, no-nonsense, straight to the point, and there was never enough of that to go around.

She stood. "I'd like to drop by from time to time, touch base, since I'm kind of the de-facto liaison from the spooks to the computer nerds. I'll call before I show up."

He grinned. "You'll be welcome any time, Marissa. A pleasure to have made your acquaintance."

"You, too, Tommy."

Normally, he didn't much care for that nickname, but it didn't sound so bad coming from her.

A few minutes later, his secretary beeped him. "Sir. General Howard and Colonel Kent are here to see you."

"Great. Send them in."

4

Samuel Cox sat staring at his desk, as if the solution to his problem might be found between the computer and the hard-copy outbox.

His first reaction to the phone call had been close to panic. Not because he was worried about anybody overhearing it—Vrach's voice was disguised, distorted far beyond vox-pattern recognition. The call was also scrambled, using state-of-the-art equipment. The NSA itself would bang their heads against the code if they tried to break it. After all, they had devised the scrambler, and they said their code was practically unbreakable.

No, it wasn't that he was worried about being overheard. But the words that the Doctor had spoken so matter-of-factly? They had chilled Cox right to the bone.

The Turks had given Net Force a computer disk to decode. Thus far, the organization had been successful in finding at least some of the information hidden on the disk. They had uncovered a list of agents who had worked for the former Soviet Union in the Middle East forty years ago.

Cox had merely shrugged at that part of the news. It meant nothing to him.

Ah, the Doctor had said, but there could be more, much more—including a list of Soviet spies elsewhere in the world.

When Cox heard that, he felt his belly go cold. That meant something to him.

Where else in the world? he had asked.

The irritatingly calm Doctor had spoken of it as he might the weather or a football score: Among others, he said, the United States. We think. We cannot be sure. No one seems to know how the information came to be in the hands of the Iranians, or how the Turks got it from them.

At that, the cold in Cox's belly had turned into a lump of dry ice.

He could almost hear the Russian's pragmatic shrug over the no-pix connection. There is nothing to be done. Either they will decode it or they will not. We will deny all, of course, but done is done. You should know. Perhaps you might consider buying an island in some friendly country, and moving your money there.

Cox disconnected without another word and sagged back in his chair.

So much for being a valuable, protected asset. The Russians would be sorry to lose him, but they weren't going to help him, Cox was sure of that.

Was he to be outed as a former spy? His good works since those foolish days would be ruined; he would be made into a villain, maybe even put in prison. It would kill his family. His wife would probably have a stroke. His children and grandchildren would be shamed. His friends would be astonished. But even if he held the government at bay and beat the charge, the taint would never leave him. *Sam Cox? The billionaire? A Russian spy, did*

*you hear? Hard to believe somebody with all that wealth
and power could be so stupid, isn't it?*

He stared at the desk and shook his head. He was a
powerful man. He had access to a giant fortune, he had
the ears of presidents and kings. That was a long way to
fall. A terrifyingly long way.

It couldn't happen. Couldn't. He would not *allow* it!

But—what could he do about it? They hadn't uncovered anything yet, so he had some time, but how to stop
it?

It was unlikely in the extreme that he could just send
somebody into Net Force HQ in Quantico to steal the
incriminating information. All men had their price, but
finding out what it was could be tricky. For some, it was
easy, money would do it. For others, it might be something complex, not easily determined. Attempt to corrupt
the wrong person, the almost-mythical honest man, and
that would point a nasty finger at you in a hurry. Why
was somebody offering a low-level government employee
ten or twenty million dollars to give up a computer disk?
What could possibly be on it that was worth that much?
Who could afford to make such an offer?

No, that could be a bad misstep.

He frowned. Perhaps they might not be able to break
the remaining code. Perhaps the disk would lie in the Net
Force vaults for fifty years or a hundred, long after Cox
had gone to his reward, and he would be beyond caring.

He shook his head. He could not stake his future, his
past, his life and legacy on that. If they had broken part
of it, they could uncover the rest. He had to stop that, no
matter what the cost.

Think, Sam, think!

But the desk offered no solutions, and his worry stood
there grinning at him. *Gotcha!* it seemed to say. *Gotcha!*

He sighed. This was not his forte. He had people who
knew how to manage such things. He touched the intercom control.

"Have Eduard drop by, would you?"

"Yes, sir," his secretary said.

Natadze would have some ideas. He always did.

Net Force HQ
Quantico, Virginia

Jay was, he had to admit, stumped. Worse, he was a little worried that brute force, his method of last resort, wasn't going to work, either. He wasn't ready to try it quite yet, but he was approaching that point, and if it *didn't* work, then what?

He had tried fifty variations, coming at the code from every direction he could think of, and nothing else had clicked.

"Hey, Smokin' Jay."

He blinked and looked at the door. "Toni! How are you?"

Toni Fiorella Michaels stepped into his office. "Doing great. How about you?"

"I'm not sure," he said, frowning. He gestured at his desk. "Home is fine. Saji's fine. But here . . ."

Toni smiled. "Hasn't it always been that way? And won't it always be?"

Jay shook his head. "Thanks. Just what I need to hear. You and the boss about ready to push off?"

"Yep. Got the van mostly packed, and we're on the road first thing in the morning."

"It's a long way to Colorado."

"You're welcome to drop by anytime," she said. "You should be able to hook a ride on some Net Force or military jet going that way pretty much anytime you want."

He nodded. "We'll still miss you," he said.

"Yeah, I know. We'll miss you, too. But things change when you have a child to look out for, Jay. With my *silat,*

I always felt as if I could handle myself in most situations when push came to shove, but after that situation at the house, with Tyrone and that psychotic, I realized I couldn't stay in this business. You don't call trouble to your family."

"I hear you."

"So, how's the new guy?"

Jay shrugged. "Okay, I guess. You ever met him?"

"No."

"I don't think he likes me."

"You'll dazzle him, once he gets to know you."

"Maybe. Guy is richer than Fort Knox, he invented all kinds of computer stuff I grew up using, and is pretty much the smartest person in any room he walks into— and knows it. I don't think he will dazzle easily."

She smiled. "What are you working on?"

He returned her grin. "Can I tell you? Are you still cleared?"

She looked at her watch. "If you hurry. My resignation starts officially in about twenty minutes."

Jay explained about the Turks and the Iranian disk.

"I'm still hacking at the rest of it," he finished. "I've got the Middle Eastern part down, and some of the South African parts, but what I think will probably turn out to be North and South America is still closed. It's like the guy who wrote the code had a personality change and went off in an entirely different direction. I can't get a pattern."

"Maybe the NSA crackers might help?"

"I'd cut out my tongue before I asked them, especially after that thing with the California druggie. They don't much like us anyhow. They'd love to show us up, and frankly, I don't think they've got the chops. But just our asking for help would have them grinning from ear to ear, even if they couldn't break it."

"I'm sure you'll manage."

"I have the CIA, the regular feebs, and the Turkish

ambassador all looking over my shoulder. Plus the new boss, of course." He shrugged and gave her a weak grin. "The usual."

She grinned back. "I have to run," she said. "I just wanted to come by and say good-bye in person. Stand up."

He frowned. "You're not going to hit me, are you?"

She laughed again, and when he stood, moved in and hugged him.

"You're a good man, Jay. Give my love to Saji."

Then she was gone, and Jay felt a hollowness in the pit of his stomach. He never used to feel that when he moved around, or when other people did. His life had been in hardware and software, and people came and went, no problem—he was happier in VR than in the real world. This time, however, he really was going to miss Toni and Alex. They were his friends, and he didn't have so many he could afford to lose any. He would have to make an effort to keep in touch. VR, RW trips, com, whatever it took. He really would.

"Anything else I can do for you, sir?"

Kent looked at Julio Fernandez. They were in his temporary office, just off the corridor. "No, Lieutenant," he said, "that will be all, unless you have something I need to know?"

Fernandez smiled. "Well, sir, as it happens, I do have something. I expect General Howard would ordinarily go for it, but he's told me he won't step on your prerogatives for long-term acquisitions."

Kent stared at him.

"I have to show it to you, Colonel. It doesn't tell all that well. We need to go to the motor pool."

Kent glanced at his watch. "All right. Lead on."

"Why am I looking at a recreational vehicle, Lieutenant?" Kent asked.

Fernandez smiled. "Not exactly your typical RV, sir, though this *is* a Class-C motor home chassis—a Class-A looks like a Greyhound bus; the C's have that cab over-section shading the truck-style front end." He nodded at the vehicle. "But we aren't talking about something a rock star would tour in, or that Winnebago you'd take the wife and kids out in for a weekend to Diamond Lake. If you'll follow me, sir."

Fernandez approached the vehicle, which appeared to be white fiberglass, with vaguely aerodynamic-looking decals on the sides in pale tans and blues. The coach entrance door was aft on the starboard side, behind the back wheels.

The lieutenant pressed his thumb against a reader and the door's lock snicked open. Two steps led into the vehicle.

Inside there was enough headroom for a six-footer in boots to stand straight.

"Head is to the left, behind this door," Fernandez said. He reached for the knob, and Kent moved deeper into the vehicle to give him room to swing the portal open. The door looked like oak to Kent.

In the head was a marine-style toilet, sink, mirror, cabinets, and a shower stall. Small, but useable.

"Enough water to take a dozen military showers, to cook with, and drink, all without refilling the tank, though it will run off shore water—you just plug in a hose outside and turn the spigot on. Same for power—upgraded to fifty amps from the normal thirty-five. Drains for gray- and black-water outside, of course."

Behind Kent was a small galley, stove, sink, a microwave oven, and across from that a refrigerator/freezer. So far, much like any other RV. But past that, it got unusual.

"This is your basic Born Free twenty-four-foot rear-bath coach," Fernandez said. "But instead of a fold-out sleeper couch over here, we have a bank of computers,

GPS, Doppler radar, FLIR, laser bouncers, and com-gear, all with hardened electronics."

A pair of captain's chairs sat in front of the electronic array.

"Over here, this little board pulls out to form a table, thus." Fernandez lifted, pulled, then lowered it, and a tabletop jutted from the wall. "Suitable for having lunch or doing map work, or playing games on your laptop."

Kent nodded.

"Up over the cab, we pull down this platform, like so, and there is sleeping space for two operators—three if they like each other real well. Even comes with a ladder.

"There's a big Onan generator installed, and if you aren't plugged into shore power, this switch right here over the driver's seat will crank it up. It is sufficiently large to run all the electronics for as long as you have fuel, which in this case means the vehicle's fifty-five gallon gas tank. This is a Ford chassis and engine, your basic six-point-eight-liter V-ten engine, which, with its special beefed-up suspension and shocks, will give you approximately three thousand pounds of useable payload. That will include, with the installed equipment, three operators and their gear, and full fuel and water tanks, it will get nine or ten miles a gallon of unleaded if your driver doesn't have a heavy foot, and climb anything you can take a sedan up. Cruises at seventy all day long."

"Interesting."

"Yes, sir. And it gets more so. The thing is built like a Swiss watch. You can stay out in the woods, if you have sufficient supplies, a couple-three months. The air conditioner is enough to cool the electronic equipment to safe operating range in ninety-five-degree heat, the furnace will maintain warmth in subfreezing weather. It's a little tight, but there's not an inch of wasted space in it."

Julio led Kent to the driver's compartment. "Here's the real fun part. That bank of switches, there? Watch." He lifted the switch covers and pressed three buttons. There came a hum of power, and as Kent watched, a pair of dark gray plates folded in from above and below over the windshield, coming to a sharp angle in front of the glass.

"Stealth gear," Fernandez said. "Extrudable spun-carbon fiber sheets and plates that give you some nice radar-shielding angles. You get an exploratory ping on your detector, you turn toward the source, hit the buttons, and you turn invisible, more or less."

"Very interesting," Kent said.

"Yes, sir. What with domestic and international terror-ists getting more and more sophisticated with their own surveillance gear, this vehicle is the perfect Command-and-Control Center for mounting operations in a hurry at a far remove."

"I assume this hardware is not cheap," Kent observed.

"No, sir, but it is reasonable. If we supply the electron-ics, the maker will build it to our specifications, and our cost is less than a hundred thousand per unit, delivered."

Kent raised an eyebrow. "Really? That seems very rea-sonable."

"Yes, sir. Company is in Iowa, American to the core, good Christian family-value kind of place. Sure, if we let it to the lowest bidder, we might get units cheaper some-where, but they won't be made as well. See those ridges, there, there, and back there? Those are steel roll bars. This is the safest RV you can ride in. In the forty-odd years the company has been making them, they've never had a single fatality in an accident. Not one."

"That's interesting."

"Yes, sir, I thought so."

"And you are telling me this because you think we should have some of these vehicles."

"Yes, sir. They are portable. Stash five or six around the country, we'd have one a few hours away from any situation we'd need covered. They run about eleven or twelve thousand pounds in this configuration, so if we borrowed a big transport plane from somebody, we could haul one to any air base in the world where we could land one of the big honkers, like a C5A."

"I can't see one of these on the back roads of Afghanistan or Iraq," Kent said. His voice was dry.

"We're not supposed to go to those places anyway, sir; it's against our charter. But from the outside, this could belong to Ma and Pa Retiree out to see America, and even without the stealth gear, it would give us advanced operations capabilities in places we couldn't sneak into otherwise. Nothing like a fleet of camouflaged military trucks full of guys in uniform rolling down a desert highway in Utah or the woods of Idaho to draw attention."

Kent considered it. "Do we have room in our budget for this?"

"Yes, sir. With a little creative swapping, I believe we can manage five units, maybe six, no problem."

Kent gave him a tight nod. He knew all about wheeler-dealers. If Fernandez could horse trade as well as he talked—and John had always said that he could—it was a done deal. "And you say that General Howard wants this to be my decision?"

"Yes, sir."

"All right, Lieutenant. Make it happen."

"Yes, sir!"

"What are you grinning at, Lieutenant?"

"Permission to speak freely, sir?"

"You've been with John Howard since he was a shave-tail, correct?"

"Yes, sir."

"I can't imagine he kept you shut up. Fire away."

"I was just thinking how reasonable the Colonel is, for a, uh . . ."

"—a jarhead?"

"Yes, sir. My thought exactly."

"We might have a reputation for respecting history and tradition, Lieutenant, but we aren't stupid. We would rather have our people in top-of-the-line gear when we can get it."

"Yes, sir."

"Go do your deal, Lieutenant."

"Sir." Fernandez gave him a crisp salute. Kent just shook his head.

5

It was late when Thorn walked into the empty gym. He had his equipment bag with him—it was too big to fit in his locker. He looked around and smiled. He had hopes of eventually turning this into a regular *salle d'arms*—mirrors on the walls, racks of swords lining the room—but first he better make sure he was going to be here long enough to warrant the change.

It was after nine P.M., long after he should have left for home, but he needed to work out. The exercise relaxed him, helped to clear his mind, and after these past few days, he needed both.

He'd met everyone at this point, and it looked like a good team.

General Howard had impressed him, so much so that Thorn would be sorry to see him go. Abe Kent seemed competent enough, and might turn out to be a better man even than John Howard, but right now Thorn would prefer Howard's humor—and especially his experience—while he settled in to his own new role.

Gridley? He wasn't sure about him yet. There was no question Jay knew his stuff, or that he could handle just about any net-based problem. He'd shown that with the progress he'd already made with the Iranian disk. Still, there was something . . . *young* about him. He was certainly full of himself, and he had that type of cockiness that made Thorn wonder just how severely he'd been tested. Was he really that good, or was it just that he hadn't run into a situation hard enough to knock the strut out of him?

Had the ground truly quaked for him yet, as Thorn's grandfather, a full-blooded Nez Pierce, would have asked.

He smiled at the memory of the old man, and the quake reference brought up another recollection: What do you do in case of an earthquake? Go to the Bureau of Indian Affairs. Why? Because nothing ever moves at the BIA. . . .

He shook his head. Enough thinking. He'd come down here to get away from thoughts, after all. Now it was time to move.

He started with stretches. He'd learned to fence in high school, and had stayed with it. It had earned him some flack as a teen—typical "Red-man-with-a-long-knife" kind of crap—but he'd eventually earned a B rating in épée, and that had shut a lot of that down. He had been respectable at the national level, but he was not quite serious enough to pursue it beyond that.

He'd wanted something more than mere strip fencing. He'd needed a challenge that extended beyond the narrow metal piste. Oh, he still enjoyed it, but it was not the be-all it had once seemed.

He moved slowly into a lunge to stretch his hamstrings, and felt a little twinge. Used to be he never bothered to warm up or stretch. He'd always tried to bring a sense of reality to his game, going more for touches that would have counted in the real world rather than just lighting up the scoring machine. And in an RW setting, no opponent was going to give him time to loosen up his hamstrings before launching an attack.

Of course, in a real-world setting, it wasn't likely he'd be carrying a sword anyway. . . .

He could still fight without stretching if he had to, he knew that, but he also knew that he'd pay a price for it later, and limping around for three or four days just wasn't worth it.

Warmed up after a few minutes, he pulled his protective gear out of his bag and slipped it on. Without an opponent, he didn't really need the padded plastron under his jacket. For that matter, he didn't really need the jacket, mask, or glove, either. But fencing was, first and foremost, a sport of tradition. Courtesy ruled—at least until the director called *allez!*—and the uniform was a part of that tradition.

Besides, if Jay's little surprise worked, the feel of the jacket and plastron would be necessary.

Thorn took his épée out of his bag, picked up Jay's mask in his left hand, and went out to the fencing strip he'd earlier outlined with tape on the wooden floor. At the *en garde* line, he saluted his imaginary director and opponent, then he took a deep breath.

"All right, Jay," he said softly. "Let's see how good you are."

He pressed a button on the back tab of the mask and then slipped it on.

As the mask settled into place, Thorn looked up and saw his opponent standing on the opposite guard line.

He smiled.

Jay hadn't had much time to play with the programming. He'd mentioned that, given a few days, he could work up VR versions of any historic fencer, from the American saber fencer Peter Westbrook to the Italian épée expert Antonio D'Addario—as long as there were video archives and other data banks to pull details from.

For now, though, all he'd been able to do was put together a sort of composite fencer, taken from various video clips and a few manuals. He'd gone for breadth rather than depth, programming in skills in multiple weapons and styles—or so he'd said, anyway—and promised more development soon.

Jay had also coded a director for the bout, even though they were fencing "dry," without the electrical hook-ups. Thorn didn't need the lights for this; he didn't even need the director; all he needed was an opponent—and the opponent didn't even have to be very good. He was looking for exercise, not a challenge.

He sketched another quick salute and dropped into his guard position, knees flexed, right toe pointed at his opponent, left toe pointing exactly ninety degrees off to the left, right hand extended almost completely, shoulder height, sword point aimed at his opponent's chin. His left hand floated easily like a flag above and behind him.

His opponent mirrored him.

"Et vous pret?" the director asked.

"Oui," Thorn and his opponent said as one.

"Allez!"

Thorn started with a ballestra, a quick, short step to close distance followed immediately by a strong lunge. Normally, he was a counterpuncher. He liked to let his opponent take the first move and then react to it. But he could attack, too, and he was anxious to see how well Jay had done.

As he lunged, he feinted toward his opponent's face mask, eyes unfocused, looking at nothing but seeing everything.

There! He felt his opponent's blade begin to come up in a parry.

Thorn smiled. In épée there were no rules, no right-of-way. It didn't matter who launched the attack. It only mattered who struck first. If both struck simultaneously, both would score a point. With electronic gear, the equipment was sensitive to one twentieth of a second. With VR, there was no limit.

He hadn't been sure how his opponent would react. It wouldn't have surprised him to see the other blade come toward him in a counterattack, especially one aimed at his right wrist or forearm. If that had happened, he would have tried to bind it, capturing the point and corkscrewing down the blade until he drove his own tip into his opponent.

This was better, though.

As the other blade came up to meet his, Thorn dropped his hand and sent his point streaking toward his opponent's right toe. It was a risky shot, since it took his own blade far from any sort of defensive position, but in épée the entire body was a valid target, and a shot to the toe counted the same as a hit on the mask.

Against a human, Thorn would probably have thrown this as a feint—if he even tried it this early in the bout. He likely would have reversed direction with his point one more time, as quickly and as tightly as he could, starting high, feinting toward the foot, then darting high again, aiming the final thrust at his opponent's right wrist.

This wasn't a human, though, and he wasn't so interested in scoring as in moving—and in testing—so he didn't turn this into a feint.

He should have.

As his point dropped, his opponent shifted his weight slightly, drew his right foot back, and then leaped into the air.

Thorn's point crashed harmlessly into the floor. His opponent's point, however, came down solidly on his mask.

"Halt!" the director cried. *"Touché."*

Thorn nodded and acknowledged the touch.

"Nice one, Jay," he said.

He returned to his guard line, saluted his opponent, and came to guard.

"Et vous pret? Allez!"

Thorn smiled and moved forward.

He maintained his guard, more cautious now. He looked for an opening, a weakness, anything.

There wasn't much. Jay had done a good job, coding in all the basics and also giving his construct good reaction time. That would make it hard to fool him.

Good.

Blade extended, his right hand and wrist shielded by his bell guard, Thorn began testing his opponent. He engaged his point, throwing a fast beat at his foible, the weak part of the blade near the tip, to try and open up his wrist. He followed that with a quick thrust at the bell guard, hoping to slide off and pick up part of his cuff.

The move didn't work, but he hadn't really expected it would. He'd throw that shot again and again, setting up an expectation in his opponent's mind. With a real opponent—a human one—there was the chance that he would tire and start to get sloppy on his parries, and leave an opening for Thorn to slip through. He didn't think that would happen here, unless Jay had programmed in a fatigue factor.

He threw the beat again, working the interior of his opponent's blade. Did it seem as though he was a trifle strong in his counter? Thorn nodded. He thought so, and that was something that could be exploited.

He made the beat a third time, but now it was a feint.

Instead of hitting his opponent's blade, he came up and pressed it to the outside. As soon as he felt the counter pressure, he disengaged, dropping below his opponent's point and circling, coming up on the outside. He pressed and added momentum to the parry—

His opponent's point drifted in just a hair too far, and Thorn extended, aiming for the outside of the wrist. He caught fabric, and felt the point of his épée sink home.

"Halt!" the director cried. *"Touché."*

Gotcha!

He had a sense of his opponent now. He could work

with this. Give Gridley credit, it was a good simulacrum.

He returned to his guard line, saluted, came to guard, and waited for the director's command to begin.

Now they were having fun. . . .

Cal's Bistro
Manhattan, New York

Natadze took a sip of the beer—some kind of dark ale—and nodded. "Good," he said.

Cox waited. The place was crowded and noisy, they were in a booth in the back, and the lunch crowd's babble was probably a more effective protection than debugging his office once a week was. The food and beer were good, but Cal's, there for forty years, was on the verge of being "discovered." Another couple of weeks and Cox would have to stop coming here because he would start running into people who knew him. Too bad.

"I have considered the matter," Natadze said, after another sip of the dark brew.

Cox waited, knowing that the man would get to the subject in his own time. Part of having a highly trained expert was allowing him to present what he was being paid to present in the manner he thought best. You don't hire Michelangelo and then try to give him lessons on how to paint a ceiling.

"This information will be restricted," Natadze said. "It will not be 'Net Force' working on it, but a man or perhaps a small team of men within the organization."

Cox nodded. "Right."

"The team leader, if there is more than one man, is the key. He will know how much progress has been made, who has made it, and any other pertinent information related to it."

Well, of course, Cox thought. *Any idiot could figure*

that much. But Cox refrained from saying such aloud. Let him go where he wanted to go.

"Therefore, we need only to secure this man's help."

"Are you thinking about bribing him, Eduard?"

"No. *Collecting* him."

Startled, Cox looked around. Nobody was watching them. "Kidnapping?"

"It is the simplest solution. The data remains at all times within their headquarters, and a building like that will have wards. Getting inside and collecting data, while not impossible, would be complicated. It would require documents, either stolen or forged. It would require an agent who would likely be scanned, photographed, or otherwise recorded. On top of that, even with a proper disguise and identification, simply gaining admittance would not be enough to guarantee finding and securing the data. It is very complex."

Cox nodded. "I understand."

"But the man who works upon the code? He comes and goes. He will be unprotected away from his workplace, or, at worst, will have a bodyguard or two. Much easier to deal with. There are many options. His home. In transit to or from work. Recreating. We gather him in, question him, and with the information he provides, we will be in a much better position. Maybe he takes his work home. Perhaps there are but one or two copies of it, which he can tell us how to collect. He will hand us a lever; with it, we can pry what we need into our hands. Not difficult at all, really." He shrugged, reached for his beer.

Cox shook his head. The thought had literally never occurred to him to kidnap a Net Force operative. This was why Eduard was so valuable to him. He easily walked down roads that Cox would never even consider taking, roads he would never even know were *there*.

"Can you find out who the operative is?"

Natadze held his beer up to the light and examined it. "I already know that."

"How?"

"We live in an age of information, sir. There are many public records available—news media, government reports, Internet and web material. Certain names appear in these records with regard to their areas of expertise. The head of Net Force's technical section is a man named Gridley. I have a researcher gathering information on him. Shortly, we will know all there is to know about this man—or at least all that is publicly available. Once I have this, it is simply a matter of choosing when, where, and how to best approach him."

Cox reached for his own untouched beer. He took a sip. It was warm, slightly bitter, and smelled of hops or yeast or something, but that didn't matter. At the moment, suddenly, the taste was wonderful. "We are in something of a hurry, Eduard."

"It should not take long to determine what we need. A day or two at most to set it up and we will have him."

Cox nodded. "Do it."

"Yes, sir," Natadze said. "I will."

Natadze left first; Cox waited for a few minutes. Could it be this simple? God, he hoped so. If they could wipe this threat away, he would sleep a lot sounder than he had in a long time. Yes, indeed. There would still be the Russians, of course, but the status quo was something with which he could live. He was still more valuable to them free and untarnished, and while they might not go to the mat to protect him, they wouldn't toss him away as long as he was useful. The Russians were nothing if not pragmatic.

And if this worked? Maybe it would be time to send Eduard to find the Doctor and have a little talk with him, as well. If they could determine who knew what over there and eliminate them? That would make his life just about perfect.

He grinned. He would have to give Eduard a nice bonus. A man like him was worth his weight in diamonds.

He raised his glass in a toast. "Go get 'em, Eduard."

6

University Park, Maryland

The house Thorn had bought was in University Park, just south of the University of Maryland, in Prince George's County. The homes were more stately than spectacular, many of them built in the 1920s and '30s, and most of his neighbors were either professors at the U, well-off business types, or political staff. The streets bore large pin oak and pear trees, and an occasional elm that had somehow managed to survive all the years of blight that seemed to seek out that species. There had been people living here since before the Revolutionary War, though the town itself was much younger. According to the realtor, crime was low, tiger mosquitoes sometimes got bad in the summer despite efforts to eradicate them, and just about all of the single-family homes were occupied by their owners. Upscale, but not ostentatious.

From the outside, Thorn's house was a two-story home, solid, and there was nothing to distinguish it from most of the others on his street, which was exactly what he had wanted when he set the real estate agent to looking.

Inside, there was still work being done. The four-bedroom house was much larger than a man alone needed, and he was having the living room and parlor converted into a fencing salon. One of the joys of being rich was, if you couldn't find exactly what you wanted for a home, you could have it built.

Eventually, he would have fencing masters come to his house to teach him. He had been looking into the Japanese arts *kendo* and even *iaido*, with the live blade.

Not that he wanted much other than that. Coming from a poor family had taught him early on to value people and small things. Yes, when he'd sold his first major piece of software and been handed a huge check, he had run out and gotten himself a bunch of new toys, ranging from top-of-the-line computer systems to fast cars to five-thousand-dollar suits. He had even bought his parents a house in Spokane.

But that was long ago and money no longer burned a hole in his pocket. These days, he had a driver, so he didn't need a car. He ate well enough, though he wasn't a gourmet, and he didn't buy his clothes at the Salvation Army Thrift Store. His one expensive hobby was collecting swords. Aside from working foils, épées, and sabers by such makers as Vniti, Leon Paul, Prieur, and Blaise, he had a collection of antique weapons ranging from Japanese *katana*s to Chinese broadswords to Civil War sabers. He would have these hung on the walls of the *salle* when it was done, and a monitored alarm service installed to keep sticky-fingered thieves from helping themselves to the weapons. Other than that, his fortune was not something he used all that much. He did like to fly first class, for the leg room, but he could have easily afforded a private jet, and first-class was a lot cheaper than that. . . .

He smiled at himself as the driver opened the car's door and he alighted at the new house.

"Good night, Mr. Thorn."

"Good night, Carl. See you in the morning."

Thorn ambled to the door, carrying his equipment bag. He thumbed the door's lock and pushed the front door open.

Inside, the smells of sawdust and fresh paint greeted him. He put the sword bag down and went into the kitchen. He didn't feel like cooking, it was late, and a heavy meal before bedtime was an invitation to nightmares, but he was hungry, so he grabbed an Aussie pie from the freezer and stuck it into the microwave, opened a bottle of beer, a Samuel Adams, and went to watch the late news on the television. So far, the new job had been easy enough. He had good people, there were a few more he would eventually bring in, and he hadn't run into anything he couldn't handle. Of course, he didn't expect he would run into anything he couldn't handle.

He sipped from the bottle as the TV lit. It was a little disappointing, really. Sure, there was always a newness factor in any kind of job. Big projects brought their challenges, but it never took him long to get up to speed, and once he did, well, then it was just a matter of time before it got boring. Most of the time, he had to invent his own challenges, and now and then he would have liked to be in a position where he had to stretch a little to keep up. Mostly, that just didn't happen.

The news flared on, the end of a story about another crisis in the Middle East.

When he'd been a kid, Thorn hadn't realized that everybody wasn't as smart as he was. A problem would come up, he'd see the answer, and he'd assumed that everybody else had seen the answer, but for some reason he couldn't understand, they'd pretend they hadn't. Eventually, he realized that wasn't the case—that in virtually every mental race he ran, he was way out in front when he crossed the finish line.

He took another swig of the beer. The weather was up next, and it was going to be cool and rainy in the District tomorrow.

A big part of his life had been a search for equals, people he could run with, but those were few and far between. Oh, they were out there, and it was a delight when he found one, but he no longer expected to simply run into them the way he once had. Once upon a time, he had lived with a woman who was actually smarter than he was. Sharp, funny, sexy, they liked the same music, the same literature and movies, mostly, but it hadn't worked out. She'd had her career—she was a physicist—and he'd had his, tinkering with computerware, and one day they'd looked up and realized they weren't connected anymore. They couldn't point to any major break. They still exchanged Christmas cards, smiled and hugged each other if they met, but their paths had diverged and neither of them could see a way back. Sad.

In sports, the NBA basketball season was in full swing. Looked as if one of the new expansion teams he hadn't realized even existed was on a roll, ten straight victories.

The microwave *ping*ed. He flicked off the television and headed back to the kitchen. He'd do an hour or so on the web, check his personal e-mail and the fencing newsgroup, and then go to bed.

Another exciting evening in the life of Thomas Thorn.

Washington, D.C.

Natadze watched from inside the rental car as the target turned into his driveway and stopped his own car, a three-year-old Volvo.

Following the man had been easy enough, and even if he had lost him, he had known where he was going. He had committed all the statistics to memory. He knew things about Jay Gridley that the man probably did not know himself—his driver's license and credit card numbers, his medical ID number, along with his phone number, address, birthday, and his wife's maiden name.

Proper planning prevents piss-poor performance. Knowing as much as possible about the subject was an important part of that.

Gridley got out and walked to the door of his condo, where his wife, who taught Buddhism online, would be waiting. According to her latest medical records, she was pregnant.

Well. If Gridley did as he was told, he would live to be a father. If not . . .

Natadze put that thought from his mind. It was not good to dwell on failure. Yes, you did whatever was necessary to assure that such a thing did not happen, and that meant considering all the variables and planning for them, but you did not give them power. Failure was not allowed. Only success got you approval.

He looked automatically at his watch, mentally marking the time. Normally, he would follow the target for days, a week, to establish his patterns, but there was a time constraint this time and he would not be allowed that luxury on this mission. He did not like having to hurry, but it was the nature of the assignment, and one made do as best one could, given the parameters. He would do it tomorrow, when the man left work and drove home. It should not be difficult. The target was a white-collar worker, a chair-warmer who was not particularly adept physically. Natadze would use the gun, he would intimidate the man, and that would be that. Have him call his wife and tell her he would be working late. That would give him some time before he was missed at home or work, more than enough to find out what he needed to know. A piece of cake.

He drove past the target's residence. Time to go home. To relax and to practice. The highlight of his day.

University Park, Maryland

Thorn logged onto UseNet and into the newsgroup Rec.sport.fencing, where there were sometimes interesting exchanges ranging from technique to politics. Threads—follow-ups that began with a single post—tended to stay on a subject for a while, assuming they weren't stupid to begin with or an insult to the FAQ (frequently asked questions). After twenty or fifty responses, if the original subject was sufficiently covered, then the postings in that thread tended to veer into other areas before dribbling to a stop.

In this group, people came to discuss the French versus the Italian grip; why the Spanish grip should be allowed in competition; or where to buy the best blades and furniture. Many of the people who wrote in were knowledgeable about all aspects of fencing. Some were tyros who didn't know an épée from an elephant. And some posters were flat-out trolls.

A troll was somebody who logged into a newsgroup and posted something provocative purely for the sake of generating attention or starting an argument. The term supposedly came from fishing, wherein lines were set to troll for fish. Some said it came from those mythical beasts who lived under bridges and menaced passers-by. Either way, a troll on UseNet was a waste of time and space. They were almost always anonymous, posting insults under screen names so as to be insulated from reprisals, and sometimes they went past merely being annoying to offering libel online.

Some trolls were more clever than simply shouting obscenities into the faces of anybody around; they would pose a question or comment in such a manner as to seem serious. But clever or merely loud, trolls were an annoying fact of net life.

Sometimes very annoying.

Thorn had attracted a couple of these pests in his years

on the net, both as a programmer and as a fencer, and
when he opened the thread on pistol-grip handles versus
straight-grips that now ran to forty-three messages, he
found that one of the more irritating trolls of recent
months was there, dogging him again.

Thorn had posted the question: *Has anybody had problems with tendonitis using the straight grip that switching
to a pistol grip has helped?*

There had been several helpful replies, a few more that
were interested, and, invariably, the idiot who tried to hi-
jack the thread to serve his own ends. The troll—he had
several pseudonyms he hid behind, but his current netnom
was "Rapier"—had entered the building:

*Tendonitis, Thorn? Must be you're gripping your blade
wrong. Or, wait. Maybe it's just that you're gripping the
wrong blade ;-)! Is that it, Thorn? So why don't you hire
somebody to give you that kind of attention? You can
afford it, a rich guy like you. . . .*

Thorn gritted his teeth. What was wrong with somebody that the only way he could get attention was to jump
up and down spitting and cursing at people, acting like a
two-year-old? *Look at me! Look at me! See how clever I
am?*

Unfortunately, yes, we see exactly *how clever you are.
Which isn't at all.*

Responding only made it worse. These fools didn't care
what you said, only that you said something—*anything*—
thus providing the attention they craved. The best way to
respond was to ignore it. "Don't feed the trolls" was the
advice that seasoned UseNetters gave to newbies. If nobody reacts, they leave.

Which, unfortunately, was not true of the really obnoxious ones. They simply changed their netnoms and came
back in a new disguise, looking to get your goat.

Generally, as soon as Thorn recognized a troll, he put
the name into his "kill" filter. From then on, that name
would be marked and he simply didn't open the postings.

Of course, every time a troll changed names, he would slip by for a message or two.

The anonymity of the net had given rise to tens of thousands of such losers. If they said those things to a man's face, they would be looking for their teeth, but safe in their homes at a keyboard they felt free to insult the world at large. Sad that this was all the life they had.

Thorn had a huge kill file of names, and one of the worst had used a dozen aliases in the last six months. It was the same guy. The writing style—such that it was—was easy to spot. The guy didn't shout by using all caps, and his grammar wasn't atrocious, but the snideness was definitive, and the speech patterns didn't vary. And here he was yet again.

Thorn sighed, then added "Rapier" to his kill file.

Somebody ought to do something about these idiots.

Even as he thought it, he had the realization: He was now in a position where he could do something. He was running Net Force.

He smiled and shook his head. Trolls weren't illegal. Irritating, obnoxious, sometimes even pitiful or outright psychotic, but there weren't any laws against that. If they actually threatened or libeled you, you could do something, but the smarter ones would avoid going that far. They'd step right up to the edge, but not past it. Innuendo, yes, and thinly veiled threats, but never enough to take them into court to squash.

There were ways to backtrack e-mail and postings, perfectly legal ones to run through an Internet service provider to bring to their attention that they had people misbehaving. Some of the larger ISPs would kick an offender off if they got enough complaints. But some of the smaller ones, especially those in third-world countries, didn't really care what their patrons did, as long as they paid their bills. Nigeria was notorious, all kinds of conmen ran schemes from there, the most famous being one about smuggling a large fortune out of the country and cutting in people who would help. A lot of folks had lost a lot of money on those schemes, even after they had been made public time and time again.

Clever trolls could hide their identities, and some of them used anonymous machines, at libraries or Internet cafes, so even if you tracked the computer down, you wouldn't catch them. If they were dangerous, you could install key-watch software and eventually nail them, but Net Force didn't chase trolls; if they did, they wouldn't have time for anything else.

Well, it was what it was, and you just had to shrug it off. It was tempting to drop the posting into Jay Gridley's lap and tell him to find the guy, though. Outing "Rapier" on the net would feel very satisfying. There were folks who, if they knew where the man lived, would drop by and have a few words with him.

Of course, the "man" could be a thirteen-year-old precocious brat using his mother's computer, and Thorn didn't want to be responsible for some irritated stranger kicking the crap out of him. Though it would be very satisfying to have the kid's mother do it. . . .

He smiled. Enough for today. Time to get to bed.

7

Washington, D.C.

Natadze picked up his guitar and moved to his playing chair, a specially made stool with a footrest built in at precisely the right height for him. He was in a T-shirt and sweatpants, and he had a sleeve, made from a silk sock with the toe end cut off, over his right arm, to keep his skin from touching the instrument. The sweatpants were elastic—no buttons or zippers, nothing that might scratch the wood.

He did not wear a watch or rings, and the only things that might possibly damage the fine finish were the fingernails on his right hand, which were kept long and filed carefully for plucking the strings. The nails on his left hand were trimmed very short, so as not to cause buzzing on the frets.

Classical guitar was a strict discipline, and that had appealed to Natadze even when he had been introduced to it as a boy. It needed a certain position, the left leg up, the instrument's waist on that leg, the lower bout just so, the left thumb always placed behind the neck, right hand relaxed here. . . .

This guitar had been made in 1967 by the luthier Daniel Friedrich, one of the most renowned guitar makers of the late twentieth century. At his peak, there had been a ten- or twelve-year waiting list for one of his new instruments, which was not that uncommon among the best makers. The top was German spruce, the back and sides Brazilian rosewood, the neck a standard 650-millimeter scale and 52 millimeters at the nut. The finish was French polish, the tuners by Rodgers, and it had been in almost mint condition when Natadze had bought it—paying forty thousand U.S. dollars for it.

A decent concert guitar could be had for a quarter of that. This was much better than decent, though. It was superb.

He was, he knew, not a good enough player to deserve such an instrument. Yes, he could play with sufficient skill so that he probably could have earned a meager living at it. He had a fair repertoire, several memorized pieces that ran more than twenty minutes, one that was almost half an hour without repeating sections, and he could manage a better-than-average tremolo when playing Fernando Sor, even though he was largely self-taught. But his music theory was only fair, his sight-reading still slow, and he resorted to tablature when he was in a hurry to learn a new piece.

Hard to justify the Friedrich, which had a powerful, almost haunting tone that would fill a concert hall, and was mostly played in Natadze's living room. Such an instrument should be in the hands of a world-class artist, somebody who could coax from it degrees of subtlety far beyond an amateur such as himself.

He had more than enough room to grow into it—he would never be good enough to fully utilize the guitar's capabilities, certainly not practicing just two or three hours a day as he did. But he had wanted it, and he could afford it, and so he had gotten it. He had owned beautiful instruments from other expert luthiers from around the world. He had Spanish, German, French, and Italian guitars locked away in a humidity- and temperature-controlled room in his house. The last few years, he had favored American makers—he had an Oribe, a Ruck, one by Byers, a particularly sweet-toned cedar-top from J. S. Bogdanovich that had been very reasonably priced—but this guitar had, in addition to its perfect craftsmanship and construction, a history. It had been played by some of the best guitarists ever. It had called to him the moment he touched it, he could feel the sense of history, and there had been no question that he would own it.

He settled himself upon the thin cushion on the stool. He did not need a back support, since he would sit completely upright throughout the session. One did not lean back while playing classical style.

He had his electronic tuner on the music stand in front of him, though he could tune to A440 by ear after all these years. He had experimented with various combinations of strings over the years, but found that medium-tension La Bella's worked well, though some of the newer composites lasted longer.

He smiled. When you had a forty-thousand-dollar guitar, buying new strings was not a major expense.

He tuned the instrument, plucked an E-major chord, belled all six string harmonics on the twelfth fret, and was satisfied with the sound.

He began with his warm-up pieces, simple airs he had known since he had started playing: Bach's "Bouree in E-minor," the traditional Spanish piece, "Romanza," Pachelbel's "Canon in D."

Then he played McCartney's "Blackbird." Hardly classical, but a simple way to be sure he wasn't being sloppy and squeaking the bass strings. Besides, it was fun, more so than scales or *barres* up and down the neck. Now and again, he would play down-and-dirty blues, too, and while they sounded much nastier on a dobro steel body, it was amazing how well they came out of this guitar. Not as if it were sacrilege to play other kinds of music on such an instrument, though some classical players would argue that it was.

He smiled, and went to work on the new piece, one by Chopin. He hated Chopin, but he was determined to learn it anyway. A man had to stretch now and then.

All thoughts of work, of anything other than the music, left him as he became one with the guitar of which he knew he was unworthy.

Cox Estates
Long Island, New York

Most of the time, Cox stayed in the city until the weekend; he had an apartment in Manhattan, an entire floor in an exclusive co-op overlooking the park. His neighbors there were senators and Broadway producers and old oil money. He also had his current mistress, a delightful woman of thirty-four, installed in a brownstone, and if he didn't feel like going that far, could make do in what amounted to a small apartment down the hall from his office. But now and then, he'd have his chauffeur haul him out to the estate during the week, just for a change. Sometimes Laura would be there, more often not—she was active in a dozen different charities, ran a foundation that gave grant money to starving artists, and went to see the children and grandchildren with some frequency, most of whom lived within a couple of hours of here. She had her own place in the city, and, likely as not, she would be there during the week as well—as apparently she was this evening, for she was not home.

The house was much too large for just them—thirty rooms, not counting the baths, but when you were a billionaire in a mansion, servants were a given. Even when Laura was gone there would be a dozen people there—a butler, cooks, maids, gardeners, security and maintenance people, his driver.

Now, as he sat in his home office, a room paneled in half-inch hand-rubbed and waxed pecan, with a desk made from flame maple and a couple million dollars worth of paintings by various Flemish masters on the walls, Cox looked at what appeared to be a rubber stamp, and allowed himself to gloat a little.

The silicone stamp was that of a human thumbprint.

A man in his position made a few enemies along the way. When you sat at the top of the heap, the climbers who would take your place were always scrabbling their way upward, hoping you would fall, and willing to push you if you didn't.

Among the business rivals were some fairly vicious men, and one of them, Hans Willem Vaughan, of Sansome Petroleum, was particularly nasty. They had clashed more than once over the years, and finally Cox had grown tired of allowing it to happen without a response.

To attack him directly would have been dicey. But Vaughan had a weakness. He was extremely proud of the fact that his best people were beyond reproach; they were morally upright, none of them had ever been arrested, all were absolutely squeaky clean, honest, and loyal.

That was about to change. Or at least, it would seem to change, which was just as good.

Eduard had obtained the fingerprints of a third-level functionary in Vaughan's organization. The man was an assistant to an assistant, a nobody, but he had access to certain sensitive material, and, like Caesar's wife, needed to be above suspicion.

In a few days, this functionary, a married man with children, was going to be revealed as a sex addict, and not only that, a bisexual one who slept with dozens of men and women on a regular basis, who had somehow managed to divert funds from somewhere into his personal accounts, and who was living much larger than he legally could.

It was a carefully crafted lie, of course; as far as Cox could tell, the man was as honest and faithful as the Arctic summer nights were long. To no avail.

Eduard would have seen to every detail—he was like that, niggling to a fault—and a trail would have been laid that, once seen, could be followed by a nearsighted bloodhound with no sense of smell. Large cash deposits to a secret account, hotel and restaurant bills, visits to private clubs wherein hetero- or homosexual liaisons were the main business, visits to known brothels, records at call-girl organizations, massage parlors, the works, would all come to light. Some of it might be explainable to sympathetic ears, perhaps, but the entry and exit records on security computers vouched for by the man's own fingerprints? It would be hard to explain those away.

How is it, sir, that computer records showed you entered Fifi's House of Pleasure at three in the afternoon and stayed until three in the morning? Does somebody else have your thumbprint, sir? Using your name? Fitting your description, right down to the mole on your thigh, sir? Sir?

The weight of the evidence would be very heavy.

Eduard had been very careful about faking this man's attendance at these places only during times when the man had no reasonable alibi to show he had been elsewhere.

In the end, the target of these machinations would be ruined, and too bad for him, but that was not the point. He was within the group of Vaughan's workers known as the Incorruptibles. And obviously as corrupt as all get-out.

At this level of the game, the appearance was more important than the reality. It would not be a fatal, or even particularly damaging, blow; Vaughan's business would not be affected, save for a point or three dip in the price of his corporate stock for a few hours, if that. But that wasn't the goal. The goal was to wound the bastard where he was the most smug. To show the world that he wasn't infallible. A chink in the armor, however small, would do that.

Like a single drop of black paint in a vat of white, not even visible to the human eye, Vaughan's organization would henceforth forever be ever-so-slightly *gray*. And he, Cox, would know that he had been responsible. He would never let on. Gloating over his rival's misfortune? Never—not in public, at least. He would be sympathetic in the extreme if it ever came up. What a shame. Nothing is sacred anymore, is it? What's the world coming to? Tsk, tsk.

Cox leaned back in his chair and smiled at the image of Vaughan being interviewed on national television, defending himself for the actions of an employee that he likely couldn't remember, if he had ever even *met* him.

Of course, Cox had his own worry, and it was much worse than some flunky he employed being caught with his pants down, but Eduard was on that, and Eduard was his man, to the bone. Somehow, Cox had always won the day, and he was beginning to feel as if he was going to win this day, too.

Net Force Shooting Range
Quantico, Virginia

Abe Kent found his way to the shooting range. It was late, but the range was open until 2200.

"Good evening, sir," the range officer said. He did not salute—they didn't hold with that indoors and uncovered unless the setting was deliberately more formal, but the man did straighten up to what might be called attention.

"At ease, Master Sergeant. I haven't had a chance to

get by sooner, but I wanted to introduce myself and see how your operation is set up here."

"Sir. Pretty standard stuff. We have twenty lanes, backstops are tank-grade armor plate behind fire-resistant treated polywood baffles, the armor angled to kick spent rounds down into a steel trench filled with fire-retardant. We can handle small arms, pistol, subgun, and rifles, as long as they are non–armor-piercing and in calibers less than .50 BMG. Our targeting computer system is an Ares Mark V, full-spectrum holographics with positional sensors. Runs pretty well most of the time. We use the Martin Ring system for all issue arms. Is that your personal sidearm, sir?"

Kent shook his head. "Not likely I would be hauling it around if it wasn't, is it, Sergeant?"

The man grinned. "An old slabside like that, I know it's not issue."

"It was when my grandfather carried it."

"Regulations say you have to keep your carry arm coded to the ring, Colonel. I can issue you a Beretta in nine or four-oh and a matching broadcast code-ring, or, if you want, I can convert the Colt for you."

"I think I'll stick with the forty-five."

"Yes, sir. You going to shoot while you're here?"

Kent considered that for a moment. "Yes, I believe I will. It's been a while."

"Sir." The man produced a box of forty-five hardball. "You want headphones or the plugs?"

"Headphones will be fine."

"Take lane five. It's quiet this time of night, only a couple other shooters here. If you leave the Colt with me when you go, I'll have it ready tomorrow. You can take a loaner—I've got a SIG in .45, if you like the caliber."

"That would be fine, Top."

"Everybody still calls me 'Gunny,' sir."

Kent headed for the lanes, donning his headphones to

block out the noise before he stepped through the sound-proof door.

He walked down to lane five.

In lane six was Lieutenant Fernandez. The younger man saw him, nodded, and kept firing until his gun clicked dry.

"Evening, sir."

"Lieutenant. You're here late."

"Sir. My wife took my son to visit an old friend, and she's out of town for a few days. Since I got married, I lost interest in my own cooking, so I figured I might as well get some practice in before I stopped for Chinese take-out."

Kent nodded. His wife had died six years ago, and he had never really thought about getting remarried. He'd had a few dates, but being single suited him okay—nobody would ever be able to replace Christine.

There was a pause. Fernandez said, "You pretty good with that old Colt, sir?"

"I manage to qualify passing scores now and then."

Fernandez grinned.

"Something funny, Lieutenant?"

"Well, sir, in my position as General Howard's good right arm, I had occasion to view the Colonel's personnel file when it came through."

"I see."

"Just the public record stuff, sir."

"And your point, son?"

"You and General Howard have something in common. He carries a sidearm whose design was old before he was born, too, though I finally managed to get him to upgrade a little. Your comment about your shooting ability sounds a lot like a pool hustler's setup, sir, since I happen to know you qualified 'Expert' with that antique you carry."

Kent couldn't help but smile a little at that one. He said, "And as your new commanding officer, I also had occasion to read your file, Lieutenant—all of it, including the nonpublic material. I know you can shoot that Beretta at 'Expert' level, as well."

"I guess that makes us even, sir."

"Only on paper, Lieutenant." He nodded downrange.

Fernandez grinned real big at that. "I wouldn't want to embarrass the Colonel his first time at the range, sir."

"I wouldn't worry about that, son, not in the least. Let's see what you got."

"Yes, sir."

8

Thorn sighed and stared into space. It looked as if today was going to be one of remedial education. He'd had two visitors so far, and both of them had more or less made him feel stupid—something to which he was not the least bit accustomed.

First, it had been the CIA liaison Marissa Lowe, who had dropped by to check on Jay's progress with the Turkish thing. The conversation had started off fine, he really liked her, but then he had ventured to say something that, in retrospect, wasn't particularly bright.

He had mentioned that his gripe with Senator Herumin of New Jersey, who had been blathering on that morning on the news about something to do with computers, was that the man was unable to see the big picture. This was a problem he had run into before, he told her.

Folks didn't understand that it was something of a curse to be able to see such things, as Thorn himself could. It really wasn't easy at times.

He was half-joking as he said it, but only half, and she picked it up like an oyster cracker dropped into the middle of a flock of hungry ducks.

"Are you complaining about being smart and fore-sighted, Tommy?"

Surprised, all he could think of to say was, "No."

She sighed. "Yes, you are." She shook her head.

"Marissa . . ."

"Let me tell you a story, Commander. One of my study partners in college got into your business, sort of. He was a brilliant dude, sharp, funny, majored in English lit, be-came a professor at an Ivy League school, wrote a couple of well-received textbooks, was doing okay. Let's call him 'Barry.' "

"Okay," Thorn said, though he wasn't sure where this was going.

"So, Barry got married, had a couple of kids, a dog, and was living a solid middle-class life. When he was about thirty-five, Barry discovered he had a talent for coming up with video game scenarios. One thing led to another, and the next thing you know, he's quit his job teaching, moved to Texas—Austin used to be a real hot-bed for that kind of thing—and he started making big bucks coming up with things like Death Eater and Moon Fighters."

Thorn blinked. He knew those old games, he'd played them in college. He didn't recall the creator's name, but he did seem to remember there was something about the guy . . .

"All of a sudden, within the space of a year, he goes from being a dull young college professor, to a hot, rich computer whiz. He and the old spouse split—he's way too cool for her—so now he's on his own. He turns around in a few months and marries a gorgeous high-maintenance trophy wife. He starts buying other toys—big house, fast cars, home theaters. Thinks nothing of dropping a couple hundred bucks on lunch, he's blowin' and goin', partying all night, sleeping half the day, working an hour or two in the afternoon. He's a golden boy, and can't do wrong."

Thorn nodded. He'd met plenty of guys like that.

"We kept in touch, Barry and I. He was basically a nice guy, but he had this one little flaw that used to drive me crazy: He was a whiner."

She shook her head, frowning. "I'd get a call from him whenever somebody opened a car door in a parking lot and put a scratch in the side of his new Ferrari. Or if the idiots at the game company wanted him to do some little thing that was beneath his talent. His Christmas bonus was only a hundred grand and he was expecting *two* hundred. And you know what he'd say after he'd lay this on me? 'Why is my life so much harder than everybody else's?' "

Thorn stared at her.

"I mean, here's Barry, he's clearing better than half a million a year, six, seven times what I'm bringing home *before* taxes. He's got a sultry young wife who steams up every room she walks into. He's got a Ferrari, a Viper, a Porsche, and a Rolls in his garage—and room for two more cars. He has a pool and a maid and gardeners and personal trainers coming to his home gym, he's got every toy he ever wanted. He plays stupid *games,* and makes more money than the President of the United States."

Thorn had to smile at that one.

She continued: "I've been in third-world countries where the average wage was twenty dollars a month. I know people in this country who would kill for any *one* of Barry's perks, and he's got 'em *all*, but he's whining and complaining about how hard his life is." She let that sink in.

When nothing else was forthcoming, Thorn said, "All right. So he didn't really have anything to complain about. So?"

"So? Right after he turned thirty-nine, he started having trouble breathing. Turned out he had developed some rare

form of emphysema—and he never smoked a single cigarette. Six months later, he couldn't move without having
to wheel around a bottle of oxygen. The game industry
had another revolution and the stuff he was writing went
into the toilet. He couldn't come up with any new ideas
that worked. He lost his big house, the cars, the hired help.
His high-maintenance wife bailed without a backward
look. Barry wound up filing for bankruptcy. Moved back
in with his parents. So here he is, on his fortieth birthday,
and he's gone from being rich and on top of the world,
to he can't walk to the mailbox without having to stop
and rest. He's broke, he's alone. And the kicker is—none
of it is his fault. He couldn't control any of it."

She shook her head again. "The point, Tommy? The
point is, *now* he's got something to whine about. Now his
life *is* harder than everybody else's."

"Yeah."

"You don't want to tempt fate, Tommy. You never
know but that God might be taking a coffee break and He
will hear you complaining and give you something to
show you the difference between nice Italian shoes and
no feet."

Thorn smiled and nodded. "Point taken."

"Good. Maybe there's hope for you. Listen, I hate to
slap your hand and then run, but I have to go. You take
care, all right?"

After she had gone, Thorn had thought about what
she'd said. She wasn't an intellectual, but despite the fact
that he probably had twenty IQ points on her, she had
nailed him dead on. Which made you stop and think.

Then, not five minutes later, Colonel Kent had stopped
by, and because that bored deity must still have been
hanging around, God had helped Thorn put his foot back
into his mouth again. There were a few problems, the
colonel had said, but he was working on them.

He had finished his report, and was about to leave.
Thorn said, "Don't worry, Colonel, I know you haven't

had time to bring in your own people yet and get up to cruising speed. I know you have to work with the tools you have, and sometimes they just won't cut it."

The ex-Marine blinked and looked at him as if he had just turned into a giant beetle. "No, sir, that's not valid."

Thorn shook his head. What had he said? He was just trying to give the guy a way to save face, and now the man was busting his chops? "I'm not sure I take your meaning, Colonel."

"Sir, with all due respect, a man who blames his tools is a poor workman. You recall that sniper in Colorado a couple years back? Shot sixteen people in the space of a couple of days?"

"I remember."

"Do you recall how he was stopped?"

Thorn searched his memory. "Shot by a civilian, wasn't he? A farmer?"

"Yes, sir. Only the civilian was Duane Morris, a retired Marine, a twenty-year man, and a former member of the USMC pistol team. He drove his pickup truck into Denver to collect a relative at the train station, so he was across the street when the killer got out of his car with his assault rifle.

"Soon as he saw the shooter, retired Master Sergeant Morris jumped back into his car and pulled out a Thirty-eight Special snubnose revolver he kept under the seat there. This gun has crappy sights, no more than a groove on the top strap, a two-inch barrel, and is generally thought to be ineffective past across-the-table range by a lot of folks. Outside of five yards, they say, you might as well *throw* it as shoot it, because you will more likely hit your target that way. It would not be the weapon of choice in a long-range gun duel.

"Sergeant Morris stepped out of his vehicle just as the shooter cranked off his first round, taking a fourteen-year-old-boy in the leg. He snapped that snubby up, and as he did, the killer saw him and swung his rifle around to take him down. Morris aimed and fired before the killer could get off a second round, and his bullet impacted the scumbag in the forehead, an inch to the left of being centered right between the eyes. Dropped him dead before he hit the pavement."

Thorn nodded. "Yes. And . . . ?"

"Morris was sixty-four years old, wearing glasses as thick as Coke bottle bottoms, using a tool not designed for the task at hand. The investigating police officers paced off the distance between Morris and the sniper. Fifty-eight yards. That, sir, was one hell of a wide tabletop. Easy with a rifle, not quite as easy with a long-barreled target pistol with a scope, highly unusual with a gun having a pipe just a hair longer than the middle joint of your forefinger. A fluke, a lot of folks said, but it was not. Morris practiced with that little handgun often. He could hit a pie plate at fifty yards all day long. The tool had the capability, and the man using it had the ability to use it properly. That's what made the difference."

Thorn nodded. "All right. I see your point."

"Yes, sir. I hope so. We have the tools. The main limiting factors are the people we set to use them. Properly taught, they can accomplish any job we need accomplished. If I can't cut a piece of string with the knife I'm holding, then I need to sharpen it, not blame the knife for being dull."

Once *he* was gone, Thorn decided that maybe it might be a good time to go to the gym. However, given the way his day was running so far, he might just stab himself in the foot. He shook his head. Well. He certainly hadn't impressed these folks with his wit and wisdom today, had he? Maybe he'd better cancel his appointments and stay in his office where he wouldn't say or do anything foolish for the rest of the day.

Washington, D.C.

Jay readied his assault on Hugo Hellbinder's secret base from behind a fat-boled banana tree. The infrared laser of his silenced .45 HK Mark-23 painted the hapless guard to the left of the entrance with a foreshadowing dot that Jay, with his specialized night-vision gear, could see, but was otherwise invisible to the human eye.

The guard on the left had to go first because he was closest to the alarm. There'd be maybe a second or two to take the other guard out after the first fell. No problem.

The humid night air of the jungle was warm and full of distractions. One of the guards slapped at a mosquito, and the other leaned over to tie his shoe.

Now . . .

Jay took the shot.

There was a soft *whap* as the subsonic .45 hit the unfortunate guard on the left, the invisible infrared giving way to hot blood as the guard's spine shattered. The other guard cried out, "What? Not *me!*" He started to roll to the side, his animation flexing slightly as he blended into the wall behind him for a second before Jay's second shot ended his worries.

Sorry, pal. The rules of the game. Spear-carriers get wiped out fast.

He'd lifted the scenario from an old vid he'd played as a teenager, one of his favorite spy games. The weapons, the sounds, even the imagery—including the occasional computer-glitch blending of enemies with the landscape—was just as he'd remembered it.

It should be, after all the time I spent reverse-engineering it.

Sure, he *could* be using VR to simulate some static mind puzzle, some way of more accurately mirroring the RW activity he was engaged in, but as always, that wouldn't be nearly as much fun.

He readied himself for the rush to the entrance. There

was a camera on the inside of the doorway—it had warned them he was sneaking in on one of his early attempts. A quick shot upward before stepping through the door, and it'd be gone. Then he'd work his way back to the underground bridge, to see if he could fight his way across.

Sooner or later he'd complete the game mission and at that point, the second part of the code would be cracked. In theory.

He retraced his steps perfectly, taking out guards and cameras, not missing a shot. Everything was going well until, abruptly, the scenario froze.

So did Jay.

A doorway opened into the space, right in the middle of the bridge. Time stalled: Bullets hung frozen in the air, a guard tilted at a forty-five-degree angle in the process of falling, his video-game body painted with pixelated blood.

Through the door stepped Saji.

He frowned—she *never* bothered him at work—particularly when his don't-call-me was on. She was one of only two people who *could.* He'd given the codes only to Alex and Saji.

I'll have to remember to give them to the new guy, he thought, before he wondered what was so important that she would actually *use* the access codes.

Something wrong? Somebody sick? Or, worse, somebody dead?

There was certainly *something.* She had that look to her, a determined set to her VR character.

"This is nice," she said in a voice that meant exactly the opposite. She waved at the frozen blood spray from the back of the guard.

"I'll put something else on." Jay started to switch to a more neutral scenario, but she shook her head.

"I've got one," she said, indicating her doorway.

He followed her and stepped into a zen garden. There

were rocks, bonsai trees, and a beautiful stream gurgling in the background.

The detail was amazing. A mosquito buzzed by, and was eaten by a bird that swooped down to catch it. Eddies and currents in the stream moved in endless, almost-random patterns. A cool breeze touched his cheek, and the smell of pine needles wafted over him.

She indicated a bench, and he sat on it, a smooth wooden surface that had been there so long that the front edge had been worn smooth.

"Nice VR. This is great—even I don't usually get this detailed. Where'd you get it?"

She smiled, and his heart stilled for a moment—if she could still smile at him like that, the news couldn't be that bad.

Unless she's dying. She did have a doctor's appointment today.

His stomach lurched.

"I'm glad you like it—it's mine."

He almost forgot to be worried. Saji had done this? Where had she been hiding her abilities? The VR they'd worked through during his therapy had never been this sharp. This was *good*.

"Really?"

She laughed. "Yes really. It's my meditation spot. I've worked on it for years."

"It's great," he said. "Amazing. Really."

She grinned. "Glad that the top VR jock at Net Force approves!"

Then: "Because I've got something to tell you."

This was it. What could be this important? What could be such serious news that she'd come to work and get him—in VR—and show him her most private meditation?

"Saji? Is everything okay? Are you all right?"

"I'm fine. You might need to take a deep breath, though."

"Me?"

His face must have shown his confusion, because she smiled, and then took his hand. "Well, yeah. You're going to be a father."

He felt an immense sense of relief—she was *okay*—

And then: *Me? A father?*

It was like being hit in the head with a hammer.

He realized she was waiting for him to say something—anything.

"Wow," he said, stunned. "I mean, *wow!*" he added, putting some excitement into the word. "That's . . . that's . . . *great!*" He grinned.

Saji seemed relieved. She grinned back at him.

She took his hand and squeezed it.

"I wanted to wait until you got home, but I just couldn't. I'm so excited, Jay! We're going to have a baby!"

He grinned back at her, enjoying her excitement.

He wasn't completely sure about his own, but he knew he'd rather take this leap with her than anyone else.

A baby. He was going to be a father. Whoa. Talk about unreal scenarios.

9

Risks were unavoidable in Eduard Natadze's line of work. He knew that and accepted that. What he would not accept were unnecessary risks—especially those caused by sloppiness or overconfidence.

He expected no trouble from his current target. He knew Jay Gridley's habits backward and forward, and knew that the computer jock posed no challenge for him. But still he took no chances.

He had made sure that he was not carrying a photo of Jay Gridley, or anything else that would connect him to Net Force's top computer jock. The only thing he did carry was an electronic receiver, but even that was simply a standard player with a couple of nonstandard tunings he could wipe with a touch. He didn't expect to be stopped and searched—they did not do such things here in America—but still, he took no chances. Besides, he did not need any photos. He had already studied his quarry and would know the man when he saw him. He would recognize the automobile the man drove, its license number, and he knew all the likely routes from Net Force HQ to Jay's home.

He was prepared, at least insofar as he could foresee any problems. He had a transmitter on Jay's car, a bug stuck under the vehicle's rear bumper with a powerful magnet, out of sight, to be sure he wouldn't miss him. He knew where his target was going. If he lost Jay before they reached the operations area, he would just hurry to the secondary pickup point and catch him there.

Natadze was two hours early, just in case, and parked in a place where no one would bother him, in a lot outside a shopping area. He wore a fake moûstache, not an obvious one, a pair of thick-rimmed glasses, and had a Band-Aid on his chin, all things that a potential witness would notice, and none of which would be any use to authorities. He would not have to keep a close watch; the bug would tell him as the man approached. It was, as the basketball players said, a slam dunk.

As he waited, Natadaze mentally played a favorite guitar piece, Tarrega's "Recuerdos de la Alhambra," a composition generally used to separate the men from the boys when it came to demonstrations of tremolo virtuosity, that multiple strum on a single string with machinelike speed and precision. He liked Eduardo Fernandez's version, perhaps because they shared a similar first name. Certainly he was not in that man's class when it came to execution, but on a good day, he could get through it without too many bobbles. And, of course, in one's imagination, there were no dropped or slurred notes, no nail noises or string squeaks.

It was much easier to be perfect in the theater of the mind.

Jay was still not quite able to get his thoughts around the concept of being a father. Yes, they had discussed it in theoretical terms, but the sudden and unexpected reality of it was simply too slippery to grasp.

Him. Jay Gridley. Some small person looking up at him, holding out his arms, saying, "Daddy, Daddy, pick me up!"

The term "mind-boggling" was way too mild. This was astounding. Earth-shaking. A tsunami of emotion.

When he passed the gate, the on-duty guard may have waved—Jay didn't notice. He was running on autopilot, replaying the scenario with Saji over and over again, trying to put it into perspective. He kept enough of his attention on the road, once he started driving, so as not to hit anybody, but traffic patterns on the way home were the least of his concerns.

A child was a major responsibility. He knew he didn't have a clue about how it would really be, but it seemed like, all of a sudden, his life was going to change in major ways, and that was a disquieting idea. He liked to keep things under control, to have a handle on life, and a baby was a variable that might not be so easy to deal with.

A baby. A little human being that he and Saji would make. It was an amazing thing every time he came at it again.

He was halfway home, on a slow stretch of road with lots of stop-and-go traffic, red lights, creeping along as fast as maybe twenty-five before he had to slow down again. A car in the next lane suddenly swerved in front of him and slammed on its brakes.

Jay shook himself from his mental fugue. He hit his own brakes and skidded off onto the shoulder, heading toward a call box on the side of the road.

Jay screeched to a halt, barely missing both the call box

and the other car. The other driver pulled to a quick stop in front of him. Breathing hard, feeling the sudden sweat on his palms, Jay got his first good look at the other car.

It was a dark maroon full-sized sedan. As it rocked to a halt, the driver's door opened and the driver hopped out. A medium-sized man with a moustache, he wore black glasses and a bandage on his chin. He was dressed in jeans and a sweatshirt.

The guy's expression was bland. Jay couldn't tell if he was coming to apologize or to take a swing at him, but he undid his seat belt and opened his own door.

Then he noticed that the man heading his way had a gun in his hand, held low by his leg.

For a heartbeat, Jay froze.

He had long ago been issued a taser, a high-voltage hit from which would knock a pro wrestler on his butt, but it was in a drawer at the office.

He had enough presence of mind to grab his virgil and thumb in the emergency code, even though Net Force would never be able to get anybody here in time to do Jay any good. Then he slammed his door shut and threw the car into reverse.

The gun man was ten feet away as he spun the wheel and stomped on the gas pedal—

Rubber burned, smoke spewed from the spinning tires. The car slewed sideways, glancing off the call box behind him with a solid *clunk*—

The gunman raised the revolver and pointed it at Jay—

The hole in the barrel looked as big as a cannon—

The man lurched, as if he had lost his balance, and fired—

The windshield starred, and the world went red.

Net Force HQ
Quantico, Virginia

Somebody ran into Thorn's office in a big hurry. The man in uniform said, "Sir, we have a distress beacon. General Howard and Colonel Kent are in Situation Control and they request your presence immediately!"

Thorn followed the man.

In SC, a room he had seen but never been in, people were busy. He saw both John Howard and Abe Kent, on handheld Coms.

Kent was closer. "Colonel?" Thorn said.

Kent waved him to silence. "Yes, yes, got it."

Across the room, Colonel John Howard looked up from his Com and over at Kent. "Two minutes ETA, General."

"Copy," Howard said. He went back to his Com.

Kent discommed and turned to Thorn. "Sir. Jay Gridley's distress beacon was activated two minutes ago. That spot, there, on the computer holoproj, that's his location."

Thorn looked at the map. "That's only a couple of miles from here. On the road."

"Yes, sir. We have a copter with a tactical team on the way."

"A car wreck?"

"Unknown, sir. But it's nearly impossible to trigger the virgil's beacon by accident, and protocol says you don't do it unless it is life or death. General Howard is on the horn with the state patrol."

Thorn nodded. "All right." Not much else he could do. This was the military arm's area of expertise. Best he not get in their way.

Howard discommed and came over to where Thorn and Kent stood.

"Commander. VSP is en route. No reports from the scene yet. We don't have a sat in position to footprint it. Our team will be there in a minute. All we can do is wait."

"This happen very often?" Thorn asked.

"No, sir," Howard said. "It's not something Gridley would have done for a minor accident."

"Lord. I hope he's all right."

"Yes, sir," Howard said. "Me, too."

In his car, leaving the scene, Natadze cursed long and loud in his native Georgian. The smell of gunpowder clung to his clothes, sharp and acrid. His ears still rang—he hadn't worn plugs, there wasn't supposed to be any shooting.

Damnation! It had gone so unbelievably wrong. He hadn't expected the man to try to run—it was not in his character, he was a photon pusher, a desk jockey. As soon as he saw the gun, he should have turned into a stalked rabbit and been unable to think. He didn't have anywhere to go, anyhow, the box had been almost perfect—

He had aimed at the front tire, to try and stop the car, but in an incredible bit of bad luck, at that exact instant, he had stepped on something on the shoulder of the road, a rock, a crushed can, something—and his ankle had buckled just as he fired. The gun went off on the upswing as he tried to regain his balance, and he saw the windshield take the round, saw it crack as if in slow motion, saw the subject's head snap to the side as the bullet or some fragment of it hit him. Saw blood welling. Stood there stunned long enough for Jay's car, his foot still spasming on the accelerator, to lurch around and into traffic and get T-boned by a pick-up truck, which was then rear-ended by an SUV. Tires squealed, traffic snarled to a stop, and Natadze's chance to grab his target was over.

He shook his head, disgusted with himself.

Hauling a dead or dying man away made no sense. The subject wouldn't be doing any code work, but neither was he going to be telling anybody what he had learned. Natadze had failed.

He was screwed. He had to get out of here before the authorities showed up. He quickly tucked the gun away—most people wouldn't know what they had seen, but he couldn't hang around long enough for anybody to regain their wits.

Quickly, quietly, he got in his car and drove off.

Kent took the call from the tac team, and he put it on the speaker:

"Sir, Operative Gridley has been wounded, looks like a single gunshot to the head. A lot of blood, he is unconscious, but still alive. Our medic says vital signs are stable. We are in the air en route to the nearest medical facility, ETA three minutes."

"Copy, Sergeant. Continue."

"No sign of the shooter. The state police arrived as we lifted, and Corporal Scates remained on-site as liaison. I can patch him in—"

"Not necessary, Sergeant. Tender sitreps as necessary."

"Sir."

Kent looked at Howard and Thorn.

Howard looked grim. "I'd better call Saji," Howard said. To Thorn's blank look, he said, "Gridley's wife."

"Ah."

Well, wasn't this a great way to end the day? One of his people shot by some loon in a fit of road rage. Thorn shook his head and moved over to a corner. It was going to be a long wait.

10

In the back of the limo, the hour long past dark and late, Cox stared at Eduard, stunned by his news. The limo was secure, swept for bugs daily, and it was just the two of them, parked in Cox's ten-car garage.

"You *shot* him?"

"A mistake," Natadze said. "It should not have happened."

"You are damned straight about that! My God, Eduard!"

Natadze nodded. "I am sorry."

Cox sighed. "Is he dead?"

"Unknown. He was hit in the head. If he lives, he will not be doing any work in the near future."

Cox glared at him. "Oh, yeah, that'll work out great! Every time Net Force brings in another replacement, you just shoot him in the head! That won't make them suspicious at all!"

"I am sorry," Natadze said again. "The error was entirely mine. I will find a way to rectify it."

Cox shook his head. No point in beating a dead horse, done was done. And at the least, Eduard was right—a man shot in the head wasn't likely to be doing much in the way of code-breaking anytime soon. Bullets in the brain tended to interfere with things like that.

And Cox doubted that anybody would make the connection to what Jay was working on—as far as anybody knew, it was a case of some driver being pissed off at another and unloading on him. That's what it had said on the news. It happened all the time. The U.S. of A. was a violent society, and armed out the wazoo. You never knew if some crazy was going to step out of his vehicle and start shooting because you didn't use your turn signal when you changed lanes.

"All right," Cox said. "Find out about his condition, follow up and see what's what. See if you can figure out who will take over for him. Get what you can, then we'll decide what to do from there."

"Yes, sir."

Natadze looked so miserable Cox felt a need to cheer him up. "Don't take it so hard, Eduard. Mistakes happen. That's why they put erasers on the ends of pencils. It's not the end of the world. Let's learn from our errors and move on."

"You are too kind, Mr. Cox."

Nobody had ever accused him of that before. He had to smile at the thought. Well. At least his secret was safe for a little while longer. Like the folks from AA said, you had to take it one day at a time. In the end—well, in the end, everybody was dead. Getting as far as you could before that happened was kind of the point, wasn't it?

After Eduard was gone, Cox went to have a drink. Once again, he had the house to himself, save for the servants, and given the recent events, that was probably just as well. He doubted that he would be particularly good company tonight.

Brooklyn, New York

Midnight had come and gone, and Natadze stood in the rented machine shop in Brooklyn, alone. The place was small, but it had more than sufficient tools for his needs. He had arranged to use it after hours, and it was costing him a thousand dollars, more money down the drain, but it was necessary.

First, he used a screwdriver to disassemble the Korth. He shook his head as he did so, marveling at the fitting. You could hardly see the joins in the revolver, so carefully fitted and polished they were. He disassembled the weapon to the frame and component parts. Then he clamped the barrel into a vise and used a hacksaw to render it into two shorter sections. It was hard work—he wore out a blade, had to replace it halfway through, and pretty much ruined the second one, too. The Rockwell on the weapon had to be around sixty. He developed a healthy sweat sawing on the thing.

A double penance. He would also miss guitar practice tonight to deal with this.

There was a heavy steel crucible, lined with some kind of protective ceramic. He put on heavy gloves, a welder's mask, and lit the oxyacetylene torch. He fined the flame down and it was but the work of a few seconds to reduce the wooden stocks to ash. He dumped in the smaller parts—screws, springs, and so forth, which melted slowly under the steady play of the pale fire, flaring now and then as they went from dull red to cherry and yellow-orange to blue-white and then fluid.

To this, he added the barrel segments, the frame, and the cylinder. It took a lot longer to finish these, especially the fat cylinder—this was not a smelter, and not what the torch was designed for, but it developed enough heat to do the job, eventually. When the steel was roiling liquid, he shut the torch off and poured this into three small molds that looked like pyramids with their tops sheared off.

When the molds had cooled sufficiently, he removed the blocks of steel, and put them into a water trough to steam and hiss and cool further.

He took the little chunks of steel and put them into a small leather sack. A five-thousand-dollar handgun, reduced to high-grade scrap metal.

Nobody would be comparing rifling patterns to any bullets fired from the Korth.

He would cautiously and carefully drop these blocks into the East River later, where they would spend however many thousands of years it took before they rusted away. Even if they were found, nobody would ever be able to connect them to a weapon used to shoot a federal agent. Just more junk at the bottom of the river, good for nothing, of no concern to anyone.

What an awful shame it was to do such a thing to a weapon like the Korth.

On the Beach Primeval

Jay stood in the sand, watching the surf come in. Everything was gorgeous: The waves lapping at the shoreline were a deep blue, the sun overhead gave the sand a glow that made it seem pure gold, and a gentle breeze caressed his skin.

After a few moments, he realized he must be in VR.

This is too good—it's got no teeth.

The phrase had originated with his instructor in VR 101, an undergrad course that had been new when he'd been in college. The old man had always said it: "Reality bites. Nothing is perfect. Remember that."

Even the most beautiful beaches had sand mites, stinking seaweed, or rotting fish that marred their perfection.

A good VR programmer would include details like this,
little teeth, to at least nibble a bit at a VR viewer and thus
make it seem more real. Well, except for fantasy VR
guys—in those, reality wasn't *supposed* to bite.

Had he accidentally jacked into someone else's datastream? Grabbed an old datafile he'd used for research by
mistake?

He reached out with his mind, flicking the off switch
which would take him out of the scenario.

Nothing happened.

He frowned. What was going on?

Had his hardware glitched? Maybe an interface problem? The neural stimulators were so good these days it
was possible to forget you *had* a body. One of the new
guys he'd hired over the summer had gotten stuck one
day when he'd removed the safety and alarm on his stims.
That was strictly forbidden, and hard to do without some
skill. The poor kid might have stayed there all day if he
hadn't had a dentist appointment and they'd called looking for him. Jay had done a hardware shutdown to pull
him out of the figure eight. A bit of bad programming
that could have been serious, and a lesson learned: Don't
shut off the safeties.

While Jay didn't run his stims that high, he *did* get
focused so intently that the effect was sometimes the
same.

Well. No matter, he'd break it off now.

He focused on becoming aware of his body; he reached
out to feel his index finger, crooking it slightly toward the
cutout sensor he knew was there.

Got it. . . .

But once again, nothing happened. The scene stayed
on, the waves lapped inward, and a few seagulls, their
feathers pearly white, flew by overhead.

Well.

Whatever was happening definitely had his attention
now. He'd been feeling a little funny, kind of unfocused

when the scenario started, but that was fading fast. His mind searched through alternative fixes for the problem.

Time to try software.

He'd route to an outside link, contact someone to go check on him in the lab. If someone had been messing around with cheap software in *his* VR rig, they were going to be sorry they had ever been born.

He couldn't find the link. A moment of panic enveloped him.

Wait a second, hold on. Maybe he wasn't *in* VR?

Could he be *dreaming*?

It was an occupational hazard that VR programmers often developed extremely realistic dreams. All the time that they spent coding sensations into a scenario wore a groove in their own heads. He looked at the perfect sunset and frowned. He'd like to think he'd dream something better than *this*.

There was an easy way to find out. He reached into his back pocket and pulled out his wallet.

Which is there because I programmed it? Or dreamed it?

He'd taken the idea from an old book about lucid dreaming. Lucid dreamers were people who were aware that they were dreaming. Once this synaptic jump was made, they could control their dreams, a very attractive proposal prior to VR. The dreamer would carry a card around in his wallet that said, "If you can read this, you're not dreaming."

The wallet trick worked because, in a dream state, your brain had a hard time keeping text together. Lucid-dreamer wannabes would pull the card out in their dreams and read it. When the text didn't work—usually it slid around the page, or faded out—they'd know they were dreaming.

Jay had used the technique to separate himself from his dreams several times and had offered it to other VR jocks he knew. He'd done it often enough that he'd actually managed to have a few lucid dreams as well. VR without the hardware.

He looked at the card.

If you can read this, you're not dreaming.

Well, that answered that.

He glanced away from the card and then looked back to be sure.

If you can read this, you're not in VR, either.

A chill frosted his shoulders.

Uh oh. What was going on here?

He tried to remember his day. . . . It had been calm—he was going to see Saji, and then—

As if the thought had conjured her, he suddenly saw his wife across the beach, almost at the opposite end.

Saji! He felt a sense of relief. Saji would know what was going on. He'd talk to her, see what kind of VR he was stuck in.

As he drew closer to her, he could see that she held something. A little white bundle.

The wind on the shore suddenly carried to him a thin cry over the crash of the surf.

The baby!

What was going on? She'd just been diagnosed—well that wasn't the right word, she'd . . . *found out* she was pregnant, just a few days before.

Something was *wrong*. He looked over toward Saji, and noticed that even though he hadn't been moving slowly, she seemed to be farther away than before.

And in the same glance, he noticed that the water had pulled back from the sand—way back. Fish were flopping in the suddenly empty bay, seaweed and kelp beds were exposed, out past the coral reef.

He looked far out to sea and it was as if his vision had suddenly turned telescopic.

A huge swell moved toward the shore.

Tsunami!

Jay had gone on a holiday a few years back and had

seen a sign on the shoreline: TIDAL WAVE ESCAPE ROUTE. The words had cast a shadow over his short foray on the beach—that and the fact that an old man had looked at his pale skin and asked, "Where you from, boy, Alaska?"

When he returned to the hotel, he hit the net and did a little studying on tsunamis. Shortly after that he moved to a hotel farther inland. The power of the water in a tidal wave could wipe out entire villages in seconds, and you never knew when one was just going to show up and swamp everything before the warning could do you any good.

And there was Saji and his *baby* right in front of one.

No way. VR or dream, or whatever. He was *Jay Gridley*, he was not going to let this happen!

Jay ran, using every trick he could think of to alter the scene: imagery, focus points, meditation, and VR conjurations.

Nothing worked. The wave kept coming.

He ran faster, figuring that at least his body—or what passed for it, wherever he was—was operating with a set of consistent physics.

But he wasn't going to make it. He got closer, though, close enough to see little fingers grasping his wife's shoulder as she started to breast-feed.

She doesn't see the danger.

The sound of the water coming had grown, and there was a feel of imminent threat, death coming, everybody out!

"Saji!" he yelled, as loud as he could, "Get out of here! *Run!*"

He kept yelling as he ran, getting closer and closer. He thought about what he would do if and when he reached her. Run with her toward high ground, or at least try to find some kind of shelter—

He glanced to his left and saw it. The swell had jumped up in size, the seabed forcing higher as it approached. He had seen some surfers once on TV, riding on sixty-foot waves, monsters that dwarfed them, making them look like toys.

This wave was bigger.

A lot bigger.

He screamed Saji's name again, and this time she heard him. She looked over, her eyes widening in surprise, and a smile beamed across her face.

No, no! Run! Run!

He gestured frantically toward the sea, and finally, chillingly, she looked.

Her face went pale, her eyes wide, and her mouth opened to scream. She turned away from the oncoming wave, tried to shelter the baby, but it was useless—

They were swept away—

Jay braced himself as best he could as the wave hit. He expected to be crushed, but some freak variation of the shoreline must have saved him: The water thundered down, tossed him into the air, then carried him away, but somehow, he came to the surface, alive, uninjured.

Except for the emotional horror of it all. His wife and new baby hit by a wall of water! And him unable to do a thing about it!

It wasn't real. He clung to that small solace. It couldn't be real—but . . . what *was* it? It certainly wasn't VR as he knew it.

His face felt as if it had been set in stone. This was not good. He was supposed to be in control.

He floated in the water, the taste of salt harsh in his mouth.

What was happening?

11

Thorn didn't want to go home. The doctors at the hospital where Jay Gridley was lying in a coma had told him there wasn't much point in hanging around. Gridley was in no danger of dying—at least they didn't think so—and if he awoke, they would call.

Jay was alive, but the doctors didn't know when—or if—he would come back. The man who had shot him was still at large. Witnesses had described the man and his car, but the police had not found him.

By the time he left it was already past two A.M., and there didn't seem to be much point in going home. He would barely have time to get to sleep before he'd have to get up and head back to Net Force HQ. Besides, he was too wired to sleep.

Hospitals did that to him, ever since his grandfather had passed away. At the end, the old man had checked himself out of the hospital and gone home to die in his own bed surrounded by his family, but he had spent a week full of tubes and needles before he'd had enough, and Thorn had spent much of that week there with him. The smells, the look, they came back every time he had to go to one of those places.

Halls of the dead and dying, his grandfather had called hospitals, and if he was going to die anyway, what point was there in spending large amounts of somebody's money to do it?

No, Thorn didn't want to go home to an empty house, but, outside of his Net Force office, he didn't really have anywhere else to go. Heading to his house, he opened a beer and went on-line, hoping for a distraction.

He found one.

His mailbox was stuffed with more than three hundred e-mails.

He opened the first one. It, and most of the others, were from his troll.

Wonderful.

Rapier, the troll who haunted him, had apparently generated a repeating message that was, if unchecked, eventually going to fill Thorn's hard drive with his drivel:

"Hahahhaa, Thorn! Touché!"

That was all it said, repeated fifty times per message, and continuing to come in one e-mail at a time every few minutes. If Rapier had tried to dump more than two megabytes at once, Thorn's filters would have stopped it, but dribbling in as short e-mail with different return addresses—all false ones, Thorn was sure—the spam- and size-filters let them pass.

Thorn took a sip of his beer and glared at the screen. Given how the rest of his day had been, he did not need this.

He deleted the e-mails, reset his filters to stop anything from the e-mail server Rapier was using, and decided that maybe hunting this guy down and getting him tossed off his server was the least he could do.

The basic process was fairly simple to start. First, you did the obvious check—the sender's e-mail return address. Thorn had noted several of the ones Rapier had used, all from the same IP.

Thorn blipped a quick message cc:ed to the addresses he'd noted. After a few seconds he got a bounce from the server, in this case, boohoo.com, that his messages were undeliverable.

Big surprise there.

He pulled up the troll's most recent posting to the news-group and checked the header, next to the HELO sig. There was a ten-digit number, broken by dots, that identified the sending machine. Of course, that couldn't be relied upon, since there were ways it could also be faked, but it was a place to start. Next to that was the receipt date that the ID'd server showed, followed by the routing info as the posting was shuttled into UseNet.

Thorn logged into the Internet registries, starting with the American Registry—ARIN. From his language and spelling, Thorn figured that Rapier was an American.

Once on the ARIN site, he ran a WHOIS search on the IP address and sure enough, the address was in the ARIN database.

The WHOIS came up, and at least it was a legitimate addy—the inetnum, netnam, and description showed it to be a small server located outside of Chicago, BearBull.com. What he was looking for were the contacts for the IP, and there they were, two of them.

Using his official Net Force address, Thorn fired off an e-mail to both:

> Dear Sirs,
>   I am seeking your assistance in locating a client of yours who has apparently violated federal law regarding use of the Internet. I would appreciate any assistance you might render in this matter.

He listed the particulars of the e-mail, and then he signed it, "Thomas Thorn, Commander, Net Force."

This was a big hammer to use. Yes, technically the troll was breaking the law—stuffing a mailbox was illegal, under the denial-of-service statutes, though hardly something Net Force was going to go after, and if the IP didn't want to provide the information, Thorn wasn't going to run to Legal and get a warrant. Then again, he'd probably get a reply in a day or so, and maybe—

His e-mail program *chinged!* and an incoming message header appeared: From BearBull.com.

Look at that—must be an automatic response—

Nope, apparently the BearBull Webmaster was a night owl:

Commander Thorn—
   Sir, our records indicate that the machine you
asked about belongs to Access & Eats, a cybercafe
located west of Chicago in the Oak Brook Mall,
in the city of Oak Brook. The owner's name is
Dennis James McManus. . . .

There was a phone number, e-mail address, and a webpage listed under the name, along with an offer to do anything to help Net Force that they could.

Thorn shook his head and smiled. Well, so much for tracking down his troll. The guy was clever enough to use a public computer, and that made it a lot harder to finger him. Of course, had he been a real terrorist, Thorn could have called upon the FBI to trot field agents out to the mall to find the guy, but for a troll? No way. Not a good idea to start one's tenure as head of a law enforcement agency by indulging in a personal vendetta. . . .

Then again, there was nothing wrong with asking questions as a private citizen. He could drop Mr. McManus an e-mail, ask him if he had a regular customer who maybe talked about fencing. Certainly Rapier spent a lot of time on-line, he must be in and out of the cybercafe often enough so maybe somebody would have noticed him?

As Thorn recalled, the University of Chicago had a pretty good fencing team, at least it had been back when Thorn had been competing in college. He'd gone to a tournament there once, got to the semifinals in épée before he lost to Parker King, which had been no shame, since King had gone on to win the NCAA finals and, eventually, a Bronze in the Olympics.

Maybe somebody there knew Rapier?

He shook his head. *Say, do you know a troll who bugs people on UseNet, calls himself "Rapier?"*

For all he knew, anybody he asked could be the guy, and wouldn't that be an unpleasant experience? Having Rapier field his call and know he had gotten to him?

Of course, it might scare him off, getting a call from Thorn, but then again, maybe not, and he didn't want to give the troll the satisfaction of knowing he had rattled Thorn's cage.

Time to give it up, Tom. You have other things to occupy your time. It's just a troll, a pathetic man with no life. Let him stew in his own juices.

Before he shut down, he tapped in the URL for the cybercafe's webpage.

The splash page came up, with a directory, and Thorn clicked on the biography for the cafe's operator.

Dennis James McManus was a slight, fair-skinned redhead, balding, about Thorn's age, a serious, almost scowling expression on his face. He leaned against a dark wall, arms crossed, practically glaring at the camera.

An unhappy man, Thorn reflected. Looked familiar, somehow, though Thorn couldn't place him. Oh, well.

He was about to log off, had, in fact, hit the quit button on his browser, when he noticed a word in the bio, just a quick flash as the page blinked off:

Épée.

Hello?

Thorn quickly logged back on and read the bio.

Apparently, Mr. McManus had been a collegiate fencing champion in Ohio.

Well, well, well. How about that . . . ?

Gotcha!

Walter Reed Army Medical Center
Washington, D.C.

John Howard was talking to Julio when he looked up and saw Alex and Toni Michaels heading toward them.

"Alex, Toni. I thought you were in Colorado."

"We almost were," Michaels said. "We caught a flight back as soon as we heard. How is he?"

"Julio talked to Saji a few minutes ago—she's in the ICU with him."

Fernandez nodded. "No change. He's unconscious. The bullet apparently broke apart when it hit the windshield, and about a third of it glanced off his forehead, just above the right eye, dug a bloody groove, but did not penetrate the skull. It hit him hard enough to rattle his brain, and he is in shock. Everything else seems to be working okay, but he hasn't come around and nobody is quite sure why."

Michaels nodded. "What about the guy who shot him?"

Howard shook his head. "No sign of him."

"Why did he do it?" Toni asked.

Again, Howard shook his head. "We don't know. We've got some witnesses who said a car cut him off, a guy hopped out and headed for Jay. He had a gun. Jay tried to back his car away and the guy opened up on him. One shot—ballistics says it looks like a Thirty-eight Special or Three fifty-seven Magnum round, from the pieces they dug out of the car."

"Road rage?" Toni said.

"Looks like," Howard said.

"Cops have any idea who they are looking for?"

"A tall-short-fat-thin-blond-brunette-white-black guy," Fernandez said. "Joe Average, wearing glasses, moustache, had a band-aid on his chin."

Michaels said, "Anybody thinking that maybe it wasn't some angry commuter? Maybe somebody targeting Jay in particular?"

Julio and Howard glanced at each other. "The thought had crossed our minds. We've got somebody going over Jay's e-mail and phone log, checking on all the projects he was working on, like that. Thing is, Jay isn't the kind of guy whose enemies pack guns—most people who'd be after him would use software at ten paces."

"Anything we can do to help?" Michaels asked.

Howard shrugged. "The new Commander was here— the doctors told us all to go home, and he did. We're running down everything we can think of now. We were just fixin' to head out ourselves."

"Can we see him?" Toni asked.

"Yeah. Check with the nurse's station, he can have two or three people in at a time. I'm sure Saji will be glad to see you."

"Who's watching your son?" Fernandez said.

"Guru," Toni said. "He'll be fine."

Howard smiled a little. The old lady they called "Guru" was the woman who had taught Toni the martial art *silat*, at which she was a deadly expert. The woman had to be pushing ninety, and Howard wouldn't want to mess with her if he had a ball bat and a knife. That little old lady could kill you with either hand and never work up a sweat.

"We'll go check on him," Michaels said.

"You need a place to stay?" Howard said.

"Hadn't thought that far ahead."

"You can stay with us. The guest room hasn't got too much crap stored in it at the moment."

"Thanks, John."

As he watched them head for the nurse's station, Howard found himself pleased. They didn't have to be here. It would have been easy for them to say they hadn't heard about it, or that they had to get settled in their new lives, that they couldn't do anything anyhow. But that's what friends did—when you had trouble, they came to offer their help.

To Julio, he said, "Make sure whoever is going over Jay's life looks real close. I want the man who did this. Before I leave, after I leave, whenever."

"I hear you, John. But you'll have to stand in line behind me to have a chat with him."

12

In the Forest Primeval

Jay woke up with a headache. At least, "woke up" was the best term he could think of to describe it. It was as if he'd been dozing, only vaguely aware of his surroundings, until something brought him back to a more active mode of being.

Weird.

The scenario had changed—if indeed it was a scenario—the beach had given way to a dense northern forest with moss on all sides of some of the trees, huge primeval ferns, and pine needles scattered under the canopy of the great woods.

He'd never been here before, yet he had the strangest sense that he had *made* everything—had seen the trees come into being, watching them sprout and grow into their huge adult forms, had seeded each bush, eroded the soil shapes in the ground, all over an immense time.

As if he were God Himself. God with a headache.

He stood there, zoning out, staring at the trees, each leaf a perfection of fractal form, replicating the entire tree on a small scale. He probably would have stood there all day, except the sharp stabbing pain in his head kept dragging him back to action.

Headaches weren't something you got in VR. Stim units only affected the sensory nerves. Pain from something inside of his head shouldn't be possible. And even if it had been, not something he would have inflicted on himself—what would be the point?

He frowned. A thought seemed to come close to the surface of his consciousness—something important about that. . . .

The pain intruded on his focus, and he shook his head, letting the thought slip away. It didn't matter *why* he had a headache, only that he *had* it.

He was nearing the edge of panic. He could not tie down where he was: dream, VR, or . . . reality?

He was *almost* certain nothing was real. The scenes changed too rapidly, days into night, trees into flowers, the beach into this forest.

And he hadn't felt hungry or needed to eat.

But the headache—you just didn't get headaches in VR.

Unless it's some experimental technique?

He remembered something he'd seen in an MIT chatroom. A grad student had claimed he could generate a realistic internal pain by simultaneously stimming acupressure points while keeping surface nerves stimmed to provide a focal point for whatever location he wanted. The problem was that the sensation was entirely subjective and hard to replicate from person to person.

Okay. Go with that idea.

If it wasn't real, then it *had* to be either VR or a dream.

What if this *were* real? What if he'd . . . gone insane and was hallucinating all of what he'd seen, mixing it with reality?

Maybe he was stumbling around in a forest somewhere, brain damaged.

He shuddered.

But he wasn't a forest kind of guy, generally. How would he have gotten there?

Another possibility occurred which was almost as terrifying: Perhaps he'd been kidnapped by one of Net Force's many enemies and was being softened up for torture? Not particularly smart, since he couldn't give them much except how to run computers. Most of what he did wasn't particularly top secret—at least the process wasn't.

There was something about that, enemies, but he couldn't quite reach it. . . .

Drifting again. *Keep it together, Jay.*

"Hey!" he called out. "If you want me to talk, I'll talk! Let's go!"

The scene shifted suddenly, and he stood on a dock near the waterfront. He wore a black trench coat and a long red scarf. A fedora was pulled low over his eyes.

Now what?

He remembered this scene, though. It was from a VR module he'd used to track some of CyberNation's money a while back.

He looked at his hand. There was the girasol, an opal, he'd created to cloud men's minds in the pulp-fiction-based scenario.

But there was no one to use it on, and his mind was cloudy enough, thank you.

He looked at the jewel for a moment. Maybe he could hypnotize himself, maybe figure out where he was. He pulled it away from his face, but it *changed*.

The opal became the glittering, nickel-plated barrel of a Colt Single-Action Army revolver. He looked down at himself again and saw chaps and spurs over blue jeans. He was wearing a silver star.

The cowboy scenario. It *had* to be VR. This was another one of his.

The transition had been flawless, completely without

flicker, no sense of data upload, no shimmer, a perfect cut.

He looked up and saw that the docks had become a ghost town. There was a frightening sense of bleakness, isolation. He was alone.

He shook his head again. Even *ghosts* would be welcome about now—

Wait a minute. What if I'm dead?

He looked around at the scene and frowned.

Shootout at the pearly gates?

The pain behind his eyes intensified and he figured if he hurt this much he couldn't be dead yet.

He walked around the town looking for something—*any*thing that would give him a thread, a clue, something that would give him an idea as to why this was all happening.

Through the swinging doors of a saloon he saw a carpet bag on a plain wooden table. He glanced around once, then approached the bag, his spurs jangling with each step. The bat wing doors creaked behind him in the wind.

In the carpet bag was a hardback book by Rudyard Kipling.

A sudden, mouth-drying fear came to him. He really didn't want to open this book. Really.

I've got to know. I've got to find out.

The book was an old one, with baroque, detailed color illustrations on the left side of the page at the beginning of each story.

He flipped through the pages and stopped to look at a painting of a jungle, with thick banana plants and lush greenery surrounding dark tree trunks. The artist had done a good job of rendering: There was an almost hyper-real, photographic quality to the scene, yet the colors were reminiscent of watercolor, vivid and clear.

As he admired it, his sense of worry grew stronger. He was staring at a portion of the jungle, a hanging vine that had been painted on a tree to the left of the illustration, when he noticed the frame of the picture grow larger, opening wider, and wider. As he stood there, amazed, the borders expanded past him, closing, swallowing him into it.

He was *in* the jungle.

And there, way in the back between two fronds, was a slice of orange color. Not the color of a fruit, but of fur.

Tiger!

It was the tiger that had gotten him before, the one he'd seen in the VR scenario during his involvement with the quantum computer.

Jay turned and ran, screaming, and while the pain in his head pounded with each step, that didn't matter. He had to get away.

He climbed a tree that seemed to stretch as he climbed, bark chipping under his fingernails, his fear driving him. It was as though he were climbing a conveyor belt in the wrong direction, carried down as he tried to climb up. Eventually, through a sheer burst of terror, he made it onto a large branch.

The tiger, the tiger!

Jay stared down at the jungle floor, but the creature had vanished as silently as it had come.

That's the tiger that got me before!

The last time it had left him near death in a coma.

Coma . . .

The word resonated in his head like the sound of a giant gong, and the headache pain he'd felt all morning intensified.

Suddenly, Jay was terrified.

What if I'm still in that coma? All the other stuff—Saji, the baby, Alex and Toni retiring—what if none of that ever happened? What if I'm still lying in a bed, dreaming?

The thought was scarier than anything he'd contemplated yet.

The silent jungle seemed to close in on him, and Jay

clung to the tree as his ancient ancestors might have, hoping against hope that he was wrong—

And wondering how to figure it out.

New York City

Cox was on a roll. The calls, the e-mails, the faxes, those never stopped, and whatever else was going on, there was business to conduct, business at which he was expert and experienced. You didn't get to sit around and wring your hands in his world when problems arose, no matter what they were.

You kept moving or the jackals would pull you down.

Jennie, his secretary, spoke over the intercom. "President Mnumba on line five."

Cox touched a button. The man's image appeared on his computer screen, just as his own visage would on Mnumba's monitor thousands of miles and halfway around the globe from here.

"John Simon, how are you? Good. Family okay? Good. Listen, reason I called, it's about those leases. Yes, yes, I know, but listen, John Simon, that's how it has to be. If I don't get those, I can't go forward, simple as that. Yes, I understand. I appreciate your position, and naturally, I wouldn't want you to do anything that makes you uncomfortable. Yes. Great to hear that, Mr. President. Have your man call mine when they are ready. You take care."

Cox smiled at the image of the African on his screen as it faded.

"Bertrand on four."

Cox touched the control again. No image this time, Bertrand was on a vox-only phone.

"Sir. We have . . . collected the material we wanted."

"Excellent. No problems?"

"An omelet's worth, nothing major."

Bertrand was in the Baltics, doing some industrial espionage. Odd as it seemed, the Croats or the Serbs or somebody there had come up with a new petroleum flow process that was more efficient than the industry standard. Cox had to have that. An omelet meant there were a few broken eggs—or broken heads. All the same to Cox.

"Good. I look forward to seeing the new material." He broke the connection.

The incoming e-mail alert *ping*ed, and it only did that when there was something of import from somebody who had the private address.

"Jennie, I'm on-line!" he yelled.

"Sir." She would start cycling and rerouting phone calls until he was done.

He logged onto his mail server. There was a single message, sent from a public machine, no signature.

"Cleaned up," it said. "Moving forward."

Eduard. Good. Cox nodded to himself.

"Off-line!"

"Ambassador Foley on three."

"Jim, how are you? Your daughter have that baby yet?"

This was what Cox lived for. The game, the hunt, the wheeling and dealing that kept the engines rumbling, moving forward. Sometimes he had to take a detour, now and then, even stop occasionally, but mostly it was onward, ever onward. He'd never get to the destination, he knew that, the road never ended, it would circle back on itself, like an equator, but that didn't matter. As long as he was in control, driving it all, that was the thing. That was the important thing.

Net Force HQ
Quantico, Virginia

Thorn pushed back from his desk and stood. One of the crew had just called from the hospital—no change in Gridley's condition.

He shook his head. Terrible thing, a man being shot like that.

So far, the state police hadn't come up with the man who had done it, and apparently the witnesses weren't much help. The shooter might never be found. Meanwhile, Net Force's best computer jock was in a coma, and nobody knew when—or even if—he was coming out of it. Lord.

Other than that, things were pretty quiet.

Thorn decided to take a walk around the building. He still wasn't quite used to this all being his domain.

He wandered down the hall, nodding at passersby.

After a while, he found himself outside Colonel Kent's office. He stepped inside, nodded at the receptionist, and through the open door saw that the colonel was hanging a *katana* on the wall behind his desk. At least that was what it looked like to Thorn—he was no expert when it came to the Japanese samurai blades, but it seemed to be the right shape and length. Might be a *daito*, which was a little longer, but it was one or the other.

The blade was mounted in a plain wooden sheath, painted in black lacquer. Kent set the curved sword edge-up onto the two hooks he had affixed to the wall behind his desk, then stepped back to look at it.

"Interesting," Thorn said. "You study the sword, Colonel?"

Kent turned. "Commander. Not really. My grandfather was a Marine. He brought it back from the campaign against the Japanese in the Pacific. Took it from the dead hand of an officer who held out alone against the American forces for twelve days on one of those nasty tropical islands. The soldier kept moving from cave to cave, hiding in the trees. When he ran out of ammunition for his sidearm at the end, he made a final charge against two squads with nothing left but this sword. Straight into a wall of rifle and submachine-gun fire, and he kept going after he should have been knocked down. My grandfather had no love for the Japanese—his brother went down on a ship sunk at Pearl Harbor—but he respected bravery in an enemy."

Thorn nodded.

"When he was getting on in years, my grandfather—his name was Jonathan—took it upon himself to do a little research on the sword. The Japanese had buyers traveling around the U.S., going to gun shows, putting ads in magazines and whatnot, trying to buy back a lot of the things G.I.s had brought home from the war, so he figured he might have something valuable."

Kent reached up and retrieved the sword, then tendered it to Thorn.

"Take a look."

There was an etiquette for this, the proper way to accept and remove a Japanese sword for viewing, but Thorn had only the vaguest notion of how it worked. He gave the colonel a short, military nod, took the weapon, and slid the blade a few inches from the sheath.

The steel gleamed like a mirror, and there was a faint but distinct swirly temper line along the edge. Thorn knew that the smith put clay along the edge during the tempering process so that it would be harder than the body of the blade, which needed to be more flexible. When the blade was polished, the harder portion became whiter than the rest of the metal, which was usually folded and hammered flat many times, making a high quality, fine-grained "watered" or Damascus steel. The Turks had a similar process for swords, as had the Spanish, and even the Norse.

Kent said, "The furniture—the handle, guard, spacers,

and such—are World War Two issue. The blade is a family heirloom, dressed down so the officer—a lieutenant, my grandfather said—could carry it into battle. The blade itself is more than four hundred years old. Probably worth twenty, thirty thousand dollars. Under the handle, chiseled into the steel, it tells the name of the smith who made it, when, where, and for whom it was made, the temple where it was dedicated, and the result of the cutting test. You know about the test?"

Thorn shook his head.

"After a blade was finished, and the furniture put on, it was used on condemned criminals to check for sharpness and durability. Sometimes they were already dead, sometimes not. They were piled on top of each other, and a man with strong arms took a whack at the pile. The measure was how many bodies the blade could cut through before it stopped. A one-body sword was not much, a two-body sword okay, and a three-body sword excellent. This is a four-body sword, according to the inscription."

"Man," Thorn said.

"Maybe they were all skinny. It doesn't say. Apparently, condemned criminals who had a nasty streak would sometimes start swallowing stones a day or two before their scheduled execution. They'd fill their belly with rocks so that when the executioner came to try his blade he had a good chance of breaking it when he cut through them."

"Lord."

"Yep. A different culture over there. Makes you wonder what would have happened if they'd won the war."

Thorn stared at the mirrorlike steel.

"My grandfather found all this so fascinating that at the age of sixty-four he took up the study of the thing from a Japanese expert in San Francisco. There are two main arts—*kendo*, with the bamboo and armor and all, and *iaido*, practiced with the live blade."

Thorn nodded again. Yes, he knew that much.

"When I was a boy, my grandfather showed me some of the basic *iaido* stuff. The old boy used to practice this for an hour or so every day, rain or shine, cold, heat, whatever. It seemed to steady him, somehow, made him calmer. He was pushing ninety when he passed away. He did his sword work that morning, went in and took a nap, and died in his sleep."

Thorn slid the blade back into the scabbard and offered it to Kent, who took it. "You still practice, Colonel?"

The man shrugged. "Now and then. My grandfather taught me a couple of forms."

Thorn said, "I do a little fencing. Western-style, foil, épée, saber, like that. Maybe you could show me some of the *iai* stuff sometime."

Kent regarded him, as if suddenly seeing him for the first time since he'd come into the office. "Yes, I could do that. Meanwhile, what else can I do for you, sir?"

"Well, to start, drop the 'sir,' business, Colonel. I'll answer to 'Thorn,' or 'Tom,' or 'Hey, you!' but I was appointed to this job, not elected."

Kent almost grinned. "All right. I can manage that. Any word on Gridley?"

"Still in a coma."

"Terrible thing," Kent said.

"Yes."

13

In his office again, Thorn considered the matter of Jay Gridley. There were technicians going over the man's work, but some of it was inaccessible to them. Gridley, like most computer whizzes, had encrypted passwords and retinal blocks on some of his files—even though that was against Net Force policies precisely for the situation that now existed: What if something happened to an operative and nobody could get at what he'd been doing?

Gridley was good, very good, but Thorn was better. Besides, he had a big advantage—there was an override, a back door built into Net Force mainframe software that would allow the Commander to get past most of the wards. Thorn could call virtuals of any of his operatives' retinal scans; he had the encryption codes for Net Force's main locks, and he could probably figure out Gridley's private codes using the Super-Cray's breakers. Having access to that was a computer nerd's delight—more powerful than a speeding bullet, able to leap tall buildings in a single bound. . . .

At the very least, even though it was probably not connected, he could take a look at what the man had been working on.

"No time like the present," he said to himself.

His office wasn't rigged for full-VR. Gridley's was. He'd go there. Besides, there might be something in the office that would help. You never knew but that Gridley might have his codes written down on the inside of a desk drawer.

He smiled. Top programmers didn't do anything that stupid, though he had once known one who had used his own birthday as a password. Guy had said that nobody would be so stupid as to expect that. He'd been wrong— there were plenty of stupid people in the world, for whom subtlety was not possible. It was almost always a mistake to make that kind of assumption.

New York City

As he was tightening the G, twisting the tuning machine to raise the pitch, the string broke. The nylon went *bing!* as it snapped, right at the tie block, which was where they usually let go. The thing was, Natadze hadn't broken a string on his instrument in years—he changed them regularly and never let them get so old and worn that it was apt to be a problem. These were only a couple of weeks old. It must have been defective.

He quickly grabbed the loose nylon to make sure the broken end didn't accidentally scratch the French polish finish. The French polish was better than other finishes for tone, but it was not the most durable. A lot of luthiers had started limiting it to the front of their instruments, while using lacquers of various types on the sides and backs. The sound was much the same, but the lacquers wore much better.

Practice would be delayed. He had to change out the remaining five—replacing one at a time was, for him, something better left only for emergencies. The other

strings should be good for another month before they
started to sound dead, but he was a believer in the idea
that birds of a feather sang better together.

It was well known that wooden instruments, at least the
good ones, got better with age. A guitar's tone, like a
violin or cello, would improve with playing. Cedar tops
did it faster, spruce took longer but grew in volume as
well as tone; everybody knew that.

While there was no proof that strings needed to be the
same age to vibrate well together, Natadze believed that
this was the case. Change one, change all was his philos-
ophy.

He fetched his winder, slipped it over the low E tuning
peg, and began slackening the string. He had tried different tuners on his instruments, and he preferred those made
by the late Irving Sloane. Rodgers's and Fustero's were
prettier and much more costly, though on an instrument
as expensive as this a few hundred dollars for gearheads
was nothing. But the Sloanes seemed smoother, they gave
an absolute lock, and they lasted forever. He had gone to
them on all his guitars, save for the collectible ones that
shouldn't be altered.

Likewise with strings, he had tried all the major brands,
mixing and matching the wound basses with the trebles,
and eventually came to realize that D'Addario's Pro-Arte
Hard Tensions gave him the best sound on this instrument, even though the medium tensions he normally used
were a bit easier on the fingers. Interesting, because they
were far from the most expensive ones.

Once he had removed all the strings, he wiped the fretboard with cleaner and then lemon oil, wiped it dry again,
put a piece of cardboard below the bridge to protect the
finish, and began to re-string the guitar. He used a variation of John Gilbert's method, melting a tiny ball on the
ends of the nylon trebles before running them through the
tie-board and looping them, starting with the high E and
the other nylons, then jumped to the low E and other two

basses. In theory, this gave the trebles time to adjust as you strung the wound strings, but in practice, all the strings went flat quickly for a few days until they had time to properly stretch out.

The process took half an hour. He clipped the long ends, using a small pair of blunt wire cutters, retuned all the strings, and ran a few scales. New strings, while not staying on key for long, did sound great, the sound cleaner and much more alive. Once the sweat from your fingers began to work, the strings had a limited life. You could take them off and soak them in cleaning solution, or even boil them to remove the grime, but that was troublesome, and it was much easier just to install new ones. If you had a guitar that cost as much as a new car, stinting on fifteen-dollar strings seemed fairly foolish.

Finally, after retuning for the fourth time, he was ready to play. He'd have to retune every few minutes, but that was unavoidable.

He might have screwed up his work a few times of late, but there was no reason why he couldn't at least *practice* playing well. With the would-be kidnap victim in a coma in the hospital—he had checked that out personally—he wasn't going to be causing any problems for a while. And the road rager who had shot him? Gone and no way to track him.

As he began to run his scales, a sudden unexpected thought burst into his brain, a nasty and unwelcome visitor, and one that stunned him with the force of its arrival.

Oh, no! How could he have been so stupid?!

Walter Reed Army Medical Center
Washington, D.C.

In the small waiting room on the eighth floor, John Howard sipped at a really bad cup of machine coffee and shook his head. Julio Fernandez also nursed a paper cup of the vile brew, but seemed less bothered by the taste.

"I'm going to check with the doctors once more. If there's no change, I'm heading out," Howard said.

Fernandez said, "I can stick around for a while. Joanna and the boy are still at her friend's in New York, no reason to go home except to sleep, and I can do that here."

Howard laughed. "You can do that anywhere. I believe I once saw you fall asleep eating a bowl of hot soup."

"Did I finish it?"

They sipped coffee.

Fernandez said, "So, tell me about Colonel Jarhead. Why'd you put him up for the new honcho?"

"Ah. Back when I was still a light colonel and in the RA, and you were probably being busted back to corporal the second or third time, you might recall that I did a rotation teaching ROTC at a U down in Georgia."

"Yes, sir, I recall that. Goofing off at the student union, eyeballing the coeds, and grading papers. Hard work."

Howard shook his head. "Abe Kent, a full-bird colonel, had been rotated out of the latest middle east conflict where he'd served with distinction, and stuck in charge of a shiny new Marine officer training facility outside Marietta. I'd bumped into him a few times before, various places."

"That's the Marines' idea of R and R—a couple months out of the war zone teaching officer wannabes."

Howard nodded. "So Abe is down South, dealing with the best and brightest of the jarheads."

"Which ain't saying much," Julio observed. "And a full-bird back then?"

"Keep listening. One of the trainees is a very smart kid—let's call him 'Brown'—a champion swimmer in college before he dropped out, a black belt in karate, and sharp as a warehouse full of razor blades. He apparently joined up primarily to piss off his father, who was a millionaire, well-known U.S. Representative—and a major antimilitary dove. Guy had been in Congress for ten or twelve terms, and would go on to be reelected half a dozen more times before he retired. He had amassed major clout by this point."

Julio nodded again. "Lemme guess—the kid had an attitude?"

Howard grinned. "Can't get anything past you, can they, Lieutenant?"

"Smart people can."

"Better shooters can, too."

Julio held up his hand. "Pick a number between one and five. Sir."

Howard ignored him. "So Brown is setting the grading curve for the recruits, first in the classroom, first in PT, kicks ass in the unarmed combat course, even outshoots the country boys on the rifle range."

"He sounds like the perfect Marine—except for the smarts," Julio said.

"Yes. It was too good to last, of course. Eventually, trainee Brown ran into some boneheaded hillbilly career DI who'd dropped out of the third grade to work his daddy's moonshine still and joined the Corps the day he turned seventeen. Words were exchanged. Things got physical. Brown decked the sergeant quite handily, and decided that if he had to take orders from dillwits like that, he wasn't going to play anymore."

"He washed out?"

Howard shook his head. "No, he saw Colonel Kent and informed him that he was not only leaving Officer Candidate School, he was leaving the Marines altogether. It had been fun and all, but, after careful consideration, he couldn't continue on, what with the morons with whom he'd have to serve."

Julio laughed. "I bet that went over real well with a decorated colonel just back from combat."

"Abe Kent informed officer-trainee Brown that, while he could bail from OCS if he so chose, he *would* be serving the remainder of his hitch in some way, shape, or form, period."

"Lemme guess again: Brown dragged out his father's clout and clonked Colonel Kent over the head with it?"

"That came later. First, he took a swing at Kent."

"He didn't."

"He did."

"What happened?"

"Kent had spent a big part of his career in combat zones and sleazy bars around the planet. He was not impressed with a would-be shavetail karate expert throwing a punch. As I understand it, he, uh, sat the boy down in his chair with some force—banking him off a wall and a file cabinet in the process. Some medical attention was required, having to do with teeth implants and resetting a broken arm."

Julio laughed.

"Brown then informed the colonel, and with a bit more respect, I imagine, that his old man was rich, influential, and that Colonel Kent would be very sorry."

"Got Kent's back up," Julio said.

"Yes. He threw the kid into the brig for decking the sergeant—he didn't mention the altercation in the office— and told Brown that he could spend the rest of his hitch on the line or in the stockade, it was all the same to the Marines."

"So what happened?"

"What do you think happened? Daddy sat on some big committees. He had favors to extend, money to grease anything squeaky. Even so, it took him six months to pry Brown out, and even with all his clout, the best he could get his son was a general discharge and not an honorable one."

"Should have been dishonorable."

"In my opinion, yes."

"So Colonel Kent stood against the kid's rich and powerful old man in career harm's way all that time," Julio said.

"Exactly. He's a man of principle. He'd been around long enough to know the chain of command is only as bright as the dumbest link in it, and that sooner or later the kid would be sprung. But he fought every inch of the way."

"Which is why he's still a colonel," Julio said.

"Yes. He resisted pressure from people with long memories. They couldn't throw him out—he was a decorated war hero in five different theaters, and had worked his way up through the ranks—but they could make sure he never went any higher."

Julio said, "Bastards."

"No question. But even knowing it was going to cost him his star, he did it anyway, because it was the right thing to do."

"Brave. Maybe not so clever."

Howard chuckled. "And we both know we'd rather have a brave man willing to go against the odds covering our asses in the field than a clever one."

"Amen."

"So, that's the reason I put Abe Kent up for the job. Net Force operations aren't always by-the-book, and this job requires a man willing to go out on a limb for his people. Whatever else you might say about him, Colonel Kent is not a man ever going to be shot in the backside."

Julio said, "Thanks for telling me, John."

"Does it make any difference?"

"Well, he's *still* a jarhead, but at least he's *my* jarhead. For as long as I'm stuck with him, he'll get whatever I can give him."

"I knew that all along, Julio."

Both men smiled.

"Sir? General Howard?"

Howard looked at the doorway and saw a young FBI agent he thought he recognized come into the room. What was his name? Rogers? Not a field guy, but a tech. What was he doing here?

"Sir. We transferred Operative Gridley's car from the state police and went over it, just a matter of routine."

Howard nodded. "And?"

"Sir, we found a wireless transmitter affixed under the automobile's rear bumper."

Howard exchanged a quick glance with Julio. "A bug?"

"And not one of ours, I take it?" Fernandez said.

"No, sir, Lieutenant. Not one of ours."

Fernandez said what Howard was thinking: "So we're not talking about road rage. We're talking about a stalker."

The agent said, "We don't know that. Could be a co-incidence."

"You believe that?" Howard asked.

"We tend to look askance at coincidence in the labs, General."

"I want to know everything there is to know about this bug, and I'd like it yesterday."

"Yes, sir. As soon as we know, you will."

Howard stared into the distance. A stalker. What had Jay been up to?

Outside Spokane, Washington

The fall day was sunny, a hint of chill in the autumn air. The alder leaves were beginning to turn, and there was a scent of wood smoke in the breeze.

Thorn, dressed in a T-shirt and Gortex windbreaker, blue jeans, and running shoes, walked the narrow trail next to the rushing water of the shallow Oregon river. It wasn't Gridley's scenario, it was his own, and one he liked to use. His grandfather had taken him for hikes in the forest a lot when Thorn had been a boy, and they were happy memories. He had invited a couple of people into the scenario at various times, usually women he had started dating. Their reaction to it usually gave him a good idea of whether there was much chance of the relationships going anywhere.

One woman he'd met in college had laughed and wanted to know why he wasn't wearing moccasins and buckskins, him being an Indian and all. Another had walked for ten minutes and said, "Borrring."

Both women had been drop-dead gorgeous and ready to spend serious time in the sack with him, but he had shut them down after that. A woman who didn't enjoy a walk in the forest, no matter how sexy or smart she was, just wasn't going to pan out in the long run. Not for him.

He spotted some bear scat just off the trail ahead. He stopped, squatted, and used a small stick to poke at the dung. Fairly fresh, still moist, still pungent. He smiled at the old joke that popped up in his memory: How do you protect yourself from grizzly bears when you are in the back woods? You wear little bells on your shoes to warn them you are coming, and you carry pepper spray in case they see you. And how do you tell grizzly scat from black bear scat? The grizzly scat has little bells in it, and smells like pepper spray.

This was black bear—there weren't any grizzlies in these woods, virtual or real world, and hadn't been for years. A black bear was much smaller and less likely to give you any trouble, but they'd go a couple hundred pounds, had teeth that could snap your arm or bite your face off, and you didn't want to mess with a momma and cubs or a male in mating season. Most people didn't realize that bears could outrun people in the short haul, and could climb, too.

At least he was on the right path. Gridley's passwords were down this way, and maybe he wouldn't need the big Cray to figure them out when he found them.

He stood and started back down the trail.

A deep voice drowned out the sound of the river bubbling over the big rocks: "Emergency override, Commander. General Howard calling."

Thorn stopped. "End scenario," he said.

Net Force HQ
Quantico, Virginia

The incoming call had visual—Howard was using his virgil, so it must be important.

"General. What's up?"

"The FBI found a bug on Jay Gridley's car."

Thorn digested that and considered the implications. "You think it might not be road rage." It was not a question.

"Somebody was tracking him. It would be passing coincidental if it was somebody else other than the guy who shot him."

"You tell the lab guys to hit it hard?"

"Yes, sir."

"State police know about it?"

"I expect so."

"Keep me in the loop."

"Yes, sir."

After Howard discommed, Thorn went over the new input. Somebody was after Gridley in particular. Why?

Could be personal, though that didn't seem likely. A lot of effort to bug his car and track him, then try an assassination on a major highway with witnesses all around. Did Gridley have enemies like that? He'd been here for years—nobody had said anything about him having hassles. Thorn could check with the man's wife, but that scenario, that Gridley had personal enemies, just didn't feel right.

So that left work. Who would want to knock off a Net Force op?

Possible answers: somebody who had suffered at his hands? Or maybe somebody who was *going* to suffer because of something Gridley was doing?

Now it was really important to get into his files and see what he was working on. Other than that thing for the Turkish ambassador, Thorn didn't have any idea what the man had been up to. A supervisor needed to know what his people were doing.

Best he find out. Time to go for another walk in the woods.

"Computer, restart scenario from exit point."

14

On the Beach

Jay paced, his thoughts fragmented. He was back on the beach where he'd started his nightmare. But he had a theory, now.

I'm in a coma.

Like most answers, it was incomplete, just a tiny bit of information that resolved only a part of the larger questions: *So how did I get here? And what now?*

He didn't have to worry that he'd been kidnapped by the enemy, he wasn't in a dream, and he probably wasn't crazy. All good news. On the other hand, he couldn't wake up, was trapped deep inside his body, and couldn't be sure about whether he was in a new coma or the one that had nearly crippled him before.

What if everything that had happened since the tiger was all part of a delusion? What if he had never come back? That Saji, work, his life, none of it had actually happened?

That thought terrified him. The idea of waking up to find that Saji was not part of his life, that he was not about to become a father . . . That would be unbearable.

He had made some progress, however. He'd gone from "Where am I and how do I get out of here?" to "I know where I am, now how do I get out of a coma?" One of his college professors had said something along those lines a few times during a software app class: "When you move from 'what' to 'how,' you're on your way."

Of course he didn't know *where* the way was, in this case.

He looked at the water and willed it to stop, picturing each wavelet stilled in motion, a sudden death to the motion of the sea.

The scene flickered for a minute, but water kept flowing, rolling in as before.

He frowned, but nodded. Something, anyway, but not enough.

He was in his own body, his mind was his own—should be a piece of cake, shouldn't it? He should be able to control his environment like he'd done in dreams before. But it didn't work. Which meant that something was wrong.

What?

Two answers presented themselves, neither pleasant.

The first was that his head had been hurt so badly that he couldn't focus his will sharply enough to create solid images.

Which is bad, but—

The second was worse: Maybe some part of his consciousness didn't want to have control. That idea, extrapolated, meant that he didn't really want to come out of it.

Whoa.

Why wouldn't he want to wake up?

Nothing occurred to him. He had the best job in the world, a great relationship with his wife, was happy—assuming that was all true and not just a dream he had within this coma, there was no reason he could think of why he'd be afraid to leave this place and head back to reality.

In his dream research, Jay had found many theories for why people dreamed. Wish fulfillment, clearing the slate, making sense of the day . . . No one really understood the total why of dreams. But he wasn't really in a dream. That was part of the problem. He steered his mind back to the topic.

What do I really care about why I can't affect things here? I just want out!

He started struggling to control the environment again: He tried freezing one wave, imagined a seagull in the air, turning some of the sand into salt. Again, nothing happened. Frustrated more than he'd ever been in his life, he sat on the beach, the warm sand making him drowsy.

How was he going to get out of here?

What's wrong with my brain?

He stared out at the waves, watching them ebb and flow. There was an almost perfect rhythm to them, the up and down, the amplitude of each crest to trough a perfect curve.

Wait a minute . . . Something there . . .

Jay remembered something he'd read after his coma— at least he thought he'd read it, assuming he wasn't still *in* that coma.

Brain waves.

There were four basic types: Beta, Alpha, Theta, and Delta, each one operating at a different frequency. Beta were the most active—the waking mind, the *thinking* mind. It ranged in speed from ten to thirty hertz.

Alpha waves were the meditation ones, the relaxed state of being. They produced a general feeling of reduced anxiety and well-being. These were slower, between seven and thirteen hertz.

Theta were even slower, the brain waves most commonly found during REM sleep, the time of dreams, at about five to eight hertz. Hallucinations—Dreams "R" Us.

The really important ones, at least to him *now*, were the Delta waves—produced during deep, deep sleep, or comas, when the body repaired itself. Deltas were slow— between two and six hertz.

I just don't have the power, Captain.

In a coma his brain was too slow to generate the waking state of mind he needed to control things. It wasn't his will, just his will*power*.

I've got to speed things up.

But *how*?

It wasn't as if he could suddenly snap out of it—that was the whole point.

Jay let out a breath he hadn't realized he'd been holding and felt himself relax. It explained why he'd been so unfocused. The latest theories suggested that there were some levels of thought going on during Delta waves, and he could certainly attest to that now—if he got out of here. It wasn't his fault, after all. Now he just had to figure out how to speed up the frequency of his thoughts.

Yeah, simple.

He pondered the problem, turning it over from one angle and then the other. How to increase his thought power? If his mind were like a computer's CPU, he could just overclock it—increase the voltage, or alter the clock settings for the bus.

Was there anything he could do that would work like that for his brain?

Jay lay back on the sand and closed his eyes. Whatever low-level consciousness he had now, he didn't want to squander it on the beach illusion anymore. He'd need every shred of thought power to try what he had in mind. The programmer pictured his memory as filled with hundreds of doors and began searching for anything he'd ever learned about brain function.

Biofeedback. He'd considered it before meeting Saji—using a machine to monitor his brain while he worked to try and reach one state or another. Over time, using creative visualization, people could use a biofeedback device to figure out what they were doing to get to a particular state of consciousness, and learn to do it without a machine. Biofeedback gave people the ability to focus better by teaching them to create more Beta waves.

Well I don't have the machine, but I can visualize.

He wouldn't be able to objectively monitor what state of being he was in precisely, but gauging the level at which he could control his environment would give him a clue.

Jay considered several other benchmarks he could use to test his consciousness level. If his memory got markedly better, he might be in a Theta-wave state. If he suddenly felt more at ease and relaxed, he'd be in an Alpha-wave state. And when things got the most active, and he felt more in *control*, he'd have moved to Beta.

Well, they aren't exactly numbers on a monitor, but they'll have to do.

Jay relaxed on the sand, picturing it warmer, heated by the sun, and then even hotter. Things moved faster in a hot environment, so he figured that might help. If his real body got warmer as well, it might physiologically help his brain with improved blood flow, too.

With his eyes closed, he thought of heat, a vein of lava running under the sand. He felt warmer and imagined sweat rolling off himself.

At the same time, he began to think of his brain as a spinning top. He pictured it, gray and twisted, uncoiling and spinning faster and faster until it was a huge ring, the neurons more and more excited.

He remembered what he'd been doing just before the accident. He'd been thinking of flowers for Saji, to congratulate her about the news. Pink was one of her favorite colors, and he'd been debating whether or not he should go with a bouquet or something more symbolic, like three flowers to represent himself, her, and the baby.

And the car had come rolling at him, fast.

Theta. Memory's on-line.

His brain twirled, as if in a centrifuge, the gray matter pressed up against the side. He pictured the centrifuge itself set inside an amusement park ride, spinning ever faster, wheels within wheels. The lava under him had moved closer to the surface, and he was baking now, his body on fire as he sped up.

A wave of knowledge hit him, and he had ideas, all kinds of them.

The Alpha-Theta border?

People in this state of mind were supposed to suddenly gain great insight as their thoughts passed from the seven- to eight-hertz range. He had a flash of memory about the Schumann resonance, the resonant frequency of the ionosphere, 7.5 hertz and multiples. In a flash of inspiration he saw another direction to go.

He dropped the heat and spinning visualizations and imagined himself in a bed. The images were coming faster now, and more clearly. It was like stepping from a black and white world into color. Everything was more intense.

I'm in a hospital bed.

Jay pictured the bed, the room quiet, made up of the same nondescript decor and hardware found in hospitals all across the nation. He could almost hear a beeping sound, and he imagined it might be an EKG keeping track of his heart. He tried to imagine the feel of the cool sheets on his skin, the whisper of an air conditioner nearby, the click of heels on a floor.

"He's coming around!"

"The monitor's going crazy!"

Voices! He heard voices!

Beta, here we come!

But, in that moment, the voices faded, and he felt a heaviness wash over him. A moment later, he was back on the beach, sun shining mercilessly, sand under his butt.

He cried out in anger, then calmed himself. He had made progress, he was sure of it. He had a goal now, a direction, and he was going to beat this thing. It was only a matter of time.

He was Jay Gridley. He was not going to roll over and give up.

No way.

15

Howard heard the *spang!* as a jacketed assault rifle round ricocheted off the concrete wall a foot above his helmet. He ducked instinctively—too late, of course. You don't hear the one that kills you, he knew that. But if you hear one, that means somebody has targeted you, and there will probably be more on the way. There were men who never bothered to duck at all when they were in a fire zone— they figured the one with their name on it would get them no matter if they were hunched over or standing upright, but Howard always figured that the smaller the target the less likely you'd get tagged. Might be more than one with your name on it—no point in tempting fate.

The tiny village was typical for the Mid East—a lot of adobe and concrete-block construction, some of the older stuff probably going back a thousand years. The streets had been made for pack animals—donkeys, camels, whatever—and not automobiles, and until recently the buildings had been designed to fit the terrain and not the other way around. The result was a third-world town that might have been created by giant rats, full of twists and turns, low overhangs, and alleyways no wider than two men walking side-by-side could traverse even without the garbage bins.

There were also a McDonald's, a Starbucks, and even a Gap store.

"Able One, bring your aim to bear on that sniper in the second-story window on the northwest corner of the hotel," Abe Kent said.

Despite the intermittent gun fire and occasional grenade going off, Howard didn't have any trouble hearing the colonel's clipped commands over the LOSIR headset built into the helmet.

"I want to see a metal hailstorm filling that aperture in five seconds. When it does, I want Baker Two's AT man to cross the street and into that Starbucks. Everybody copy?"

"Able One copies."

"Baker Two copies."

"On my mark—five . . . four . . . three . . . two . . . and fire!"

Eight subguns spoke as one, and anybody in or around the mosque's window who didn't duck better be bulletproof.

Howard peeked around the edge of the Dumpster, a nice, thick, bullet-stopping steel-plated one, and watched as Baker's antitank man scooted across the street, dodging and stutter-stepping, ending in a dive and roll. The man had some speed.

The subguns went quiet.

"Baker Two AT, put a rocket through that hotel window at your convenience."

There were undoubtedly civilians in that hotel, and Kent wanted very much to minimize any unintended or "collateral" damage. But they were taking fire, and the first rule of engagement was always the right to self-defense.

Three seconds later, a new JAM-II antitank antisniper laser-guided smart rocket *whooshed* from a shoulder launcher, zipped the hundred yards from the Starbucks to the mosque, still gaining speed as it went through, and turned the room inside out in a fiery roar. The precision of the weapon meant, however, that the surrounding rooms were all untouched.

Adios, sniper.

Howard smiled. He was just here as an observer, and while he might have done it differently, there was no arguing with success. Abe Kent had been in combat as often as any man of his rank, more than most, and when you wanted the job done, he was your go-to guy.

"Nice shot, son, I owe you a beer. Able One, recon and report."

Howard pulled his head back to cover and looked at Kent, who sat on his heels in a squat he had learned in some Southeast Asian jungle years before.

"Very neat, Colonel."

"All in a day's work, sir. Not like I haven't been in this general vicinity before." He waved at the street.

"Are we done?"

"Pretty much."

"Computer, end scenario."

Net Force Military Computer Training Center
Quantico, Virginia

Kent pulled off the headset and looked around the darkened training room. It wasn't necessary for the troops to be here, they could have been anywhere in the country and logged into the communal VR scenario, but Kent liked his people together, so that he could talk to them face-to-face before and after a sortie. The center would allow sixty players to gear up at once, though there were only eighteen of them here now—Howard, Kent, and the two eight-person squads. Net Force seldom had large numbers in the field, though it was possible—they were much more like a Delta or SEAL team: small, portable, fast, hit-and-run and get out in a hurry.

Howard had done all right with them. Had some good officers and sergeants, and the troops were pretty sharp—their pay was better, and they had money for training—though he never trusted a VR scenario the same way he did reality. When you got shot in VR, you shook your head and tried to do better. When you got shot in combat, it wasn't so easy. The map was never the territory.

Still, it was a good exercise, and it did instill enough sound and fury to keep you on your toes.

Howard would be gone soon, and it would be Kent's command, and he needed to know what his people could do.

Colonel Kent went over the exercise with the troops, telling them what they had done right and what they had done wrong. Howard sat quietly in the background, nodding. That was good. It always helped if a superior officer backed you up. It wasn't absolutely necessary if you knew you were right, but it was nice to have the acknowledgment.

When they were done and the troops had filed out to consider their performance, it was just Howard and Kent alone in the room.

"Anything new on the Gridley matter?" Kent asked.

"FBI has some info on the bug; they are sending it over. I figured we'd read it, then go show it to the Commander—if that's all right with you."

"Still your show, John."

"Not really, but I'll stay around long enough to see this one through. I like Gridley, he's a good kid. But even if I hated him, he is one of ours. I want whoever did this to him to get nailed for it."

"I understand."

Quantico, Virginia

Natadze rolled past the impound yard. He avoided the
temptation to look directly at the entrance and perhaps
straight into the fiber-optic security cams surely hidden
there. Who could know if that data might someday be
strained by some curious and perceptive agent alert
enough to recognize that a wolf had passed?

Part of preparation was eliminating such possibilities.

And he was prepared this time, better than before.
Should he be noticed, he would appear to be a tourist;
rental car in a phony name, travel tickets from Los Angeles, even a camera on the front seat, the perfect example
of a patriotic citizen come to visit the capital of his great
country.

Nobody to worry about.

He wanted very much to recover the tracking device
which he had foolishly left on the target's car. Like an
amateur, his shock at the time had clouded his thoughts,
and he had left *evidence* that the attack on a member of
Net Force had been deliberate. Unforgivable, that.

In his hand was a device that resembled an MP3 player,
and could be used as such. But if certain buttons were
pressed just *so,* the liquid-crystal display on the face of
the device would change, revealing an indicator that could
be used to lock onto any one of a number of transmitters
on varying frequencies.

The device was yet more complex—it had the capability to receive GPS signals so as to track a transmitter
across the globe. He could have punched a control on the
tracker and had it send code out to the bug to activate a
feature that would give its longitude and latitude to him
to within a twenty-foot radius, anywhere in the world.

He wasn't using that setting now. Since the mishap on
the highway, and his mistake, Natadze had decided to go
back to the basics. The fewer machines the better. Had
the feds found the bug, they might decide to check and

see if anyone beamed a signal to it, and then backtrack it to the originating transmitter. Such a thing was possible, if they were alert and ready.

So he was operating passively, relying on the sensitivity of his receiver to indicate if it were near. Since he wasn't sending anything out, he couldn't be caught—at least not that way.

He'd found the impound yard, and had driven there. If the target's car suddenly started moving, he wasn't going to follow it where any watch might take note of him.

There were two possibilities, and he was prepared for either. The first was that he'd get a strong signal from the bug, indicating that it was still in the impound yard. If that were the case, he would go to the entrance and present a different set of credentials, showing him to be an insurance adjustor. A car of similar make and color to his target's had recently been involved in a hit-and-run accident. No one had been hurt, but the car had been impounded, and a follow-up visit from a claims adjustor who had forgotten to take a measurement wouldn't be out-of-line.

He had caused this to happen, and that automobile was in this yard somewhere.

He would remove the device while he took the measurements, and all would be as it should have been. And if he were questioned about getting the wrong car, it would be easy to believe a mistake: Darkness was drawing near, he had only seen the car once, and it had been a busy day. He knew that most people were so sloppy that they believed in the possibility of infinite mistakes. His story would hold under all but the most rigorous scrutiny, and if it came to that, he would simply not allow himself to be taken.

This was not only about survival, but being professional, clearing up all the loose threads.

The other possibility he had to consider was that the Net Force operative's auto had been taken elsewhere, per-

haps to an FBI lab. This would mean they'd found the
bug, or were shortly going to do so—they were thorough
about such things, he knew. No harm done: The car he'd
staged would be left here in this lot, he would drive on
and write it off. He had been careful to wear a disguise
when he'd purchased the device, during a busy time of
day. There would be no way to trace him.

He was good, but going after the car inside a Federal
facility, with their suspicions alerted, would not do.

He tapped the switch, listened. There was a faint chirp
from the MP3 player, and a tiny lower response, like an
echo. But the sound was weak; even without looking at
the signal-strength meter, Natadze knew the bug was not
here.

Too bad, but it was done, and beyond his control. He
had to assume that the FBI was trying to track the bug,
see what it could collect. He touched the player's controls,
returning the device to its ostensible use. He tapped PLAY,
and the tiny FM transmitter inside beamed a digital re-
cording into his radio, that of Rimsky-Korsakov's "Flight
of the Bumblebee," arranged for guitar and piano.

He had another piece of business to attend to—checking on the target. Since Jay had seen him, and there was
always the chance of being identified, however small, he
had to consider permanent removal as an option. It wasn't
what he would like, but given the choice between killing
Jay now or allowing him to live and ending up in jail, he
would choose the former.

*If it comes down to you or me, my friend, it must be
you.*

In his mission preplanning, he'd studied the area he
used for the attack: He knew where the police stations
were, estimated response times, and also where the hospitals were.

He'd considered the latter in case the target had hurt
him, but knowledge was knowledge. The nearest major
hospital off the Beltway at that point was Walter Reed

Army Medical Center. The center didn't serve civilians such as himself, so he'd needed to locate a second hospital.

Jay, not being technically a civilian, *had* wound up in Walter Reed. Having his target in a facility full of military personnel could made things more difficult, so he wanted to take a look.

He pulled onto I-495 and headed for town.

Natadze took Exit 318, Georgia Avenue South, and rolled down the street. It wasn't far to the hospital.

The medical center was huge, and set well back from the road, looking like some kind of giant bunker. The war on terror, begun years before, had resulted in several pillboxes that were thinly disguised as welcome areas.

It was not a sight to inspire confidence.

He could pass as military and could probably get in, but if an alarm were raised, getting out would be difficult at best.

Taking the target would require either a massive strike on the building with a great deal of collateral damage, beyond his ability to accomplish alone, or a carefully researched and planned strike through multiple levels of security.

He didn't like either idea. If they had found the bug, they already knew the attack was not a case of road rage, and would be wondering why Jay had been targeted. Very likely, there would be armed guards, and success in an assassination at the cost of his own life was more than he was willing to pay.

He would have to come up with another way.

He shook his head as he listened to the music. Vynograd, the Russian chasing the bumblebee, had fast hands, no question. Two hundred forty beats per minute at the peak, and on an eight-string, no less, using his *chin* to fret the bass notes, that was something to see. Even though you needed at least a piano for the accompaniment, the guitar part was a very nasty test of hand speed. It was a showpiece, of course, something you would play for a jury, and, naturally, a lay audience would love it. Classical guitar competitions were always full of such things— there would be a fugue by Brouwer, or one of Nikita Koshkin's pieces, "Rain," for instance. While technically demanding and impressive for that, such pieces were not as impressive to another competent player as, say, a careful rendition of the "Concierto Aranjuez," by Rodrigo. This was played in concerts perhaps more frequently than any other classical work around the world, save maybe for "Romanza," and against an orchestra, but it offered places where a player could make things more interesting or less, depending on his skill. The first part ran just over six minutes, the second eleven and a half minutes, and the third part a little more than five minutes. Natadze could manage this work, but not as well as he would like—and he figured when he could play it as well as Romero or Fernandez or Bream, then he would be in good company indeed.

Yes, and if he could flap his arms hard enough, perhaps he could *fly* like a bumblebee.

He sighed. It was easier to think about the guitar than his job at the moment. But now it was time to get back to work.

16

It was getting late, well past quitting time, and Thorn was ready to head home, when he looked up to see Marissa Lowe standing in the doorway of his office.

"I should have called," she said. "I'm sorry to hear about Gridley," Marissa said.

Thorn waved her in. She plopped onto the couch.

"Yeah," he said. "The doctors say they don't know when he'll come out of it. Or if he will. He has an old trauma—apparently he got his brain zapped a while back, had an induced stroke—and there's a worry that the previous injury might somehow be causing problems." He noticed a slight hint of musk in the air—her perfume?

"You trace the bug?"

"FBI knows where it came from—it's a commercial unit, nothing real esoteric, sold retail in New York three months ago—but no record of who bought it. A cash sale, and no security cam in the store—which, of course, is a selling point with their customers. Could be anybody."

"So what now?"

"We're running through Jay's files, as best we can. Haven't found anything worth shooting him for yet."

She shook her head, glanced down at her watch. "Well, I was just in the neighborhood, and I've taken more of your time than I should. I ought to run."

He paused. He was intrigued by her, he had to admit, and maybe more than intrigued. A part of him wanted to ask her to stay, ask her to dinner, ask her home for the evening, but there was already too much happening too fast.

So, "All right," was all he said. "It's been a pleasure."

Net Force Obstacle Course
Quantico, Virginia

Kent was not a fanatic about exercise, and he didn't expect that a man his age was going to be able to run with twenty-year-old jocks; still, he believed that sitting behind a desk didn't mean you should turn into a slug, either. He made it a point to hit the obstacle course a couple-three times a week, and to do enough physical training so that if he had to run up a flight of stairs, he wouldn't keel over from exhaustion. He wasn't in the shape he'd been in thirty years ago, but he could keep up with any man his age, and some a lot younger.

This particular evening was drizzly and cold, and the steel chin-up bar was wet and rough under his hands. There were the usual die-hards out, even in the gathering darkness, but a lot of the fair-weather athletes were foregoing the pleasure.

His arms burned as he finished his set of chins, and his breath came and went faster than he would have liked. If he lived to be as old as his father, he had another twenty-five years, thirty if he made it to Grampa Jonathan's age.

He was on the downhill slope, no way around that, but staying fit as long as he could was important. His grandfather had been spry until he died of a heart attack in his sleep, and his old man had gone bowling the day before he passed. You worked with what you had.

He gathered himself for his second set of chins. This new job wasn't the same as those he'd done in the Corps, but there were some good troops on hand, and the chance of getting to a hot zone leading them—that had been part of the deal. His option, Howard had told him. You can sit at HQ and direct things long-distance, or you can suit up and lead in the field. No question but that getting his boots muddy was the choice he'd make, and staying fit was part of that. You didn't want to be the guy the men were having to carry when they went into harm's way.

The second set came hard. He would have done ten more, but at eight, the burn was too much. He gutted that one out, but he was done. He let go, dropped back to the ground, and shook his head. There was a time when he would have done three, four sets, run the course, come back and finished off with another set.

He shook his head. That had been a while. Then again, a man his age who could do eighteen chins? That wasn't so bad. It was all relative, wasn't it? At least he could still hear—John Howard was sporting a hearing aid, from too many guns having gone off too close to his head. And he didn't need glasses, except to read. Best to be thankful for what you have than to complain about what you didn't.

He took a moment to slow his breathing, then made ready to start the course. It was the usual kind of thing—logs and ropes and barricades to clamber over, tire hopping, crawling under razor wire. More than you were apt to run into on any field of combat, urban or country, but that was the point.

The rain began to come down a little harder, not a deluge, but enough to soak everything. Fine. It did rain on

the battlefield now and then—he'd even been caught in a
frog-drowner of a thunderstorm in a Middle Eastern desert
once, a freak thing in which four men had been swept
away when a flash flood had caught them in a low spot.
You never knew what God was going to throw at you,
and like the Boy Scout he had been, "Be prepared" was
still his motto.

He headed for the first obstacle.

Cox Estates
Long Island, New York

The rain was coming down in buckets as the limo pulled
up to his front door. Hans, the butler, alerted by the chauffeur's call, stood on the porch with a huge golf umbrella,
and was at the car's door before Cox opened it.

Cox alighted and allowed Hans to keep most of the rain
off as they splashed through a puddle and onto the porch.

"Nasty weather," Cox said.

"Yes, sir."

Inside, Cox let Hans take his raincoat. As he headed
for the study, he saw Laura on the phone in the hallway.
She looked up, smiled and waved, and went back to her
conversation.

In his study, Cox pulled a cigar from his walk-in hu-
midor, one of the smaller Cubans, clipped the end with a
platinum cutter given to him by the Prince of Wales, wet
the tip, and used a wooden match to light it—after letting
the match's odor burn off. He puffed on the cigar. Blue
smoke wreathed his head. Ah.

"Knock, knock?"

He looked up to see Laura standing in the doorway.
She still had her figure after all these years, a handsome
woman. "I thought you had a thing this evening?"

"Aid to Rwanda Medical committee meeting," she said.

"It's been cancelled, due to the weather. The storm moving in could drop two or three inches of rain. Nobody wants to be out driving around in that. Do you have plans for dinner?"

"Not really. I thought I'd have Martina cook a chicken or something."

"I'll join you, if that's all right?"

"That would be nice." It had been perhaps three weeks since they'd had dinner together.

"I'll speak to Martina. We can catch up—I talked to Sarah today, I have the latest on little Joseph and William. About an hour?"

He puffed on the cigar and nodded. "Sounds good."

Once Laura was gone, he knocked the ash off the cigar. He'd only smoke half of it, if that. Too much tobacco and alcohol were killers, he knew that, and he only indulged himself in either infrequently. Half a stogie, twice a week, no more than one or two drinks a day. Coupled with the exercise, he felt as if that was about right.

At dinner, Laura was chatty. He heard all about the grandchildren, their latest adventures, and what his son and daughter-in-law were up to. He mentioned some of his business dealings, but as always, Laura's eyes seemed to glaze over, and her smile became fixed. She had no ears for industry, never had, even in the early days. If he was happy and enjoying his work, that was enough for her. He could have done a lot worse for a spouse, and, of course, it had been her family's company that had been his launching pad; he would always owe her for that.

He smiled as she talked about schools and science projects, nodding at the appropriate times. He had not been a particularly attentive father, and while he enjoyed seeing the grandchildren, he didn't think about them much. His passion had been the job, and through that, he had managed to provide the best of everything for his children and their children. When he was gone, they would have to work at spending it all before they died, and with even cursory management, the fortune he had amassed would last for as long as there were heirs to inherit it.

The one flaw in the perfect tapestry that was his life was this spy business. And he had decided that he was going to deal with that the way he had dealt with every other problem. Whatever it took to resolve it, he would do. He had been taking steps in that direction for some time, without tangible results, but it was only a matter of time before he had what he needed. Once that happened, Eduard would be put into play. And the Net Force people would not be outing him, either. He had a hammer that could squash dinosaurs, and if he had to use it, then that's what he would do.

He had to remind himself from time to time in this situation that he was one of the most powerful men on the planet. That he was very nearly bulletproof.

He nodded at Laura. "Good to hear they are doing so well," he said.

She smiled in return. "More wine?"

"Perhaps just a bit more."

Hans appeared as if by magic, bottle in hand, to pour. Life was almost perfect. Almost.

17

Washington, D.C.

Natadze went home. He had a nice condo in New York, but he preferred to live in the District when possible, and he considered that his primary residence. The house he used was legally owned by a series of concentric paper-corporations, with no trail to him, set up by the courtesy of Mr. Cox so there was no way anybody could know it was his.

Natadze stayed off the books as much as he could. Those few elements of his persona that had to be public were mostly false—licenses, credit cards, even magazine subscriptions. It was hard to track prey if you couldn't even identify it, and Eduard worked hard to be as untrackable as possible.

He arrived home at the same time as the FastAir Express carrier's truck. He had made an arrangement with the delivery man, claiming that evening rounds were more convenient for him, and had made it worth the man's time to provide the extra service. It was amazing how many problems would just disappear if you threw enough money at them. Another lesson that Mr. Cox had taught him.

Despite the situation with Jay Gridley, he felt his spirits lift immediately when he saw the truck: The new Bogdanovich had come!

The delivery man exited the blocky truck, carrying a large box that Natadze immediately knew to be the guitar for which he had been waiting. He met the man at the front gate, signed the acceptance form, gave him a sizeable tip, and hurried inside.

It was but the work of a moment to open the box, dump the biodegradable packing peanuts onto the floor, and get to the cased instrument. The case itself was one of Cedar Creek's custom models, a kind of hound's-tooth pattern against a dull yellow background. They made good ones, Cedar Creek, and were priced remarkably cheap. Not something you would trust to the airlines to manhandle, but then you wouldn't trust a steel *vault* to the airlines.

He hurriedly opened the six latches and looked at the guitar.

Bogdanovich was, as were some of the other underrated American luthiers, such as Schramm and Spross, doing outstanding work at very reasonable prices. He was, Natadze believed, a New Yorker who now lived in northern California. Natadze already owned one of his guitars, a spruce-front, maple-back model he had found in a San Francisco shop some years ago. That one had a tone as good as instruments costing five times as much, and he had been impressed enough that he ordered a new one custom-made for him. Fortunately for him, Bogdanovich hadn't been discovered yet, and the waiting time was still relatively short. If you wanted a Smallman, for instance, the Australian maker's list was several years deep, and Natadze was still waiting on one of those. Bogdanovich's list, fortunately, was only a few months, and to judge from the tone of the one Natadze already had, he was able to run with the best.

He picked up the guitar, turned it slowly. Built on the standard Torres/Hauser pattern, this one was western red cedar–topped, with Indian rosewood back and sides. It had a Spanish cedar neck, ebony fretboard, and Sloane tuners. It was French polished only on the front, with a harder lacquer on the sides and back. Beautiful just to look at, but the test, of course, was the sound.

He pulled up a chair, closed the case for a foot prop, tuned the guitar, and ran through several scales, going up the neck.

Ah. No dead notes, no buzzes.

He plucked an E-chord in first position. The notes were sharp, clear, warm—cedar was more mellow than spruce— and they rang with a long sustain. He plucked the E again, high up the board. Perfect. He belled the harmonics at the twelfth. Excellent!

He retuned the trebles, and played "Blackbird," one of his warm-up pieces. The guitar filled the kitchen with beautiful music.

Yes! It sounded almost as good as his Friedrich!

Well, all right, not quite *that* good, but still. How bad could things be, when such guitars existed?

He would have to send a note to Bogdanovich, but not for a while. First, he needed to play this beauty for a couple of hours.

Perhaps he could play the sonata by Nikolai Narimanidze, a countryman. People did not realize how many excellent composers and musicians came from Georgia. If they knew much about the country at all, it was usually that it was Stalin's birthplace, and that the semisweet wines were decent.

Well. That was not important now. Now, he could forget his worries for a few hours and do what he liked to do best.

University Park, Maryland

John Howard stood in his kitchen, watching the coffee drip through the gold mesh filter. Nadine was working on breakfast, still in her bathrobe. Toni Michaels came into the kitchen, also in a robe. Howard nodded at her. "Alex still asleep?"

"In the shower," Toni said.

"I hope there's some hot water left," Nadine said. "I think my son is part fish, as long as he stays in there."

"Alex won't die if the water gets cold. How is Tyrone?"

"Doing better," Nadine said.

Toni nodded and didn't push it.

Howard looked at the coffee pot. They had a bond, the Michaels family and his. Tyrone had saved their son's life—and his own—and that would never go away. He'd had to kill a very bad man to do it, and there had been some trauma connected to that, even though the boy had dealt with it better than a lot of men did.

The coffee was done and poured when Alex Michaels came into the room. He nodded at the others, and accepted a cup of the fragrant brew from Toni. He sipped at it. "Morning."

"Nearly afternoon," Toni said. "Slug."

"Eight-fifteen is not anywhere close to noon," Michaels said. "Just because you like to do crosswords at five A.M.—"

"First batch of pancakes is about ready. How is little Alex?" Nadine asked.

"Great," Michaels and Toni said as one.

Howard smiled.

"Guru is teaching him Javanese," Toni said. "And already showing him how to stand for *djurus.*"

Howard shook his head. He had met the old woman they called "Guru" several times. She was in her eighties, squat, and a master of the martial art that Toni and Michaels studied, *Pentjak Silat.*

Toni, who could toss black-belt fighters around like toys, said the old lady was a lot better than she was, and Howard believed her. He had seen her move, and had seen Michaels move, and he wouldn't have wanted to face either of them without a weapon in hand. Preferably a gun.

"Anything new?" Michaels asked.

"No."

A silence settled upon the kitchen, broken by Nadine. "Who wants the first stack? Toni?"

"Sure," Toni said. "I haven't had homemade pancakes in ages."

"You ever think about learning how to cook? You could have them more often," Michaels said. But he was smiling.

"This from a man who burns water?"

He smiled.

Howard turned the conversation to what they were all thinking about: Jay Gridley. "The FBI is trying to run down the shooter," he said. "They are interviewing people who were still at the scene when the state troopers got there. Some who came forward, some who didn't but whose license plates were caught on the troopers' car cams. It doesn't look real promising so far. The AIC, Peterson, says if it was a pro hitter, he won't have left any big clues. So far he's been right. The only thing people noticed—those who noticed anything at all about the guy—was that he had a Band-Aid on his face."

Toni and Michaels nodded, but didn't speak.

"What about you two?" Howard asked.

"We flipped a coin," Michaels said. "If Jay doesn't come around in the next day or two, I'm going to Colorado, Toni will stay here for a while."

"It could be months, or even years," Howard said carefully. What he didn't say was, *Or he might not come out of it at all.*

"Yes," Alex said simply.

"We'll see how it goes," Toni added. "If Jay is still in

there and it's at all possible for him to wake up, he will.
He's a fighter."

Howard nodded and sipped at his coffee. She was right.
He hoped.

18

In the Dream Time

Jay lay on his back on the bench and laughed as the stack of weights on the Universal Gym tried to come down and crush him. An errant shaft of sunlight from a high window played on the chrome, the glint of light harsh.

Gonna crush you, Gridley!

Not gonna happen, Iron.

Jay knew he looked like a demigod, hugely muscled, thews and sinews grotesquely rippling, power radiating from him.

Conan the Gridley. Hah!

He heaved, hard, and felt something give in the machine. The stack of weights hit the top of their range, something broke, and part of a shattered plate flew free. It arced across the room and hit the wall, *clang!* and fell to the floor with a clunk.

Pumped, he stood and *shoved* the old Universal aside, enjoying the sound of it screeching across the concrete floor, a primal testosterone buzz rolling through his body.

"Who was that you were gonna crush?" he said aloud.

He was strong. This was the power of comic-book heroes, of mythological characters.

Would it be enough?

He had managed to gain more control over his environment, at least. The gym and his other exercises were a testament to that.

But it was still weird. He couldn't program things like he could in VR. There were no objects to code, no places to do input. The illusions he created were simultaneously more real and unreal than anything he'd ever done in VR. Things acted on their own with patterns he would never be able to create with software, fractal shades of reality that came from within, unlike anything he could achieve through a program.

Like his VR scenarios, this was a metaphor. He was training his will, to increase his mental activity until he could get *out*.

The idea had come from a memory of the previous coma's rehab. He'd been weightlifting, an exercise for which he saw no use whatsoever, but had been forced into, and he'd accidentally put the pin into the wrong notch. He'd started his press, thinking it was his normal weight, and had been shocked to find it so heavy. Unwilling to admit defeat, he'd strained, inching the stack up slowly, bit by bit. It had become a test of will—no inanimate pile of metal was going to beat him!

Jay toweled the sweat off. He was as ready as he could be, and he hoped it would be enough.

To match his training metaphor, he'd entered himself into a strongman contest. He'd seen one on ESPN once while channel surfing. It had fascinated him to see these modern Samsons doing what they did.

Each event in the contest he'd planned would test his willpower, help him focus. The brain-wave states of Delta, Theta, Alpha, and Beta were going to be achieved through doing something else, just like VR.

Jay continued his preparations, stretching his legs, now

as thick as tree trunks. He was glad for Spandex.

Otherwise I'd be shredding clothes like the Hulk.

There was a musical fanfare from outside, and it was time for the contest. He headed out into a brightly sunlit arena.

"And here representing geeks everywhere, is *Smokin' Jay Gridley!*" The loudspeaker blared again, this time the theme to *2001: A Space Odyssey.*

Also Sprach Zarathustra.

Jay grinned as he stalked across the arena. Just ahead was the competition.

Alpha, Beta, Theta, and good old Delta.

Of course there was no *real* competition—only the mental activity borders between layers of his consciousness. Each had a Greek letter embroidered on his gear, making him identifiable. Delta looked weak; Jay already knew he could beat *him.* Theta looked tougher, but Jay was sure he could take him. Beta and Alpha grinned. Those were the real challenges.

Alpha held his arm up, pinched his biceps and shook his head.

Beta sneered and then pointed his index finger at the ground.

You going down, Jay.

Even though he'd seen similar behavior in many of the other constructs in his dream state, it was still impressive. None of the characters had ever used these mannerisms before, and he found their independence unnerving.

Relax, Gridley, it's all in your mind.

So he grinned back and waved at them.

I can be unpredictable, too.

Today's contest had four events. All Jay had to do was beat everyone at their own game, one-on-one, and he'd be free.

He hoped.

He and Delta moved toward rows of metal kegs, each of which weighed a couple hundred pounds. Past that, twenty-five feet away, was a platform, just over waist high. The goal was to put as many of the kegs as you could up onto the platform. All within seventy-five seconds.

Jay knew that Delta could do about four kegs, maybe five. They took their positions, and after what seemed like an eternity, the shot starting the event went off.

Jay wanted an edge in this race, so when he picked up his first keg, he tucked it under an arm and then picked another one with one hand. He heard a murmur in the crowd as he did this, and looked up for a moment at the watchers to see Theta frowning. Beta and Alpha sneered.

Go! He lurched forward, almost falling. Delta, who had just picked up the one keg, was out in front, but not by much.

Jay put the kegs down on the platform and ran back for more. He picked up two more, and saw that although he was slower compared to Delta, he was still a keg up.

Go! He picked up another pair and made it back to the platform. He ran back.

Two more. Beside him he saw Delta returning for his fourth keg.

Faster.

He picked up the pace and *pushed,* his entire body pumping, blood rushing, heart pounding, will straining. As his fifth and sixth kegs touched down on the platform and he turned back for more, he heard the buzzer go off.

"Gridley, six kegs, the winner!" called the announcer.

Yes!

Delta glared. Jay smiled.

One down.

The next contest used medicine balls. They were fifty pounds each, and had to be thrown at a plywood target. The target was big, to reduce the difficulties in aiming; the bottom of the target was a little higher than three feet off the ground.

This was Theta's event, and Jay watched him pick up a ball, lean back, and thrust forward.

The ball flew and slammed into the plywood target, a little more than halfway up. He was strong, too, no question about it.

Jay was up next. He concentrated on the sequence he'd been practicing for months—or perhaps it was just days or even hours. Time was so subjective here.

He picked up the heavy ball. He wanted to do more than win; he wanted to smash the competition, to make them worry.

I can do this.

He took several deep breaths, hyperventilating. For what he wanted to happen, he'd have to hit the target high.

Okay. This one's for you, Theta.

Theta leaned against a railing nearby, smirking.

Laugh at this!

Jay bent deep, twisted, wound it up. When it seemed as if he were going to cramp from turning into himself so tightly, he expanded.

Fire all muscle cells, this is NOT a drill!

The twist was followed by two short steps as he lined up and fired the medicine ball with every bit of his focus.

All he *had* to do was hit the target.

What he did was break it.

It was only the upper right corner. Plywood was tough stuff, made up of criss-crossing wood fibers. The chances of him punching through were nonexistent. But by catching the corner just *so,* he knew he could tear the corner off, like ripping a book cover.

He'd done it in practice, so it wasn't so amazing to him. But the audience gasped, Theta slumped, and he had the satisfaction of seeing Alpha and Beta glance sharply over at him.

That's right boys, you're next.

And then he was through Theta.

Alpha's event was tougher. It was a tire flip, with huge

tractor tires weighted with water. They lay flat on the ground, and you had to pry them up using a dead lift, raise them onto their treads, and shove them over, then repeat the sequence. Seventy seconds was the time limit.

The contest was tougher, not just because he was already tired, but because his consciousness level had climbed. It was harder to hold all of his constructs together. Things were starting to go fuzzy at the edges.

The first couple of flips went okay. He caught the balance of the water within the tire at just the right time, and it almost seemed to flip itself. He looked over and saw that Alpha was dead even with him.

And that nearly lost him the game.

He shifted balance slightly, and the water sloshed backward, almost toppling the tire backward on the next flip.

He let out a low hiss, angry with himself.

Do or die, Gridley!

He shoved with everything he had, felt the water shift, and the tire went over.

He kept after it now, pushing hard. Four, five, six, seven, eight . . .

The buzzer sounded.

He glanced over, and saw Alpha was half a revolution back. He'd won!

And suddenly things got even more indistinct. The arena shrank to a smaller size, more of a large room now, everything tighter. Alpha, Theta, and Delta were smaller, too, all standing on a platform off to the left, watching as he and Beta moved toward two huge logs set on the remaining platform.

Log press.

Each log was maybe twelve inches in diameter, with hand slots cut into it at shoulder-width. The contest was pure strength, total number of reps in seventy seconds.

This is it.

This was the hard one. He'd never beaten Beta, never made it out, didn't know if he had what it took.

Beta looked over at him as if he could read his mind.

He probably could, too.

Jay had failed every time he'd tried to win against Beta before.

So he'd trained differently this time. He'd had a realization. It wasn't about the end, it was all about the competition itself.

The gun sounded and they began.

He didn't count his reps, but focused on the feeling, the burning of muscles, the lightness of the weight. He'd trained with heavier logs than this; all he had to do was keep going.

He glanced over at Beta, and saw him straining but keeping the same pace. Jay tried to shut Beta out of his thoughts. He'd lost last time because he'd pushed harder when he thought Beta was going down. A mistake.

It's not about him, *it's about* me.

He tried not to think at all; he worked, seeking the joy of work, wanting the play of muscle, the power. It came down to that. Enjoying the contest for itself, the test of his body; the play of his skin over his muscles, the sensation of the weight rising through the air, rough bark against his hands, the pine-sap smell of the recently cut wood. Not the goal, but the moment. . . .

The air shimmered, and his reality faded in and out.

He kept going.

Born here doing this. Will live here forever doing this. . . .

The scene faded. Everything was dark now, he couldn't see a thing. But he could hear—

A faint sound, brilliantly crisp and *electronic*. The click of heels on a floor, the smell of . . . antiseptic?

He tried to speak, tried to turn his body, but succeeded only in a quiet moan.

"Jay?!"

Saji!

University Park, Maryland

There were times when Thorn did general practice—basic
forms with all three weapons: foil, épée, and saber—and
other times when he just concentrated on his footwork or
blade work alone, repeating a series of lunges or parry-
and-riposte drills. Now and then, he would concentrate on
one blade, such as he was doing today with the épée, and
one particular exercise that he felt was a weakness. Playing to your strength was more fun, of course, it gave the
old ego a big boost when you could execute a fancy series
and know that nine of ten people you faced would have
trouble handling it. But you lost matches on your weak-
nesses, and eliminating those made you a better swordsman—even if your competitive days were long past.

This morning, he felt ready to deal with one particular
chink in his armor, and decided that he was going to concentrate on his infighting.

Infighting was more of a foil style than something you
saw much of in either épée or saber, which was exactly
why he wanted to work on it. One of the big advantages
in cross-training—and this was especially true when it
came to cross-training with eastern weapons and styles as
well as western fencing technique—was that it opened
your mind to seeing each weapon in a new light. The fact
that it sometimes gave you new moves, new styles, and
new advantages didn't hurt either.

Infighting was exactly that: close-in fighting, often
standing side-by-side with your opponent, your fighting
arm twisted behind your own back, your point probing,
your parries forgotten. It was something you did, not
something you planned, and the whole concept was con-
trary to Thorn's own natural style.

He preferred distance. He had a long reach and a great
sense of timing, and so he liked to stay outside of his
opponent's reach whenever possible, drawing him out,
creating openings that he could attack into. When he

closed, it was to take advantage of something, and almost always resulted in a quick hit. He'd never been comfortable going toe to toe.

It was time to change that.

He was working at home today, in a little room he'd left clear of furniture. It didn't have the right flooring, or the racks of weapons, or the wall full of mirrors that he planned to install in Net Force's gym, but that was all right. He wasn't planning a full-scale bout with any of Jay's VR opponents.

He'd hung a number of golf balls on long strings from the high, vaulted ceiling. Each golf ball was a target. His normal work-out routine started with him addressing a single golf ball, coming to guard before it and simply thrusting at it, over and over, until he hit it fifty times in a row. It got significantly harder after the first hit, since the ball would be moving, swinging back and forth like a pendulum, after each successful strike.

After fifty consecutive hits, he would move back far enough to add a lunge to his strike. Twenty consecutive hits later he would move back still farther, adding a quick step and turning his lunge into a *ballestra.*

That was his normal routine, and he did it with either foil or épée, depending on which weapon he was concentrating on at the time. It was good for practicing aim, for developing speed, and for working on timing. Some days it was simply warm-up for other drills. Other days that was all he did. Today he wanted something more.

He raised the first golf ball, shortening its string so it hung at about shoulder height. Another golf ball hung a couple of feet behind the first one. He lowered this so that it hung near his hip. Then he stepped back and dropped into guard position.

Go!

He lunged, striking at the first golf ball, simulating an attack upon an imaginary opponent. As the tip of his épée struck home, he turned the move into a *prise de fer*, keep-

ing his point low and sweeping his guard through a hook
and lift, visualizing his opponent's blade being lifted and
carried above his left shoulder. His guard held near his
left ear, pinning his imaginary attacker's blade away from
his body; he brought his point on line and stepped forward
with his right foot, driving his tip into the second golf
ball.

He smiled at the thunk of the tip. Not bad, but that was
the easy one.

Stepping back, he waited for the golf balls to stop
swinging and then did it again. And again.

When he felt he had the rhythm down, he rehung both
golf balls, adjusting their strings so they were both chest
high.

Now for the hard one.

He came to guard closer to the first ball. In this drill,
the first ball would be his opponent's blade, the second
ball would be his target.

Go!

He beat, once, fast and hard, knocking the first golf ball
to the left with the side of his blade. In the same motion,
he stepped forward with his left foot and brought his blade
around the back of his head, whipping his point at the
second ball.

He missed. Badly.

He stood there a moment longer, feeling the strain in
his right shoulder, until the first ball, swinging on its
string, hit him in the back.

Nice one, Thorn, he thought.

Grinning, he shook his head and set up once again.

Twenty minutes later, having hit the ball only three
times, he sighed and took off his mask. He was still a
long ways from where he wanted to be, but at least he'd
made a start.

Feeling as if he had addressed the problem, if not completely solved it, Thorn went to take a shower.

19

Thorn wasn't doing anything illegal, but he still felt a little guilty as he ran the computer check on Marissa. He wasn't using his status with Net Force to gain access to any classified or secret information—he would never do that; the material he found on the web was public information, available to anybody who bothered to look. That was legal. But still . . .

Some of it he already knew, but he was definitely intrigued by her, and curious about the rest.

In her academic records, he came across a set of scores on assorted exams, for college, government service, and the like, and one of them was a standardized IQ test. Thorn had always done well on those himself, since his IQ edged into what was considered genius range on such scales.

He blinked at Marissa's number:

Five points higher than his.

She was smarter than he was!

He shook his head. He hadn't even considered that before. He had assumed that she was a feeler, not a thinker.

That she was brighter or quicker didn't threaten him—
he liked smart women, he liked to be challenged—but
that he hadn't seen it did bother him. Slipped right past
him, that did.

This was an old lesson, one he should have gotten by
now: What you see isn't always what you get.

What else was he missing because he accepted it at face
value?

New York City

It was early, the domestic market hadn't opened yet, and
Cox was attending to business that had piled up during
the night. Business never slept when you dealt with people
around the globe.

The scrambled phone rang. He knew who it was; there
was only one caller who used this line.

He pushed a blue button on the unit, picked up the
receiver, and leaned back in his custom-built Aeron form-
chair, the specialized pellicle flex-plastic shifting under
his weight. Most people wouldn't think of paying several
hundred dollars for a chair, much less the several thousand
this one had cost him.

Most people were shortsighted.

"Cox."

"Good day, Comrade."

Of course, it was the Russian, making his tired little
joke again.

Cox's tone needed to be consistent, otherwise the Russian would start to wonder. "To what do I owe the pleasure of this call?" He kept his voice dry.

Cox knew the intricate chain of events he'd set off by
pushing the blue button. The good Doctor had been most
cautious—understandably so—when he'd awakened his

sleeper, preferring to contact him by phone and infrequently. He'd been smart enough to realize that if Cox figured out where he was, that might not be a good thing for him. But if being rich had taught Cox anything, it was a special kind of patience, the ability to see beyond the present.

Patience, along with money, could buy all manner of things. The chair upon which he sat, for instance, was more than just a comfortable seat. The quality of it, the fine materials and the beauty of its design—all added to the pleasure of using it. The areté of such a fine mechanism improved his life.

It was a matter of value. His time was priceless, as it was the only thing he could not buy—although he had some tame scientists working on antiaging drugs which might pan out. The chair increased his pleasure by being well-constructed, beautiful, and functional, all at once. It gave him satisfaction. The expense was nothing. He would have bought it even if he couldn't afford it, and figured out a way to pay for it later.

So, too, had he invested quite a bit in the Doctor. He had decided that he would need to speak to the man on *his* terms someday, and had started tracing his controller's phone calls as a matter of course almost as soon as they had begun.

The demise of the Soviet Union had not, unfortunately, dulled its agents' paranoia. Even low-tech tradecraft and off-the-shelf technology could foil most people trying to trace them electronically.

Vrach—Cox didn't know his real name—had not called him directly, at least not since Cox had begun trying to find him. Instead he'd phoned through a network-access setup, encrypting his voice into an Internet datastream which could be bounced all over the world. The data would leave the network at an exit point, and be turned into a phone call.

Cox looked at an LCD inset in the desk and noted that the exit point chosen this time was Brazil.

Should the Internet data be traced to the point where it entered the network, a tracker would discover that the Russian had used a cell phone, making a trace more difficult still. And Vrach called on *disposable* cell phones, never using the same one twice. Backwalking and finding him, using electronic tracking alone, was nearly impossible.

There were, however, other ways. It had taken a team of Cox's agents quite a while to get as far back along the trail as they were now; these men were always on call, waiting to move at any time.

Vrach had been tricky, routing his communications from access points all over the world. The man could be thousands of miles away—or right next door.

So Cox's hackers had designed and distributed a computer virus specifically designed for the hardware that tracked incoming and outgoing calls on Internet-phone connections. This had allowed Cox's hounds instant access to the network where the call originated. Once they were inside the firewall, they could trace the call over the Internet back to the true origin.

"I have good news."

The only good news the Doctor could have worth being happy about would be that every record of him as a Soviet agent had been destroyed. Since that wasn't likely, Cox wasn't too excited.

"Really?"

The final, and largest problem in finding the Doctor was that his cell phone calls not only originated from different cities, but from *moving* locations: buses, trains, subways, and once even a ferry.

He could almost hear the Doctor grin into the mouthpiece.

Go ahead and grin; my turn is coming.

"The Net Force agent assigned to decode the captured file has been severely injured, in what the authorities have been led to believe was an incident of road rage. He had decoded but a small portion of the information, and you were not on it."

Cox did not feel relief, he felt irritated. That the Russian's not-so-subtle hint suggested the incident had been the Russian's doing. Cox *knew* better.

Pathetic.

Sooner or later, he would find the man. Cox had spread men across the eastern seaboard and the Midwest, at each place where the Doctor had originated a cell call. Helicopters waited in every city, and with the press of the blue button on this phone, were launched moments after a call came in, cellular-direction finders in each one.

Aloft, these copters would triangulate the calls as soon as the hackers provided the relevant information. It took time to get close, however, and even if the helicopters had found which boat, train, or bus the doctor was on, it wouldn't show them who was behind the phone, or where he lived.

Which was why an army of detectives constantly rode buses, trains, and ferries in several metropolitan areas. Those alone cost him nearly a million dollars a month.

Cox tried to imagine how it would be to have such a job, waiting all the time, on a train where he might have to track someone identified as a target.

It would be mostly boring, he decided, but that didn't matter. They were well-paid for their time. They could read, or listen to music, or whatever, he didn't care, as long as they were there when he needed them.

A text screen lit up on the dedicated computer attached to the phone. Amber letters scrolled across it:

Connecticut. Train to New York.

Fantastic. They hadn't had a hit this good so quickly before.

"This does not seem to help me much," Cox said. It wouldn't do to cut the call short.

"But it does—and it shows that we are still looking out for you, *da?*"

Cox shook his head in disgust. Vrach *was* trying to assume credit for Natadze's action. It obviously never even occurred to him that Cox would have taken matters into his own hands. The man was not nearly as clever as he thought he was. Few men were.

"I see."

Agent in place at next stop, read the text.

Excellent! thought Cox. Even with the call terminated, they would be able to find the phone—Cox didn't know how, but his technicians had told him they could, as long as it was still powered.

"I should think that this would convince you to keep helping us. There is a Senator we would like to know more about."

He could hear a rustling as the Russian talked. It sounded as if the man was moving around.

Train stopping, said the text onscreen.

Cox sighed, making it sound as if he were exasperated. "All right. Tell me his name."

The Doctor did so.

"You will do what you can?"

A green LED lit up on his caller ID box, and the display now read, "Subject Identified," as the instant message screen popped up a confirmation.

Yes! They had him!

Subject has left the train. We are tracking.

"But of course," said Cox. "Don't I always?"

"You see? I knew my call would cheer you."

Cox smiled. "You have no idea how much better I feel now, Doctor."

"We will speak later."

After the disconnect, Cox didn't even put the receiver down before he called Eduard. Yes, by God, things were finally beginning to look up. They had the Russian. And after Eduard got to him, they would have everything he knew about Cox's situation.

This was how empires were built: one brick at a time.

20

Midnight, Full Moon
The Hills of West Virginia

Thorn had a great-uncle who had been born in West Virginia, and the man, ancient when Thorn had met him, had told some wonderful stories of his boyhood. Hillbillies and moonshine stills, the incredible landscape with its hardwood and pine forests, and the days he'd gone spotlight hunting with his bluetick and red-and-tan hounds in the dark. At some point, Thorn had decided that he would go there, but he had never managed it in the Real World—though he had eventually built himself a scenario.

So it was that he now tramped through the warm summer night following a pack of baying coon hounds, in pursuit of whatever it had been that caused Jay Gridley to be shot.

He had managed to open nearly all of Gridley's files, and the one that held the most promise was the one from the Turkish Ambassador. As had many of the countries in the Middle East, the Turks had been on-again, off-again friends. Currently they were on-again, and Net Force's decision to help them had not been strictly altruistic, since uncovering Russian moles still in place was in the best interests of the United States, even though the Russians were no longer the evil empire they had once been.

Ahead, the hounds called, their deep *barrooos!* resonant under the light of the full moon. Bright enough to read by out here, bright enough to see the sparkles in the opal ring Thorn wore, the ring that had belonged to his grandfather. Thorn wore it in VR a lot, though not so much in RW—there it was only for special occasions. His grandfather had had small hands, and it just fit on Thorn's little finger.

The old man had believed opals were potent stones, full of magic. He had gone to Australia once, bought a small but gorgeous black boulder opal from the Cody Brothers, well-known for their outstanding stock, and had it set into a custom gold ring made by Rick Martin Snow Owl, a beautiful setting that protected the opal. It had been one of his grandfather's criteria for a good stone—if it shines brightly under moonlight, it's a good one.

Thorn had inherited the ring. It was an irregular-shaped red-multicolor flashfire, had blues, greens, oranges, even yellows in it, and on a sunny day, you could see the fire shining from across the street.

Not so bright in moonlight, if you wanted to keep your scenario TTL—true-to-life—but still a comforting glow. The colors reminded him of looking at a neighborhood strip mall full of neon signs at night from five hundred yards away; brilliant, electric, magic.

Opals were supposed to be unlucky, but his grandfather had laughed and told him that was a lie started by diamond merchants in London in the late 1800s. The opals were cutting into diamond sales, and what better way to discourage people from buying them than by saying they were cursed?

Thorn smiled. He missed his grandfather, a man who

had been wise in the ways of the world—and who had remained kind despite his knowledge.

The dogs began calling louder, and Thorn knew from the tones they had treed a raccoon—a bit of information he had been hunting.

He passed through a grassy meadow, skirted patches of poison ivy, and tramped back into a stand of long-leaf pine. The light from his big dry-cell lamp found the dogs, who were baying and trying to climb the fat-boled tree with no success. Thorn shined the brilliant beam into the branches.

Twenty feet up, the light reflected from the eyes of a big raccoon clinging to the trunk.

Thorn grinned. *Gotcha!*

"All right, pups, I'll take it from here. Back off, be quiet, and sit!"

His great-uncle had told him that hounds weren't that easy to train, but it was Thorn's scenario, and having dogs that would do what he wanted was simple enough to program—even if it wasn't really TTL.

The dogs, eight of them, moved away from the tree, circled around, lined up in a row facing him, and, as neat as a military drill team, sat.

"Good dogs!"

Thorn unslung the tranquilizer rifle from his shoulder, worked the bolt, inserted a hypodermic dart, and locked the bolt shut. He snicked the safety off, raised the weapon, and lined up on the coon. He squeezed off he shot. The compressed *whump!* of carbon dioxide was loud in the night.

The raccoon jumped as the dart hit it, but he stayed put.

Three minutes later, the coon lost his grip on the rough pine bark and fell to the soft and mossy ground, unharmed and unconscious.

The dogs looked longingly at it, but stayed put.

Thorn went over to examine his find.

Net Force HQ
Quantico, Virginia

Thorn removed the sensory apparatus—the headgear, gloves, and slicksuit mesh—and considered what he had found. He had the tools for this: Using cause and effect, coupled with extrapolation, he might be able to come up with a reasoned scenario that made sense. At least it was a place to start.

Jay had not broken the entire code the Turks had gotten, but those parts he had managed to decrypt had revealed spies in Africa, the Middle East, South America, Central America, and Mexico.

In that order.

Consider that as . . . inertia, and extrapolate in a straight line. Do that, and it was not that great a stretch to infer that the unbroken sections would continue north, into the U.S. and maybe Canada. Everybody knew the Soviets had fielded scores of spies in the U.S. in the bad old days, and why assume that they had all folded their tents and left when the cold war was done?

Assume for the sake of argument that the still-encrypted portion of file was going to show the names of spies in the U.S., some of whom were still here.

Not a major leap to go there. So what?

So, what if one of those spies somehow found out about the file?

How?

A leak from the Turks? Or surely the Russians must have realized pretty quick their ancient agents were being collected. Would they have tipped off the ones still at large? That would make sense, if the ones remaining had any value to them.

Why attack Jay?

That one was easy. Going to prison for treason? That would be good motivation. Or maybe it was the Russians themselves. They could have a mole somewhere they absolutely did not want to lose. Just because the Russians were currently friends didn't mean they wouldn't still want intelligence information if they could get it. Friendly countries all spied on each other. The Russians would know about the file's existence, they would know the Turks had intercepted it, and maybe they were trying to make sure Jay didn't get to some valuable bit of information?

The Russians trying to protect a valuable spy, or the spy trying to protect his own hide, either of those would be enough reason to want Net Force to back off.

But, okay, assume one of these scenarios was true, then whoever it was would have to have pretty good resources. They'd know that Net Force had the file, if they had some way of getting into the Turk's agencies, but how would they know that Jay was the man working on it? And be able to target him, get a bug on his car, and be ready to take him out the way they had? That indicated somebody with expertise, and experts cost money.

Thorn stretched. He needed a break. He decided to check his e-mail, see what had come in while he'd been working, and then get back to the problem of Jay.

It had been a pretty good day so far, considering how early it was, but when he found his personal e-mail box jammed once again with messages from the troll, he decided it was time to put a stop to it. He didn't need this irritating crap when he had more important things to do.

He emptied the mailbox and got on-line. He wanted to check something before he went any further with this, and it didn't take long to track down the stats he wanted. The amount of information on the web was incredible, things nobody would have ever dreamed of in the early days of the net.

He had wondered why the man who called himself Rapier felt such anger at him, and for the life of him, Thorn hadn't been able to come up with a reason. Yes, Thorn had made a lot of money in the computer software field, and that alone engendered a certain amount of resentment, but Rapier—whose name was Dennis James McManus, he had discovered—seemed personally irritated, and Thorn didn't know him from a hole in the wall.

What Thorn had on the holoproj in front of him were the results of fencing matches from his days in college, specifically the matches at the University of Chicago all those years ago.

It didn't take long to find the match, one he had forgotten until this very moment. He didn't have a great memory for names, and recalling the faces of the people he'd competed against was worse. But he remembered tourneys, and individual matches, the good ones, and when he saw that he had fought McManus in the quarterfinal match, before he had lost to the great Parker King in the semifinals, he recalled the bout.

The guy had been pretty good. They had fenced to "la belle"—a tie score one point away from victory. McManus's style was odd—he had a great lunge, fast and strong, but his tip control was so-so, and his riposte slow. And he liked throwing flicks, too, which were legal, but irritating. Even so, he might have won the match had he not been penalized.

McManus liked to infight—and was good at it, if a bit sloppy. Early in the match he had stepped in too close and bumped Thorn with his hip, getting his touch disallowed and earning himself a warning for corps-a-corps. At la belle, when Thorn threw a feint, McManus bound his blade and stepped in close, his bell guard high, tip landing solidly on Thorn's side, but again he came in too fast and too far. He had run into Thorn again, harder this time, and the director again disallowed the touch.

McManus had ripped off his mask to argue with the director, without asking or receiving permission. A stupid error, and inexcusable at that level of competition. When the director called him on it, he popped off and actually shook his blade at the official. McManus had been dis-

qualified on the spot. That had cost him and his team, the
match had been awarded to Thorn.

Maybe McManus could have won on points, maybe
not, but the rules were the rules.

*Could that be it? That much bile and anger, after all
these years? Because he lost a match he felt he should
have won?*

Thorn could find nothing else to explain it, but it
seemed so . . . petty. How would it be to live your life like
that? Hanging on to something that small for so long?

He considered how he was going to handle it, and decided that a simple and direct response was best. He
flipped on the voxax circuit and said into the microphone:

"You lost the match. Knock it off."

He sent that to McManus's e-mail address. It wasn't
necessary for him to say he knew who McManus was—
that he was able to send him a message told the guy that.
And that he referred to the long-ago match was enough
to show the man that he knew why McManus was dogging him. A smart man would back away. Even a fairly
thick one would see the writing on the wall.

If McManus kept sending his crap, he couldn't say he
hadn't been given a chance. He didn't want to use his
position as a personal hammer, but Thorn had the right
of every other citizen when it came to harassment, and
while he would undoubtedly get a faster response because
of who he was, he had the right to see that McManus
didn't keep bothering him. What the man was doing *was*
illegal, at least technically, and a call to his server would
stop it. If McManus switched servers and tried under another name, Thorn would still know who he was, and he
could do worse to him if he felt like it.

Given the situation with Jay, this was a minor irritant,
but at least it was one about which he could do something.
Now, back to the problem at hand.

21

Natadze had taken an early morning commuter jet from the District to New York, picked up a rental car at the airport, then driven to Cox's estate. Even though his employer's private phones were fitted with the latest in scrambling devices, there were some things they simply did not discuss except when they were alone, and in a room that had been swept for bugs.

Who was to say that the company who made the scrambler had not made a way to unscramble it at their desire? And that they had not provided that way to somebody with an interest in such cloaked conversations? One knew that the government lied to its citizens on a daily basis about so many things, and, under the guise of national security, would snoop anywhere it wished. It had been more than a decade since the United States lost its innocence and joined the rest of the world's harsher reality.

Cox's study at his home was a safe room—shielded against stray radio or microwaves, checked daily for listening devices, with triple-paned windows polarized and vibratored to thwart lasers or directional microphones that might possibly be aimed at them from miles away, however unlikely that was.

What could not be seen or heard could not come back to haunt you.

Natadze sat on the brown leather couch, Cox in one of his form-chairs.

"Do you have any questions?"

Natadze shook his head. "No, sir. I understand my mission. I am to find out what the Russians have, to the limits of the Doctor's knowledge—where that information might be found, who has it, how it might be accessed—and then I am to find and delete everything."

"Including the Doctor."

"Yes, sir."

"I don't want any mistakes this time, Eduard."

"There will be none."

Cox nodded. "Good. Have you given the matter of Net Force any further thought?"

"I have. I am considering ways to make certain no problems arise from that end again."

"Good. I leave it in your hands, Eduard."

Washington, D.C.

When he opened his eyes, Jay saw Saji sitting in a chair three feet away. She smiled at him. He could smell her, a rich, warm, musky scent. And his vision and hearing both seemed much sharper, too—the light was actinic and bright, the hum and click of the systems monitor next to his bed seemed unusually loud.

Standing behind his wife's chair was Toni Michaels.

"Hey, Jay," Saji said.

"Hey, Little Momma," he said. "Are we having fun yet?"

Her smile grew, and Toni's grin lit at the same time.

"Finally. What do you need to know?" Saji said.

"Did they get the guy who shot me?"

"Not yet."

"How long was I out?"

"A few days. More than a couple, less than thirty."

He nodded. "Hey, Toni. I thought you were gone."

"We forgot something, had to come back." To Saji, she said, "I'm going to go call Alex and John."

Saji nodded. "Good."

The door to the hospital room opened and a nurse hurried in as Toni departed.

The nurse, a short, dark-skinned woman of maybe fifty, said, "Mr. Gridley. Awake at last."

"That would be me, yes."

The nurse came over, checked the monitor next to the bed, and smiled. "Dr. Grayson will want to have a word with you. Stay right there, would you?"

"That would be me, staying right here."

The nurse took off, and Saji reached over the bed's railing and took his hand. "I knew you'd be back."

"Good that you did. I wasn't sure I was ever going to make it. I've been trying for what seems like forever."

"You knew you were in a coma?"

"Yeah. I figured it out after a while. Anything else broke but my brain?" He put his hand on his head, felt a bandage patch.

"Nope. And the head injury wasn't all that bad. All that solid bone."

Jay grinned. "How are you doing?"

"Me? I'm fine."

"But you're pregnant. We haven't had a chance to talk about that."

Saji smiled. "We will have plenty of time to talk about it," she said.

"It's weird, thinking about having a baby. A new person."

"Yes."

"But I'm happy about it," he said. "Really."

"Me, too."

They sat there for a few seconds, just beaming at each other. The door opened and Toni slipped back into the room. Saji turned to look at her.

"I called Alex. He and John are on the way. Alex said he would call work and let everybody know." She smiled at Jay. "You've had a parade of visitors in here the last week."

"All come to look at Vegetable Boy?" he said.

"Yep. Some of them wanted to cover you with fertilizer, help you grow and all."

"So, not that I'm feeling vengeful or anything, but why haven't they caught the crazed road-rage guy who shot me?"

Toni said, "Well, it turns out that it wasn't road rage. There was a bug on your car, and current thinking is that the guy was following you."

Jay paused. "Why?"

"Don't have that part yet. Maybe you angered somebody with your sparkling personality."

Jay started to shake his head, but found that hurt. "I don't believe I have any enemies who'd want to shoot me. Certainly nobody comes to mind."

"If it's not personal then it's business. Something you worked on, something you are currently working on."

Jay thought about that for a few seconds, but he was too muzzy to concentrate. And he felt tired all of a sudden.

Saji caught it. "Just rest, Jay. We'll get all the other stuff sorted out later."

"Yeah."

He breathed slowly, and tried not to think about it.

Fat chance.

The doctor arrived. She was a tall, thin woman, with

pale skin and lots of freckles that likely meant her cut-short, carrot-top hair was natural.

"Mr. Gridley. How are you feeling?"

"Feeling good, but you're the expert. You tell me, how am I doing?"

"Except for being in a coma, you are in good shape. And since you are no longer in a coma, I would say you are doing very well indeed."

"Why was I down so long?"

She shrugged. "We don't know. We believe that it was something of a carryover from your earlier incident. To be honest, though, there is still much about the brain that we don't understand."

Jay nodded slowly. "Can I go home?"

Dr. Grayson shook her head. "No, not just yet. We'd like to make sure you don't nod off again. We'll run a few more tests, keep an eye on you for a day or two. If everything checks out—and I expect that it will—you will be able to go home in a few days."

"Thanks."

She nodded. "Welcome back, Mr. Gridley."

After the doctor left, Jay looked at Saji. "Hey."

Toni said, "I think I need to go to the powder room. I'll come back when Alex and John get here. We'll knock."

Jay laughed, but that hurt his head.

22

Natadze waited until the target was in the shower before disabling the magnetic alarm sensor at the back door. He used a powerful rare-earth magnet he'd taken from the head of an electric toothbrush, sliding it between the top of the door and the inset switch mounted in the top of the jamb. The magnet would prevent the switch in the sensor from triggering when he opened the door. The setup was standard, easily defeatable with the right equipment. The PDA he carried was more than it seemed; it had a magnetometer and both an ultrasonic and an infrared sensor. Between the three he could ID most alarm triggers.

When going after a bear in his own den, one of the most important factors was the timing: It was best to catch them in a vulnerable state. Sleeping was good. In the shower was good. A tiny microphone near the water meter had alerted him about the shower.

Of course the target didn't *know* he was being watched. He probably felt he'd done enough to stay out of Cox's grasp. With an alarm system, he probably believed that he would be safe in his own house. Well, if he thought so, he was wrong, as those who thought the world was a safe place usually were.

Especially those who should know better.

The lock was simple, a standard Yale model, an easy pick. He used a torsion tool and a vibrating pick gun, and it was but a matter of fifteen seconds before he opened the door, scanning in front of him with the PDA.

The room was clean, no sensors waiting for him. He was in.

Spycraft had apparently fallen on hard times. It should not be this easy.

Then again, Natadze told himself, maybe it *wasn't* this easy. Maybe the target had tricks yet to play. The most diabolical man Natadze had ever known had been a Russian. It did not pay to generalize about such things, of course, either way, but it did pay to move with caution. Overconfidence was a killer. A simple alarm and lock might be ways to gull someone like Natadze, who, feeling cocky, would pay for it with his life.

He needed this, especially after his failure with Gridley. He needed a challenge. Most of all, though, he needed to succeed.

He was sure the target knew where the data were. In the information age, erasing backups could make that-which-had-been into that-which-never-was. He would not fail Cox again. If he was to succeed, he would have to move with care.

Now was the time to be the most precise. Like the intricate fingerwork of a long solo, every motion, every step needed to be just *so*. Even though he could still hear the shower, it didn't mean the target couldn't be alerted very quickly, or arm himself. The other half of knowing when to strike was understanding your own weakness: Realizing his vulnerability in the shower, the man might well have put some kind of weapon or warning system in place. Or both. Natadze did. He set both an IR and a motion sensor alarm when he was occupied at home to the extent he might not see or hear a prowler enter. He kept a Glock in a plastic bag in his own shower, kept another pistol at hand when he was on the toilet, and slept with a gun under his pillow. Once, during an electrical storm, a nearby lightning strike and blast of thunder had caused a window to shatter in his bedroom. He had very nearly put a bullet through the broken pane before he came fully awake. Only years of making certain of a target before pulling the trigger saved his neighbor's house from an errant round.

He walked carefully, feet close to the walls to be sure he didn't cause the floor to squeak.

The bathroom door was just ahead, the sound of the shower louder now.

The door was open slightly, and Natadze used a tiny fiber-optic lens to peer around the gap. Should the target be looking, he would see only the tiny end of a glass fiber, almost invisible. The shower door was frosted glass, inside a tiled enclosure. There was no sign of anything else, anything to worry about. Clouds of vapor rose and flowed along the ceiling.

Still in there.

Was the man singing?

No matter. There would never be a better time.

He crept into the bathroom, quiet and smooth. Before the target could sense the change in air pressure in the room, he leveled his Korth at the shower and yanked the glass door open.

The man was old, very pale, covered in soap suds, liver spots and saggy flesh making for a most uninspiring picture.

I hope I go out better than this.

The Russian jumped. To give him credit, though, the man didn't scream, faint, or attempt to run. He merely sighed slightly and wiped some soap from his face.

He muttered something in Russian. Eduard lost most of

it in the noise of the running water but it didn't sound much like a warm greeting.

Natadze nodded. He pulled the towel from the rack with one hand, keeping his gun rock-steady with the other.

"Dry yourself," he said. "We need to talk, you and I."

Washington, D.C.

John Howard talked to the Net Force guard outside Jay's hospital room. One of four who were on duty at all times guarding Jay, he was the one people were supposed to see, perched on a chair in his uniform. Another guard, in a hospital gown and bathrobe and pushing an IV roller stand up and down the hall, was considerably less conspicuous, if no less well-trained and armed. There were two more guards in strategic locations on the floor who were, for all intents and purposes, invisible, using electronics for their surveillance. Anybody who wanted to pay a visit to Gridley and who wasn't cleared wasn't going to make it.

So far, no one who wasn't supposed to be there had made any attempt to get into Jay's room, but none of the Net Force personnel had relaxed their guard in the slightest.

Behind Howard, Alex Michaels waited. When Howard had finished talking to the guard, he turned back to his ex-boss.

"All quiet on the Gridley front?" Michaels asked.

"Actually, he's talking up a storm. And even if somebody got past our people, Toni is still in there, right?"

Michaels smiled. "Oh, yeah."

Howard said, "You and she heading off soon?"

"We'll stick around until they let Jay go home. Doctor said a couple days."

"It was good of you to stay."

Michaels shrugged.

Howard said, "I talked to Thorn while you were in visiting. He's on his way over. He's also got a theory about why Jay got hit. He thinks it was the file the Turks gave us."

"The Soviet spy list?"

"Yes. The revelations were moving toward the U.S. He thinks maybe one of the moles might have gotten wind of it somehow."

"That would be a trick in itself."

It was Howard's turn to shrug. "Turkish security might not be as good as Net Force's, and the Russians are still selling everything that isn't nailed down—and some stuff that is. Maybe that information was valuable to somebody here."

"A Soviet mole who didn't want to be outed?"

Howard nodded. "Makes as much sense as anything else. We ran checks on the violent bad guys we've put away in the last couple of years. Anybody Jay took down who would likely be ticked off enough to want to shoot him is still in prison, as near as I can tell."

"We didn't get them all," Alex said. "Remember CyberNation?"

Howard frowned. "I remember. The scar still itches when it gets hot and sunny. But they would probably try to hit you or me; we were a lot higher on that list."

"Yeah. So what is Thorn doing about it?"

Howard shook his head. "Computer things. Digging in Jay's files, looking for clues. He'll probably be happy to have Gridley back in harness to help out—Jay will know more about his own stuff."

"You'll be keeping him guarded?"

"Of course. In addition to these guys, we've already got sub rosa people on Jay's place. He won't go anywhere without an armed Net Force shadow until we get this cleared. That goes for his wife, too."

"Interesting that Saji is pregnant."

Howard smiled. "That it is."

"From what Toni said, those were the first words out of Jay's mouth when he woke up."

"Good for him. Hard to think of Jay Gridley as a father, though."

"It ought to settle him down some. Teach him some patience."

Howard and Michaels both grinned. Kids did that, no question.

23

Still in his office, Thorn read the FBI report again. He had heard that Jay was out of his coma, and had, in fact, been on the way out the door to go and see him, when his computer priority-one notice had chimed. He went back to check it.

It seemed that a man the Bureau strongly suspected was a Russian spy—a control—had been found dead in his home in Bridgeport, Connecticut, only a few minutes before. The locals were working the incident, but the Russian connection had the Bureau involved. It looked like an accident, according to the very sketchy on-line preliminary report by the Special Agent in Charge of the case, but he was suspicious. There was nothing specific, but the AIC was not convinced that the man, a doctor, had slipped in the bathtub and cracked his skull.

Even if the Agent in Charge was correct and this was more than a simple accident, there was nothing to connect it to the attack on Jay. Still, considering Thorn's theories about Jay's shooter, the report bothered him.

Jay had been working on a coded file that exposed hidden Russian spies around the world, and would likely have revealed more, right here in the U.S.

A man known to the FBI as a Russian agent, and more, one suspected of being a control—one who ran other spies—had died in a freak accident? Or maybe been killed in such a way as to make it look like an accident? That was . . . odd, to say the least. Enough to stick in Thorn's mind.

The common term was "Russian spies," which is what Thorn had set his tripbot to note when new law enforcement reports came in.

This was Thorn's gift—that he could sometimes take two things that did not seem directly related and he could see a correlation. It had helped him come up with new ideas about software, it had even helped in his fencing bouts, and he had learned to trust it over the years.

These two events were connected. He knew it—in his gut, if not his mind.

But how?

The obvious thing was, somebody had killed one man, made it look like an accident, and tried to kill the other. How many assassins or would-be assassins could there be in this area?

Who could say for sure? Maybe there were dozens of them running around looking for victims. But he didn't believe that, and—

What if there was just the one?

Forget for a minute the why of it. Just run with the idea that the guy who shot Jay also killed the Russian. What would *that* mean?

Thorn shook his head. What *would* it mean?

Well, it would mean that if you found one, you found the other.

And if you got him, you could maybe find out why he had done it, and maybe who had put him up to it. . . .

A hint of something touched him, as might his opal ring catching a ray of sunlight at just the right angle to gleam with a sudden bright flash of color:

Maybe there was a way to figure out who the assassin was—by the process of deduction.

Thorn knew he had to think large, to encompass all the possibilities. First, assume it was just one guy. He was obviously dealing with a professional who wouldn't leave anything obvious with which to track him. The bug on Jay's car had been a mistake, maybe, and they had done what they could with that—the records from every traffic cam, bank ATM machine, and Homeland Security invisible in the area of the spy electronic store had been accessed for the day the transmitter had been sold, but all that had given them were thousands of faces. They had run those against the ones in the law-enforcement archives, and the FFR—the Facial Feature Recognition software—had come up with a few bad guys who happened to be passing by, but none they could tie to the assassination attempt on Jay.

Of course, it could be that the shooter didn't have a criminal record, any kind of security clearance, a passport, or even a driver's license, so maybe his picture wasn't accessible.

Can't match what isn't there.

What they needed was a cross-reference. If a camera anywhere near the dead Russian agent held an image of somebody who matched one of the faces in the electronics store? *Then* they'd have something. Neither set of images alone would do it, but together, the chances of a coincidence, of matching faces? That would be unlikely.

Gridley was awake and Thorn really needed to get by there to see him, but he could get this rolling before he headed for the hospital.

Thorn put in a call to the Intel Section of Homeland Security and got the woman in charge of the surveillance cams to provide Net Force with the Connecticut records on the day the Russian was killed.

Then he called the State Police, the Department of Transportation, and the local Sheriff's office. Finally, he got a street directory of businesses around the location, and sent a blanket e-mail, asking them for their visual records on that date. He didn't have a court order, but in these days, people felt that helping the government find somebody who was a killer and who might be a terrorist or a spy was worth doing.

The records would start to come in pretty quick, and the Super-Cray would run the matching software, looking for two identical peas in a very large pod.

There were a lot of things that could mess it up. Maybe it wasn't the same guy. Or his image hadn't been captured on one or both cameras. Or maybe it had been, but the shot was the back of his head or too fuzzy to make a match.

Those images that did look similar enough would kick out and ask for a human interpretation. All Thorn could do until then was wait. It could take weeks, or even months, and it could always come up empty.

But at least it was a place to start.

Now, to go pay a hospital visit. Maybe Jay himself had something to add to this.

Thorn had only known Jay for a short time before the shooting, but the man sitting in the bed in front of him didn't seem like the man he remembered.

He looked the same physically, but the Jay Gridley he'd first met had a brash cockiness that had grated, particularly before he'd walked Jay's VR stuff and realized Jay really *was* that good.

This man seemed a lot less sure of himself.

"Jay. How are you doing?"

"Commander. Other than being shot in the head and in a coma? I'm fine."

He didn't sound fine at all.

Thorn had arranged to have an FBI expert with identikit software come to the hospital—having Jay go into VR this early wasn't, his doctor said, a good idea.

Thorn was trying not to be too hopeful, but if he could match the face he'd yanked from the traffic cam in New York with any kind of ID that Gridley could provide, that would be good.

"Thanks for agreeing to do this so soon—I'm hoping we can get a handle on this guy."

"Me, too."

The door behind him opened. A thin man with a slightly dreamy expression entered and smiled.

"Commander. Mr. Gridley. I'm Adrian Heuser, the ID artist."

The artist sat down in one of the visitor's chairs and pulled a rolling tray over so that Gridley could see it. "I understand you had a little trauma after you saw your, ah, shooter?"

Jay indicated his bandage. "Yeah. You could say that."

I guess the lab rats don't get out much, Thorn thought.

"Normally we do this in VR, but we've got a flatscreen for you." He put a small flat panel on a stand in front of Jay on the tray, "and one for me." The second panel must have had a digitizer, because Heuser pulled out a stylus and tapped it several times.

"As much as you can, I want you to relax, and focus. I want you to go back to just before you were hurt, back to when you were watching. What are you doing?"

"Sitting in the car wondering why this jerk had cut me off."

Heuser took Jay through it, asking questions, getting Jay's input. The man's stylus danced over his tablet, tapping out menus and putting down textures and color. He asked what Jay's attacker was doing, what he was holding, how he stood, how he walked.

Jay was vague. Understandable, if frustrating.

A picture began to take shape on the flatscreen, a face with a gun alongside it. But it wasn't all that clear. It could have been any generic white man, wearing a Band-Aid on his chin and thick glasses.

Not much help.

Heuser came at it from different directions; he was very smooth, but it was obvious that Jay had given him all he had. He saved the file and said he'd pipe it over to Thorn.

"Sorry I didn't do better," Jay said.

"You did fine, Jay. Don't worry about it."

Gridley smiled and nodded. "No problem there," he said. "I'm *awake*. Not much to worry about after that."

24

Cox had breakfast with the Natural Resources Minister of one of those emerging African states that had gone under three or four different names in the last fifty years. It didn't much matter what the locals called it, only that they would be willing to deal with his companies for oil reserves they couldn't really afford to exploit themselves.

The Minister, a rotund man dressed in nicely cut Armani, had a big smile and a shaved head, and was so dark he seemed almost blue. He was willing to deal. Of course, there would be a kickback, and a little something to grease the wheels beforehand. Nothing really overt needed to be said about this, it was understood. Part of the cost of doing business.

If they got five years' worth of oil before some new group came in, slaughtered the current government, and nationalized everything, Cox's companies would make a healthy profit. And Cox had good instincts when it came to bailing. He could almost smell a coup. If he saw that coming, he would dump the refineries and drilling platforms, sell them to some second-tier petroleum company who thought they could either ride a regime change out or make a deal with the new rulers, and Cox would end up smelling like a rose.

He had morning meetings with half a dozen movers and shakers from industries associated with his. Among them was a ship-line owner eager to build a new fleet of Panama-canal-sized tankers, those that would draw forty feet or less and be able to reach secondary ports. Cox also saw the head of a drilling firm who was willing to low-bid a new contract and kick back a chunk to Cox besides. And he had a polite meeting with a bearded South American revolutionary who was willing to guarantee mineral rights to Cox when he took over the government—if Cox would front him funds for arms now.

An ordinary man might be overwhelmed by such constant wheeling and dealing, by the stress of running a multibillion-dollar concern, guiding it through treacherous seas with pirates in all directions. Not Cox. This was why he had been born. He had the power of a country's president, but a lot more money to go with it.

Better the ruler than the ruled. Always.

His private line *cheep*ed. Ah. That would be Eduard!

Southeast of Bridgeport, Connecticut

It had gone well, Natadze thought, as well as could be hoped for. The Russian had given up everything he knew about Cox, Natadze was sure of that, he had held nothing back. He had not been a particularly brave man, the Russian. His lean and idealistic days were long behind him; he had grown soft living in the U.S., had allowed the luxuries and easy life here to let him think he was in no danger. He had lowered his guard.

A fatal mistake.

The Russian had rolled over quickly, and what had to be done to make sure he was telling the truth had been done. Nothing that would show on an autopsy, of course, but effective. Very.

Natadze was not a great fan of torture. He took no thrill from using it. When it was necessary, he applied it, but it was a tool, nothing more. He hadn't needed to apply it. The threat had been enough. The Russian had known who he was, and of what he was capable. Eduard was as certain of the information the dead man had given him as he could be.

There were only four places, according to the Russian, where the intelligence regarding Samuel Walker Cox still existed: First was the old Glavnoye Razvedyvatelnoye Upravlenie—the GRU—and that piece was at the former HQ building at the Khodinka Airfield, near Moscow. They still called it "The Aquarium," and Natadze knew it well enough. You could take the purple metro line to Polezhaevskaya Station, big as you please, and stroll a short ways to the place. Getting into such a building even now would be difficult, but that wasn't necessary. They were all still broke in Moscow, despite the newest reforms, and if you had enough money, you could buy just about anything you wished.

Natadze knew hungry people in the GRU who would be more than happy to do him a favor for a suitcase full of rubles, much less American dollars. A computer crash, a small fire, and those files would be gone. And his contacts knew that to try and hold out on him for blackmail later would be a bad idea.

The second place was with the Turks, who certainly had kept a copy of the encrypted material that had begun this whole affair. There were poor file clerks in Turkey as well, and Natadze knew somebody who knew somebody who could pave a road to a clerk's door with enough money to buy those files.

The third had been the Russian himself, and he wasn't

going to be telling anybody anything unless he believed in an afterlife, and that would be the Devil who processed him into Hell. Should be there by now. If such a place existed, no doubt the doctor would wish to discuss it with Natadze when he eventually arrived there.

He smiled. He did not believe in Hell, nor in Heaven. God, if He existed, should be too busy to concern Himself with what people did on this one little mudball of a planet.

The fourth, and most problematic, was the file at Net Force HQ in Quantico. Americans could be bribed, of course, but not all of them were corrupt—and if you chose the wrong one to try, the whistle would be blown, fast and loud. An organization such as Net Force would be full of patriots, and men who valued their country more than they did personal fortunes were very dangerous. As far as he knew, Net Force still did not understand the significance of the Turkish files, and Natadze did not wish to alert them to this.

So that would be the biggest challenge. He would have to figure out a way to get to the files and destroy them. Fortunately, the man he had put into the hospital was in no position to work on them, at least for a while. He could start the ball rolling on the GRU and Turks with a couple of calls. Money was no object to Mr. Cox—an amount that would make a man rich in Moscow or Ankara was pocket change to a man worth billions.

Natadze felt good about things, better than he had since the snafu with Gridley. He was on top of the situation, he had been very careful with the Russian, the death would look like an accident, and in any event, he'd left nothing behind to follow him. Mr. Cox would be pleased with him. Thinking of which, he picked up the throw-away cell phone and pressed in Cox's number.

"You have good news?"

"Yes. It is done," he said. "No problems."

"Excellent. I'll see you soon."

"Yes."

Natadze discommed. He would destroy the phone at the first stop for petrol, and would scatter the pieces into several garbage cans at different locations. No more mistakes.

Washington, D.C.

Jay asked the doctor point-blank: "If you were me, would you stay here?"

Dr. Grayson smiled. "If I were you, I'd probably be in a circus sideshow, me being a woman and all."

"Funny," he said, not answering her smile. "And not a bad sidestep of the question, either."

She sighed. "You were in a deep coma, Mr. Gridley," she said. "After having a bullet thwack you in the head. Another day or two in the hospital is a smart idea in the long run."

"In the long run, Doc, we're all dead. And you're still dancing."

She shook her head. "If I were you and I knew what I knew, I'd stay here for another day. People are both very tough and very fragile, and we don't begin to know all there is to know about this kind of injury."

"But I'm not in a coma now, my head wound is not serious, I've got a bandage on it and all, and I can lie around in my own bed a lot cheaper than I can this one."

"Why don't we wait for your wife to come back from lunch and discuss it?"

"Oh, no, then it would be two against one. I want to go home."

"What's so important there it can't wait?"

"The guy who put me here is still out there. I can help track him down. Wouldn't *you* be perturbed if somebody had shot you?"

"If I agreed to let you go home and you had a relapse,

my malpractice insurance company would never forgive
me."

"I won't sue you."

"That's what they all say."

"Come on, Doctor. I need to be out of here."

She nodded. "It's not a prison, Mr. Gridley. You can
check out AMA if you wish."

"AMA?"

"Against Medical Advice. You sign a waiver, then if
you drop dead on the way home, you can't blame us—
though the families usually do anyway."

"Where do I sign?"

She smiled again, and shook her head. "That's what
your wife said you would say."

"Saji talked to you?"

"On the way to lunch. She said you would tell me you
were checking out of the hospital, and no matter what I
said, you wouldn't be swayed. She said she would keep
a careful eye on you."

Jay frowned. "How could she know this? I didn't discuss this with her."

"Apparently she knows you better than you think."

He sighed. Yeah. Apparently so.

But that didn't matter. He was going home.

25

Even though he knew it was theoretically possible, Thorn hadn't really believed he'd be that lucky. Now and again, it happened, just often enough to keep him from discounting it.

The Super-Cray had come up with a match on Jay's shooter and whoever killed the dead Russian.

Alone in his office, Thorn had his holoproj float the two images side-by-side. The picture on the left was from a bank ATM cam near the spy goods store—the man hadn't been using the machine, but had been walking past it in the background, behind a woman withdrawing money from her account. Forty dollars, according to the ATM's records. It was not the sharpest picture in the world, and only caught him from about the knees up, but it showed a dark-haired man of perhaps thirty-five glancing in the camera's direction. A scale running down the size of the image showed his height in centimeters, based on the known height of a NO PARKING sign on a post behind him. He was about six feet tall.

The woman, a young and attractive brunette who was visible only from the chest up and blocking most of the frame, wore a skimpy red halter top that had trouble keeping her rather voluptuous breasts in check, and if the rear view was as interesting as the front one, Thorn guessed that this was the reason the passing man was looking over his right shoulder her way. He was checking her out.

That would mean he was heterosexual.

Or maybe he was gay, she had on designer pants, and he was admiring those.

Or maybe she had a puppy standing next to her and he was a dog breeder . . . ?

Leave that for now.

The second image was taken by a traffic cam covering an intersection in southern Connecticut, the town of Bridgeport, four miles away from where the Russian spy's body had been found. A car was halfway through the intersection, making a clear right-hand turn on a red light, right next to a NO TURN ON RED sign. The traffic cam had snapped an image, showing the driver and the front of the car with its license plate, all neat for the local authorities to run the plate and mail the driver a ticket. The picture was date and time stamped.

The driver was an elderly woman, white-haired, and barely able to see over the top of the full-sized Cadillac's steering wheel.

But: Behind that car, stopped behind the crosswalk, was a new Dodge, and seated at the wheel of that car was a dark-haired man whose head was surrounded by a pulsing red circle.

"Enlarge two hundred percent. Unsharp mask, selected field, on image two," Thorn said. "Apply reasonable extrapolation generator."

The computer obeyed, doubling the size of the image inside the circle, sharpening it, and augmenting the colors and shapes rendered based on a specialized enhancement program, the REG.

It looked like the same man to Thorn, but the big thing was that the Cray thought so, too. It had a much higher accuracy rating than Thorn's eyes.

"List facial feature matches, normal tolerances."

A pair of grids showing sizes blossomed, one under each image. The computer brought the two grids together into one image in the middle. All the features that were plus or minus a millimeter lit in flashing red for a beat, then locked. There were twelve matches of the eighteen factors scanned.

Same size nose, same size right ear, same distance between pupils, same ratio of forehead to ear height to chin angle . . .

Thorn didn't need to go any further. Once you hit five major facial points, it was either the same guy or his twin brother, and Thorn didn't think that was likely.

This was the guy who had bugged Jay's car, shot him, and who had killed the Russian spy. Thorn was sure of it.

"Ha!" he said. "You are *mine,* pal!"

Unfortunately, it wouldn't be that easy. He searched the rest of the file, but there was no obvious way to identify the man—at least none that the Super-Cray had been able to come up with. The Cadillac in the foreground blocked the bottom of the car the shooter had been in, so there was no license plate visible. No other images of that car were in the traffic cam, and if the Cray hadn't seen him elsewhere in its strain, then it wasn't like a set of human eyes would do any better.

"Print images," he said.

Thorn passed out hard copies of the holographs to General Howard, Colonel Kent, and Lieutenant Fernandez.

"This is the guy?" Howard said.

Thorn nodded. "I believe so, yes. What's the word on Jay?"

Fernandez said, "He's checked himself out of the hospital and gone home. We have guards watching the house. Saji says he's planning to head back into VR and start looking."

Thorn frowned. "VR? I would think the doctors would want him to stay out of that for a while."

Howard nodded. "They do, but Jay's more stubborn than they are."

Thorn said, "I'll call him and pass this along when we're done. "I've run the driver's license databases from all fifty states through the mainframe. The Super-Cray is checking all military photo records, current passports, and federally incarcerated prisoners—nothing yet. NCIC and CopRec databases are matching the image through local and state jail and prison systems, and that will take a while even with big crunchers. If he's in the system, we'll find him. Eventually."

"You want us to go out on the streets looking?" Fernandez asked.

Thorn smiled. "The regular FBI is doing that already. They've got agents flashing these pictures in the vicinity of the spy store, the area where Jay was shot, and in the dead Russian's neighborhood."

"Good. At least that'll give them something to do," Fernandez said. "What's this on his fingernails?"

Thorn frowned. "What?"

Fernandez pointed at the picture. "Looks like he is wearing nail polish on his right hand, see?"

The picture was too small to see more than a little gleam.

Thorn tapped the computer console on the conference table, called up the ATM image, and had it focus on the right hand—the left was behind him and out of sight. The computer enlarged and enhanced the hand.

A little fuzzy, but sure enough, it looked like the guy had fairly long fingernails, neatly manicured, and they did seem awfully shiny. Kind of an odd, slanted shape, angled to one side. That didn't mean anything to Thorn, though.

"What's the other hand look like?" Kent said.

"Can't see it," Howard said. "Miz Halter Top there is blocking it."

Thorn called up the other picture, in the car. The man's left hand was on the car's steering wheel, at about ten o'clock. He had the computer magnify and enhance the image. It was grainy, not as sharp as the ATM image of the right hand, but it appeared as if the nails on that hand were much shorter and duller. Odd . . .

"He's a guitarist," Kent said.

"What?" Thorn said.

"I have a nephew, in Tucson, Arizona, my sister's oldest son, who teaches music at the local U. He plays classical guitar, and that's what his hands look like. Nails on his right hand are long, polished, and angled, and the ones on his left are clipped short—it's how you play the instrument."

The others looked at him.

"You pluck the strings with your nails, but if you have long nails on the other hand, the strings buzz when you fret them—at least that's what my nephew told me."

"So maybe he's a country-western guy, or bluegrass or folk music player," Fernandez said. "Even a rock star."

Kent said, "Could be, but rock stars mostly flat-pick, and acoustic guitars have steel strings. Fingernails simply don't hold up against those, so those guys wear curved finger-picks or have fake nails. Classical guitars have nylon strings."

"How do you know all this?" Thorn asked.

"When I was stationed outside Atlanta, one of my sergeants was a serious blues guitarist. I used to go and listen to him play at local clubs, and I picked up a few things here and there."

"And you remembered it?" Julio asked.

Kent looked at him. "Not everybody older than you is automatically senile, Lieutenant."

"No, sir," Fernandez said. "Point demonstrated and taken."

General Howard grinned.

"Does this help us?" Kent asked.

Thorn nodded. "Absolutely. If nothing else, it's another place to look. And something tells me there are not a lot of classical guitarist hit men around."

Washington, D.C.

Jay sat in the command chair of the *Deep Flight V*, and stared out at the inky black water over two miles below the surface of the ocean.

He tapped instructions on the keyboard and the deep-sea submersible tilted to the right—starboard—and headed toward an odd-looking pile of silt. At this depth there wasn't much moving except him. Vaguely nautical-sounding music played out over the stereo, and there were odd creaks and groans from the structure around him caused by intense pressure from the ocean.

Except that he just didn't *feel* it. He wasn't *there*. It wasn't *real*.

He frowned and shook his head. *I was sure this would work.*

Even as he thought it, he knew that it wasn't true. He'd wanted it to work, but he hadn't really believed it would.

He sat in the media room of the apartment he and Saji lived in, the 270-degree panorama projection screens at one end of the room lit up with images from his VR simulation. He was looking for a Spanish treasure fleet lost in the late 1500s. But when he leaned back, he could feel the upholstery of the chair, and hear the purr of the ventilation system. He even thought he could hear Saji rattling around in the kitchen, though that could be his imagination.

He frowned again.

You're going to have to do it, Gridley.

After spending subjective months inside his head, in a world similar to VR but not as controlled, he found that he was loathe to leave reality. No, more than that. He was *afraid*—if only a little bit—to leave reality. He knew you couldn't get trapped in VR. It just wasn't possible. But then he'd always believed that you couldn't get trapped inside your own head, either.

He'd devised a non-VR metaphor to break the code that had put him in the hospital. He'd built a simulation he could run from a flatscreen, a remotely operated vehicle sim that searched the ocean floor while he sat in his desk. He'd been hopeful that it might work, that it would let him wait a while before going back into artificial reality.

But it just didn't do the job. Not even close.

So he'd taken the next step, programmed the media room for near-full VR immersion, and created a sim that put him inside a submarine. That worked better. He was more engaged. But it still was not enough.

No, not nearly enough.

Jay's edge, his best trick, was using all of his senses in VR. Limiting himself to vision only, or even audio and visual, was like cutting off his arms or legs. It felt wrong.

He took a deep breath and saved his location before killing the sim. He stared at the VR gear hanging on the rack, feeling a slight chill.

Can't be a VR jock unless you do VR, Jay, said a voice in his head. Was he ready to give it all up? Not go back because he was *afraid?*

No.

Besides, he had to find the guy who had done this to him. Before he came back and found a way to put Jay back inside his own head permanently.

He called up several research databases and began to construct what he needed. He took his time, writing code segments that added to the reality of the VR, making it

more detailed than necessary. One of the things he'd realized from his experience was that most VR wasn't as
good as his unconscious—even his.

But after a while he realized he was just stalling.

"Saji," he called out. "I'm going in."

"I know." Her voice was faint from the kitchen, but he
smiled at the sound. She knew. She always knew. And
she'd be there to help him if somehow, someway he got
into trouble. Not that he would, but . . .

He closed the file window and pulled his stims off the
rack. The movement was familiar and practiced, and
within seconds he was ready to jack in. He reached inside
his desk drawer and got a large binder clip. He pried it
open and clamped it on the loose flesh behind and above
his left elbow.

Ow.

It didn't hurt too much, but the pressure was there. He
jacked in and suddenly found himself on the floor of the
ocean.

It was cold and dark. He looked down, pointing some
of the bright LED lamps on his modified Mark 27 Navy
diving helmet at the ground, and watched his feet sinking
into the muck. He adjusted his buoyancy so that he was
just touching the surface.

He'd forgotten to breathe. He inhaled sharply, feeling
a push into his lungs from the flow amplifier in the helmet. He nearly coughed, which wouldn't have accomplished much, except to push more of the Perfluorocarbon
fluid filling the helmet out of his lungs just a little faster.

The fluid he was breathing made diving at this depth a
little easier, because it didn't compress the same way a
gas would. Although it still hadn't been approved for general use, military and special research units all over the
world had started using Perfluorocarbon fluid for deep
dives once they'd solved the carbon dioxide removal and
inertia problems.

Weird.

He felt like he should be choking, but he had plenty of air, didn't feel faint at all.

The silt pile he'd identified earlier was just ahead on the right. Jay activated the deep-dive Sea-Doo seascooter he'd brought with him, and it pulled him toward the pile of silt.

As he neared it, he could see that it seemed to be regularly shaped, which gave him hope; the regularity of man-made shapes was a big part of finding salvage in the sea.

He cut the forward motion of the seascooter and let it hang in the water. Green and red lights circled it, so he could find it at this depth, even if his suit lights went out.

The cold dug at the suit, trying to get in.

His left arm was still feeling clamped, and he had a moment where he *knew* he was in his own home. For that moment, everything seemed artificial before he suspended his disbelief and let himself come back to the VR scenario as his baseline reality.

He shook his head. He was still fighting this, as bad as a first-timer exploring the near edge of VR.

Jay let himself sink toward the silt pile, careful to move slowly. He wasn't just looking for lost treasure; he was searching for a specific gold bar from a specific sunken chest—one that was shaped like an octagon. Part of a shipment of Incan gold intended for Spanish royalty, the conquistadors had chosen the mold shape to distinguish it from gold being brought back from Mexico.

Of course he wasn't really looking for gold at all. That was just the VR equivalent. He was really hunting for the man who'd shot him.

The metal detector built into his boots signaled a positive. There was metal down there, all right.

He touched down on the sea floor and took a few seconds to look around. He'd done a good job on this—there were little eddies of water moving the silt slightly, tiny, ugly lichen-like things, and a very real feeling of desolation.

He reached for the pain from the binder clip on his arm again, and suffered a slight disorientation.

He was down.

He let his feet and then his ankles sink into the silt, and before long found himself up to his knees.

Whoa, there . . .

He adjusted his buoyancy again, and once he'd stopped, he reached slowly into the silt pile. He could feel something hard in there, and heavy. He pulled it out with both hands, and saw that it was a gold bar.

But not the right one.

He let it fall behind him and reached in again. There were more bars in there, but he couldn't tell them apart.

The binder clip.

He stopped moving. If he removed the binder clip he'd be able to focus on the gold bars, and might be able to find just the right one. But of course, that would remove any connection to the outside world.

Now that I've moved some of the bars, I might lose this spot.

He'd been in such a hurry to get this over with, and so focused on the details, he hadn't built in the functionality to stop mid-program; no save point.

How bad do I want to do this?

He took a deep breath and closed his eyes. Cut off from visual, it was easier to reach over and pull the clamp off his arm. He let it drop, and imagined he could hear it clatter to the floor of his office.

Then he opened his eyes and looked at the silt pile again.

The VR seemed clearer and sharper than it had before. He reached into the muck again and fished around, feeling bar after bar of Spanish treasure. Only now, he could feel their shapes.

Rectangle, rectangle, rectangle . . .

Jay kept it up, enjoying the feel of the soft muck and the hard contrast provided by the gold.

Man, I'm good.

So when he found it, one slightly differently than the rest, larger, heavier, and shaped like an octagon, he was already grinning.

He pulled the bar out and shook the accumulated muck of over four hundred years off of it.

Gotcha!

He felt pretty good about this. Of course, he knew he'd had something to prove. Being shot was bad enough, but it was how he had felt just before the gun had gone off that bothered Jay the most: He'd been terrified. Worse, after being stuck inside his own head, he had been afraid to go back into VR—him, Jay Gridley!

Yeah, well that was then. This was *now!*

And now, Jay had *vengeance* to inflict.

Now to call and let everybody know.

He routed the Com to the office through his virgil, to make sure it was properly scrambled, and logged into a VR conference room at HQ. It only took a few minutes for Thorn to get the crew together and call him back.

Net Force HQ
Quantico, Virginia

"Okay, Jay, we're here."

Jay shifted into VR, and found himself sitting in the conference room at the virtual table with Thorn, Howard, Kent, and Fernandez.

Jay said, "I got the guy."

Thorn said, "You sure?"

"Positive, Boss."

"Run it down for us."

Virtual Jay tapped a control on his virtual flatscreen.

The images of the man they believed to be the man who'd shot him and later killed a suspected Russian spy appeared and floated holographically over the tabletop. A 'proj within a VR, nice.

"We came up empty on matches from any official government sites—no driver's license or check-cashing ID, no service record, nothing from the passport folks, jails, prisons, like that. So either the guy hasn't got any records there, or he's wearing a disguise that hides enough facial features that the Cray can't tag him. You might be able to tell, but the computer can't."

"That seems stupid of the computer," Julio said.

Jay grinned. "Said the man who hates the things with a passion. It has to do with how a machine looks at something, which is different than how people do. You see a brand new Corvette tooling through an intersection, even if you've never seen it before, and you can't read the name, and even if it isn't the same size or design as last year's model, you still know it's a 'vette, right?"

"Sure."

"How?"

"Because it looks like a 'vette."

"Right, to you. There are design elements that give it away. But if the car is longer, lower, has slightly different angles, a computer matching it to last year's model might not make the connection. It depends on what you give it for reference. Open the tolerances, factor in silhouette profile, and then maybe it does, or maybe it offers up the nearest match, like a search engine might give you. But if you give it last year's stats and tell it to match, it will miss the new car."

"So you're telling me I'm better than a computer," Julio said. "I already knew that."

Jay grinned but let it pass. "In facial recognition software, you have numbers. Put a blob of mortician's putty on the earlobes or the top curve, and the ears aren't the same size anymore. Polarizing glasses hide eye color and spacing, and part of the nose. Plugs can make the nostrils wider. If you comb your hair down, you can screw up the forehead sizing. A thick moustache and beard hides the chin and lips. On and on—anybody who knows what the computer looks for can get around it. We have to assume this guy knows that. Whatever the reason, he isn't in the system where we've looked."

"But . . . ?" Thorn said.

"But the guitar thing was the key. There aren't that many classical guitarists in the country, relatively speaking—I'm talking hundreds of thousands, and that includes everybody from guys who make a living doing it to kids taking their first lesson."

"Only hundreds of thousands?" Howard said.

"When it comes to computer work, that's nothing," Jay said. "Google or Gotcha! can scan what? Three, four million webpages in fractions of a second. And we've got better hardware."

Howard shook his head. He wasn't a big computer fan either, Jay knew.

"I did some fast research on the subject, talked in RW to an expert, and then I made some assumptions for a baseline."

"What assumptions?" Thorn asked.

"One, that the guy was fairly serious, because according to those who know, players who aren't serious usually don't bother with the fingernail thing."

Thorn nodded. "According to the FBI and cops who ran this thing, they say the guy is a pro, very careful. Only reason we found images off him is sheer dumb luck—he didn't make any big mistakes."

"One, anyway," Julio said. "Jay's still alive, isn't he?"

Jay grinned. "Maybe he wasn't planning to kill me. The more I think about it, the more I think maybe he might have wanted to kidnap me."

"Based on?" Howard asked.

"If he'd wanted to kill me, there were fifty places better

than the one he picked, and I'd have never seen it coming."

"Kidnapping you on a major highway wasn't a mistake?"

"We'd never have ID'd him from the eyewitnesses, would we? I think something happened. Maybe he didn't even mean to shoot me in the head. Maybe he was just trying to scare me."

Thorn said, "Go ahead, Jay."

"Thanks. It doesn't really matter what he had in mind, though—I just needed a place to set up shop."

Thorn nodded. "We're with you so far."

"So, we assume he's a good guitar player. That narrows it down to, say, ten thousand, people who practice a couple hours a day, at least. My expert says it's actually probably fewer than that. I also assumed for the sake of the search that fairly serious classical guitarists not only study the instrument, they keep up with related material—magazines, either treeware or e-zines, sheet music sites, guitar competitions, concerts, guitar makers, and music stores, all like that.

"Then I gridded the country and checked by region. I'm thinking that the guy must be a local—living somewhere on the eastern seaboard."

"Why?" Kent asked. "He could live anywhere, couldn't he? We have quite a national transportation system. It sure seems you're making a lot of assumptions, son."

Virtual Jay glanced at virtual Thorn, who smiled. He was a player himself, and a good one. He knew the old researchers' adage: Assumptions were the mothers of information.

Jay said, "You have to start somewhere. Did you ever work a hard crossword puzzle? Sometimes, you just have to put letters in, to see if it sparks anything. You can always erase and change things."

"All right," Kent said. "Stipulated."

Jay continued: "When you strain classical guitar mag-

azines, websites, UseNet groups, concert tickets, and luthiers—those are the guys who make guitars—you come
up with plenty of duplicates, but now we're down to a
few thousand names who recur in three or four arenas.
These are the serious folks. If we eliminate the women,
those we can ID immediately as being too old or too
young, and those outside of the east coastal states, we're
down to a few hundred serious guys. Running checks on
their pix, using national, state, and local images we can
access, gets down to twelve without easily found visual
ID's."

"Twelve?" Julio asked.

"Yep. Then we dig a little deeper, checking guitar websites, high school yearbooks, newspapers—we have their
names, so it's easier—and we have four possibles left.
Remember, we restricted the search to people who live
on the east coast, but that's just their permanent address,
not their current one. It turns out two of the four are over-
seas right now. One is a soldier stationed in the Middle
East, the other is a guy working in Japan."

He paused, enjoying the drama of the moment.

"One of remaining two is in a wheelchair."

He paused again.

"Jay," Howard said.

Jay grinned. "And the last one . . ." He touched a control on the flatscreen. A third image, full-face and a close
view, appeared next to the others, and it was obviously
the same man.

"Tah-dah!"

Julio snorted. "Why didn't you just show us the picture
in the first place?"

Jay laughed. "It's not enough just to get the *answer*,
Julio, you also have to show your *work*."

Julio shook his head and muttered softly. Jay didn't
quite catch what he said, but it didn't exactly sound like
a compliment.

Jay kept going: "This image was taken at a box office

in Washington, D.C., two months ago, by a QuikTix machine that sold him the admission to a classical guitar concert. He paid with a debit card. We have the bank and the ID on the account. The name is fake—he calls himself 'Francisco Tárrega,' which is a giveaway—Tárrega was a famous Spanish guitarist who died a hundred years ago. The address is also bogus, but he does have an active mailbox at a Mail Store in the District where the bank sends his statements. We can get a team of feebs to watch the place. When he goes to fetch his mail, we've got him."

"Great work, Jay," Howard said.

"But wait, it gets better. I also sent copies of the picture to classical guitarists and instrument makers and sellers and all like that, once I was sure he wasn't one of them. I've got half a dozen people who recognize the guy, and we have a first name—Edward. We also know he probably is foreign-born. Our witnesses say he has an accent. He sounds like a Russian, Ukranian, something like that. Nobody claims to know the guy well; they do say he seems to know guitars and can talk the talk. One shop owner in New York City says from what this guy has told him, he owns at least a few fairly expensive custom-made instruments."

At home, but also there, Jay grinned and relaxed. He felt a little better about this, but he'd feel better still once the guy was in custody.

Or on a slab.

"Welcome back, man," Julio said.

"Thanks," Jay said. "It's good to be back."

Or anywhere, for that matter.

26

Thorn stripped off the VR gear and smiled, very much pleased with himself. Jay had come up with the guy's name, but Thorn had just discovered where he lived!

He reached for the com, to call Jay at home. Jay had a personal stake in this.

Jay's face appeared on the computer's screen. "Hey, Boss. What's up?"

"We got his house, Jay."

"We did? How?"

Thorn smiled. Spoken like a true information hound—the "how" was as important as the fact it was done.

"From your info. One of the interviewees, a music store owner, said our man claimed to own some expensive handmade instruments. Said he was passionate about them, prized them highly, and knew enough particulars so that the store owner was sure he was telling the truth. The guy loves fine guitars."

"And?"

"So, I did an on-line survey of American luthiers who produce classical guitars costing more than a couple thousand dollars, and asked if any of them had shipped one to somebody with the first name 'Edward' in the New York or Washington, D.C., area in the last few months. I got three hits. On one of them, from a luthier in Portland, Oregon, the spelling was different—it was E-D-U-A-R-D. I checked with the carriers the guitar-makers used, ran down the three addresses. Two of them checked out to be people who couldn't be our man. The third one, the "u" spelling, that's our guy—I talked to the truck driver who delivers air freight to the house. He's trucked several guitars there in the past year. It's him."

"Cool," Jay said. "But I should have thought of that."

"You were just out of a coma from being shot in the head, Jay. Cut yourself a little slack getting back up to steam."

"Yeah, I guess." But it didn't sound as if he meant it.

"Anyway, we have a home address, and a last name to go with Eduard—Natadze."

" 'Not-see?' What kind of a name is that?"

"Na-*tad*-ze. He's from Georgia."

"A Russian from Georgia?"

"No, Georgia the *country*. A web search shows the name is Georgian. They have their own language, but a lot of them speak Russian, given as how it used to be part of the Soviet Union."

"Well, I'll be," Jay said. "You sicced the feebs on him yet?"

"Not yet. I've run down ownership of the house, and it's a circle of holding companies and paper-only corporations, no way to connect to him. I was thinking maybe the fewer people who know about this, the better—that maybe we should check it out further to be sure we're not mistaken, before we call in the regular FBI."

There was a pause. "You're turning Howard and Kent loose." It wasn't a question.

"Technically, I'm not supposed to do that," Thorn said. "But maybe it wouldn't hurt if somebody from Net Force did a recon and checked the situation out. Kind of a . . . training exercise."

Another pause. "And if they happened to spot this guy walking out his front door, they might feel compelled to detain him and then call the FBI field guys."

"That would seem a reasonable decision. To make sure he didn't escape."

Jay grinned. "You are going to fit in just fine around here, boss." A pause, then: "Listen, I'm not a field guy myself, but do you suppose I might ride along, as an observer?"

"I'm sure General Howard and Colonel Kent wouldn't have any objection to that. If your doctors think you are up to it."

"They do, no question. Thanks, boss. Good work."

"You're welcome, Jay."

When he discommed, Thorn smiled again. It felt pretty good to be the guy who came up with the missing piece of the puzzle. And to be the boss, too? How much better did it get than that?

He reached for the VR headset again. He hadn't done more than a cursory look at this Natadze guy, enough to ascertain that he was their suspect. Now, he'd do a little more digging and see what else he could find.

Washington, D.C.

Natadze shook the delivery man's hand again, and this time, he pressed a wad of folded bills into the man's palm, ten hundreds. "Thank you, Esteban, I appreciate it."

The man accepted the money without looking at it. "Yeah, well, you always done right by me, Mr. Natadze. This guy asked about guitars, and I told him, without thinking, you know? *Lo siento*. Least I could do was tell you. I hope it's not nothing serious."

"Let me be honest with you, Esteban, it's a visa thing. Some papers I was supposed to fill out are . . . a little late."

The delivery man, Hispanic and probably still working off a green card himself, nodded, his face grim. "I hear you."

It was the perfect thing to say, as Natadze had known it would be. Now, in that moment, they were *brothers*, dodging *La Migra*, or whatever they were calling it these days. Just honest, hard-working men being hounded by the uncaring bureaucratic machine over some niggling technical detail, some obscure letter of the law designed to keep a good man from getting ahead. Esteban knew all about that.

"What will you do?"

"I'll turn in the papers and pray for the best."

"I know a guy who knows a good lawyer," Esteban said.

"Thanks, my friend, I appreciate it. My uncle is an attorney; I'm sure he'll know how to handle it."

After the man left, the sense of panic Natadze felt threatened to roil up in his throat and choke him. Esteban felt bad, and that and the thousand dollars would probably keep the authorities from getting anything else out of him for a little while, but that was closing the gate after the horse had gotten out.

He forced himself to stand still and take three deep breaths, slowly, inhaling and exhaling through his nose. Blind panic would be fatal.

He felt only a little better as he headed for the back door. He would slip out, go over the fence into his neighbor's yard—the one without the dog—and leave the area on foot. It didn't seem likely they would have allowed the delivery man to pull right up to his door if they were out there now, watching, but he couldn't take the chance. They'd know his car.

His main regret at losing the house were the guitars in the basement. They were beyond price, some of them, but even so, it was not worth spending the rest of his life on death row to stop and pack them. He had to go, now! Somehow, he would either send for them, or make it back here some day, but now was not the time.

Maybe he could take just one, the Friedrich . . . ?

No. A man on foot carrying a guitar case was memorable.

He paused only long enough to collect his good revolver and some spare ammunition. He tucked the holstered gun under his sport coat.

It was not *possible* that they could have found him, and yet they had. Why else would somebody who claimed to be from Net Force be asking the air freight delivery man about him? He had to assume the worst—they knew who he was and they would be coming to get him.

It didn't make any sense. He was *sure* he had not left anything behind in his operations of late, neither with Gridley nor the Russian, nothing that could tie him to them, much less to this *house!*

And yet they had questioned Esteban, and they knew about his hobby, and they *knew where he lived.* It was clear that they had only wanted to *confirm* it.

There was no way they could have gotten that information, no connection to him.

Well, yes. There was *one* way.

He dismissed the thought angrily, instantly ashamed that such a disloyal idea had crossed his mind.

And yet—who else could possibly know?

Another worry, but no time to distress about it *now.* To stay here was to be trapped.

He looked through the sliding glass door into his fenced backyard. Nobody there he could see. It had only been an hour or so since Esteban had talked to the agent, he'd said. Maybe they hadn't had time to get the proper clearances and roll. There were laws in this country that governed such things. You couldn't just kick in a door and arrest somebody without a judge permitting it.

But maybe they had a tame judge, and were on the way and closing fast.

Of course, they might be sitting in a helicopter a mile away watching through a telescope, or footprinting him with a satellite, or just on the other side of the tall wooden fence, guns drawn, ready to cook him on sight.

No, they'd want him alive. To find out who he was working for, and what else he knew of value. If they were out there.

He took a deep breath, and stepped out into the yard, his hand on his revolver's butt under his jacket. He was not going to prison, no matter what else happened. And with any luck, he could take a couple of them with him.

But nobody yelled or leaped out waving guns. There were no helicopters in sight, and if they had a spysat watching him, there was no way to tell.

He made it to the fence, jumped up and caught the top, and pulled himself up to peer into his neighbor's yard.

Nobody there.

He tugged himself up and over the seven-foot-tall fence and dropped to the soft, sweet-smelling and neatly mowed grass. He hurried across the yard to the gate. A few more blocks, he would steal a car, get farther away, change vehicles, and get farther still. He would avoid public transportation, use back roads when he could, and get out of the District. Into a neighboring state, maybe one past that.

If he got that far, then he'd figure out what to do from there.

27

Kent wanted this to go by the numbers, and he was being
very careful not to do anything to screw it up. It was,
after all, his first field op for Net Force.

At the moment, he was in that RV that Lieutenant Fernandez—who was about to become a Captain as General
Howard's parting gift, though he didn't know it yet—had
scored. It was a comfortable way to sit surveillance, that
was for sure.

John Howard sat on the couch, looking through the
one-way polarized glass at the subject's house. The man
who lived there was one Eduard Natadze, a Georgian native. They didn't know much else about him, except for
the guitar material, but that didn't matter—they knew
what he looked like, they had his house in sight, and they
knew if he showed up, they were going to grab him,
which should be enough info to do the job.

Jay Gridley perched on one of the captain's chairs, also
staring out at the surveillance scene. He didn't need to be
here, but Kent understood why he wanted to be. He
wouldn't get in the way.

It was Kent himself who was the problem. He simply wasn't as comfortable as he'd like to be. He knew he didn't have any problems at all when it came to a battle-field, but this kind of operation was not his forte. Sure, he had done enough intel gathering over the years to know you sometimes had to sneak instead of stomp, but this was the first time he'd ever mounted an operation on U.S. soil, other than in training or VR exercises, and he wanted a win.

So far, everything had gone like a Swiss watch.

They were parked within two hundred meters of the subject's residence. Fernandez had an eight-trooper team scattered around the place either disguised or in hiding. There was a "repairman" working on a street light, a "gardener" clipping bushes, and others hidden inside nondescript cars and trucks, ringing the house. When the guy came home, they'd have him.

His car was there, but he wasn't in the house, they knew that, not unless he could make himself invisible to their FLIR and sound sensors, which could pick up a man's body heat and the sound of his respiration. Unless he was hiding in a freezer and breathing real slow . . .

But as the day wore into night, and eventually into day again, there was no sign of the subject. Maybe he was out of town.

As Gridley crawled out of the overhead bed just after dawn, he said, "I just had a thought. Commander Thorn talked to the guy who delivers this guy's guitars, right?"

Kent said, "That's what he said."

"Let me check something."

Gridley sat on the couch, opened his flatscreen, and began tapping the keys. After a moment, he said, "Well, that's that."

"What?"

"I tapped into the carrier's delivery logs for this address."

"And . . . ?"

"There are four of them in the last six months. All of them at exactly the same time: 1:30 p.m."

General Howard came out of the head in the back of the coach, rubbing his face. "And this means what?"

"It seems unlikely that the driver would make four deliveries to the same address at exactly the same moment."

"Yes," Kent said, "it does. But I fail to see the significance. Why would the driver put down something that wasn't so?"

Howard said, "These guitars are valuable, right? So if you were a guy paying for them, you probably wouldn't want them sitting out on the front porch until you got home. Bad weather, a sticky-fingered passerby, that would be bad."

Jay nodded. "So maybe the delivery guy has a key? So he can leave them inside?"

"If you had a house full of expensive guitars, would you give a delivery guy a key?"

"I wouldn't," Kent said.

"So maybe Natadze has some other arrangement with the guy," Howard said. "Maybe the guy only comes round when he knows Natadze will be here."

"Exactly," Jay said. "I'm thinking our delivery guy probably just scanned the guitars as delivered at some point during the day—probably on his lunch hour, which would explain why the time was exactly the same for each delivery. But he didn't actually deliver them until later, probably after hours."

"Could be," Kent said, "But even so . . . ?"

Howard picked it up. "That would be service worth a nice tip."

Kent got it. "Ah. You're saying this guy is in Natadze's pocket."

"He told the Commander about the deliveries. Maybe he told Natadze about the Commander," Jay said.

"Oh," Kent and Howard said as one.

"Maybe we better have somebody have a little talk with this delivery guy," Jay said.

It took a couple of hours, but when the FBI agent called them, he confirmed it. The delivery driver had stalled, but in the end, had confessed to telling Natadze about the query from Net Force.

Jay was right. That was that. At least for now.

"So we missed him," Kent said. "Probably by minutes."

Howard nodded, feeling the man's frustration. "It happens."

"Not to me."

Howard said. "Have you taken up walking next to the ferry when you cross the river, Abe?"

Kent's jaw muscles danced. He was probably thinking something he didn't want to say to a general, even one who was his friend. Howard understood the feeling. He glanced at Julio, who had come by to hear the sitrep. Maybe he could make Abe feel a little better.

Howard said, "Listen, a few years back, we had a shooter on our to-do list, a Russian guy who called himself Ruzhyó."

He saw Julio smile and shake his head.

"The op was out in the middle of the Nevada desert, nobody else around, the guy living in a trailer. Should have been a walk in the park. We set it up, went to collect him, by-the-book, and this one guy gave us a world of hurt. Had bouncing-betty mines jury-rigged, bigger explosives, a rack full of guns, and he was ready for us. We had troops blasted and down before we knew what hit us. Guy laid smoke and took off in his car, but we had the perimeter and he didn't have a prayer. A couple hundred yards away, his car blew up. Big explosion, body parts everywhere, and end of mission.

"We packed it up, I left a couple of men in the trailer to secure it, and we went home to lick our wounds."

"But at least you got him."

Howard shook his head. "No, we didn't. He suckered us. He was buried in a hidey-hole. The car ran on a re-mote, the body parts were a mix of an old lab skeleton and a butcher shop. After we left, he climbed out of his concealment, went to the trailer, killed the two men I'd left, and disappeared."

Kent turned to look at Howard.

"Yeah. One step ahead of me all the way. He'd been a Spetsnaz guy and a shooter for years, he had figured we'd find him one day, and he set up his scenario well in advance. He knew the terrain, knew how we would come in, and he had an answer for all our questions. We underestimated him—*I* underestimated him—and he cost me two dead and two wounded.

"You didn't lose anybody here today. The guy was tipped off before we ever rolled, before we even *heard* about it. There was nothing you could have done to make it work, Abe. He knew we were coming before we did, and he took off. It's just the breaks."

Kent nodded. "Point taken." After a moment, he said, "Knowing you, General, you wouldn't have been real happy about your Russian. That the end of the story?"

"No. We ran into him again, in England. He hooked up with another bad guy we had reason to talk to, and our second meeting ended with Mr. Ruzhyó pushing up the daisies."

"That name means 'rifle,' doesn't it? My Russian is very rusty."

"Yes. And he had one when we came across him—a little twenty-two built into a cane. If we hadn't been wearing body armor, he would have taken three of us out with that sucker—five shots, five hits. He got one round through a glove, and knocked out another shooter's weapon. He could have escaped, but for whatever reason, he didn't, he stood and fought. Hell of a gunslinger. I wished he'd been one of ours." He paused, then looked at Kent.

"Bad pennies keep turning up. You did everything right, but this guy got a pass. Not your fault. You'll do better next time."

"Damn straight I will," Kent said.

Both Howard and Julio smiled. They knew exactly how he felt.

28

Thorn jacked out of VR and sighed. Much of yesterday and this morning, he had hunted for traces of the man called Eduard Natadze, and had found nothing more useful than what they already knew. Using the new parameters and expanding the time limits, he had searched all manner of things connected to classical guitars, and found that Natadze had bought other instruments. An examination of his house already gave them that—a locked room in the basement had a collection of them, neatly cased, and a gun safe that held others, according to the portable X-ray scanner the FBI had used to check it. They left the house as they found it and set up surveillance, but nobody expected the man to return—he'd been burned, and he had to know they'd watch the place. Still, according to what they knew, the killer loved his guitars. Maybe he would risk it to recover them.

That he showed up on a couple of security cams at shops or concerts did them no good.

There were no records of him anywhere officially. If he was here on a visa, it was not under the name of Eduard Natadze or anything even remotely similar to that. Nor was his photo registered anywhere in the INS. Neither the car in his driveway nor the house itself were listed in his name; they were officially owned by corporations, holding companies, and dead ends. Nor were there any driver's licenses issued in that name or carrying that photo in any of the fifty states, the District of Columbia, or Puerto Rico.

The man was off the radar—at least as far as Thorn had been able to determine.

It did not seem possible in the information age that somebody could walk in civilized society and not leave any more tracks than this man did, but there it was. And when the Invisible Man goes to ground, how do you find him?

Maybe Jay Gridley was doing better.

Endless Summer
Modesto, California

Jay crept slowly along the strip, the murmur of the Viper's exhaust a deep, throaty rumble loud in the summer night. The cruisers were out, low-riders and candy-apple-red or green metal flake paint jobs twenty coats deep; custom rods showing their brilliant feathers, a fine display of rolling automobile iron, mostly Detroit, but a few foreign cars sprinkled in among the big machines. The Beach Boys' classic hit, "I Get Around," blared from somebody's radio—bad guys and hip chicks and driving around on a Saturday night. Easier back in the days when gasoline was leaded and thirty cents a gallon for ethyl.

His fire-engine-yellow Dodge was tiny compared to the full-sized cars, an open cockpit two-seater, but the engine was more than respectable. The Viper could scream with the biggest dinosaurs, and once you pressed the pedal to the metal, the speedometer needle went one way and the gas gauge needle went the other. A rocket on wheels, Jay liked to think, and while expensive to drive in RW, it was considerably cheaper here in VR.

Despite the admiring gazes of the girls dressed in tight shorts watching the cars grumble past in the warm summer night, Jay was frustrated.

Natadze was nowhere to be found. The scenario was entertaining, but that was all—the guy Jay wanted wasn't in it, and no matter which block he circled, he could not find the man.

Either Jay had lost a few steps, or the guy was a ghost.

And that wasn't all that was wrong. Yeah, he'd overcome his fear of VR, jumped back in the pool, and was in control again, but being shot, that feeling he'd had of utter terror and helplessness in the moment before the gun went off, that was still nagging at him like a bad back. The memory kept replaying in his mind, popping up at odd times and places. Taking a bath and avoiding getting the bandage on his head wet, he saw it: The man stalking toward his car, the gun in his hand, the flash—he didn't remember the sound of the shot, but he did remember the muzzle blast—and then nothingness.

He couldn't really recall the man's face. He had mentally filled it in, since they had the holographs of Natadze, but in the doing of the event, his features would not resolve. A faceless man with a gun. Death come to call.

In the middle of eating a sandwich at noon, the memory of being unable to run, to get away, had suddenly turned the bread and cheese into something he couldn't stomach.

Lying in bed next to Saji, the shooter got him yet again.

Since he had awakened from the coma, it had been there, sometimes just outside his perception, ready to jump in and rattle him again and again.

He had been helpless. Paralyzed with fear. He hadn't

been able to run, to fight, to do anything. It was horrible. He felt guilty. He should have been able to *do* something, but he hadn't. He had just sat there in a panic, a sparrow hypnotized by a cobra.

Buck up, Jay. This isn't helping anything.

Maybe Thorn was having better luck looking.

"End scenario," Jay said.

Washington, D.C.

Jay shucked the VR gear and sat staring at the wall.

Saji drifted past. "And are we having fun yet?"

"Not to put too fine a point on it, no. It's not like the earth swallowed this guy up, it's like he never existed except for going to classical guitar concerts and music stores. If we hadn't gotten those two accidental pictures, we'd never even have known that much."

"So you just have the FBI watch all the music stores and stake out every classical guitar concert from now on," she said, smiling to show it was a joke.

"You know, even if that was possible, it wouldn't work. He knows we know about that. I'd bet a billion against a brick bat he won't be hanging out at those places anytime soon, and if he wants to pick up a new axe, it won't be under his name, or some place that has a security cam. The man is a phantom."

"You found him once and you didn't have anything. You'll find him again. It just might take a while."

"But I want him *now*," Jay said. And as he did, he realized what that sounded like—a whine. But he had to get this guy. He *had* to.

"You will, Jay."

Then he said, "I think maybe I need to go into work. Maybe something there that will help."

"I'm surprised you aren't already gone," she said.

"It's okay with you?"

"Go and be Jay Gridley. It's what you do."

He smiled again. *Yeah. It was. At least it had been before he'd been shot.*

"I love you," he said.

"I love you, too, Poppa."

That statement brought mixed emotions. A child, *his* child. But—what kind of father would he be? What lessons could he teach a son or daughter when he had just sat and stared at a man who had simply walked up and shot him?

Work. He needed to get back to work. He would worry about this later. After he got the guy who did it.

Harrisburg, Pennsylvania

Natadze drove five miles an hour over the speed limit as he headed north on the highway toward Harrisburg. He was nestled into a line of cars all moving at the same rate. The state cops would give you some leeway if you were speeding a hair in traffic, but if you were poking along at exactly the limit and cars were piling up behind you, that drew more attention.

Natadze did not want any official attention. He was driving a stolen Ford, his third car since leaving D.C., and even though the plates on it were also stolen, New Jersey plates from a freshly wrecked Ford of the same year, make, and color, which was not all that easy to do, he would not be able to stand close inspection. He had phony identification that would pass, but the registration numbers on the car would give him away if they stopped him and did a cross-check, and they might also have a picture of him. Not likely, but possible.

He wanted to keep his profile as low as possible.

Harrisburg was not the most direct route to New York

City, but he had a safe deposit box in a bank there, in which were fresh identity papers, a sizeable amount of cash, and keys to a storage parking lot where a clean car was parked. There were similar caches in six other cities, established for just such emergencies.

He had worried at the problem considerably since he had run from his house in Washington. The authorities had been asking after him. Maybe it was no more than Homeland Security trying to chase down every foreigner as they sometimes did. Maybe it was unrelated to who he was. That was a possibility.

But he did not believe that, not for a second. That they knew who he was and where he lived was astounding. Those two pieces of information should not have been linked in any way. If they knew both, something was terribly wrong—for him.

Nobody but Cox knew where he lived.

Natadze shook his head against the disloyal thought. No, Cox would not give him up, there was nothing to be gained by that.

Perhaps his employer had somehow let the information slip? Someone close to him had picked it up and run with it?

That didn't make a lot of sense, either, but at least it seemed more reasonable. Somebody had stumbled across the data, had wanted to make points with it, something like that.

But that was still a problem. If Cox had let something slip like that, something that led the authorities straight to Natadze, then he was slipping badly, to the point where he was becoming a liability—or at least a threat. Eduard could not have that. Cox knew too much about him—was, in fact, the only vulnerable spot in Natadze's carefully crafted armor.

No, it almost didn't matter whether Cox had given him up intentionally or accidentally. Natadze had to know if Cox had been behind it, and he had to know *now,* before he went to ground, before he went to any of his safe houses. Cox knew about all of them—all of the ones in this area, anyway—and if Cox was the weak link in this chain, then none of the safe houses were safe at all.

In the meantime, he needed to find out just how compromised he was. He would have someone check out his house in New York. If the federal authorities had that covered, then he would have to take more drastic steps. He could take a trip out of the country, to the place in Brazil, perhaps, have some plastic work done, a new identity built, and return as a new man. A different face, hair color, and style, colored contact lenses, voice lessons, maybe. There were many ways to change yourself. That was no problem.

His biggest regret was his guitar collection, but perhaps, once things had cooled, he could dispatch an agent to collect those. He still had three in his New York house, not his best, but quality instruments.

They could not watch the D.C. house forever. Six months, a year from now, the authorities could not afford to keep men there long. The house was paid for, taxes paid a year in advance, and if the water and power were turned off, that wouldn't matter. They had no right to take his property, he had not been convicted of any crime. Perhaps a lawyer, hired anonymously, to make sure that his rights were protected.

While he was having the house in New York checked, he would get in touch with Cox. Five minutes with the man, face to face, would tell him everything he needed to know. Risky or not, not knowing the truth about his employer was riskier yet, by far.

His mind made up, he started looking for a good place to turn around and turned his thoughts back to his driving. It would not do to allow himself to make a simple, foolish mistake and be pulled over by a traffic policeman. He would have to kill the officer, and that would certainly draw more attention than he needed.

29

Jay sat in his office, staring at the wall. Maybe coming into work had not been such a good idea. He should be on-line, in VR, should be hunting for clues that would lead him to Natadze, but he couldn't get going, couldn't seem to overcome the inertia.

He felt . . . tired. As if he hadn't slept in weeks. Stalled.

He looked up to see the new military commander, Colonel Kent, in the doorway.

Kent said, "You all right, son?"

Jay started to nod and wave him off, but somehow, the feelings he'd been having boiled up, and before he could help himself, he said, "I've been better."

Kent raised an eyebrow. He stepped into the office.

Feeling as if he were suddenly riding a runaway horse over whom he had no control, Jay started talking. He was aghast at himself as he began to spill the story about being shot and how it made him feel—the fear, the inability to help himself.

Why am I saying this?! To somebody who is almost a complete stranger?! I haven't even told Saji!

But even as he thought this, he couldn't stop, not until it had all poured out.

When he was done, Jay said, "I'm—I'm sorry, Colonel. I didn't mean to run on like that."

Kent shook his head. "No problem, son. I've heard it before. Felt it myself. They used to call it 'shell shock,' then it was 'battle fatigue.' Now it's called Delayed Stress Syndrome. It happens to men in harm's way—soldiers, cops, firemen. After things are all over, it sets in. It's not something you can control."

Jay shook his head.

"It's true. Even in guys who have trained their whole lives for combat, career military men, it happens. The map is never the territory. It's the reason no battle plan survives first contact with the enemy. VR can be realistic as hell, but some part of you knows you won't die when a bullet hits you in a computer scenario. That same part knows when the pucker-factor is real and you could check out at any second."

Jay said, "Yeah, I guess."

Kent looked at him. "Let me tell you about my old friend Anson. Maybe it will help. Anson was D.I. I met him when I was in the Corps. He did his thirty years, then retired and went home to Kansas City. One Saturday night a couple years back, he took his date to a nice restaurant. Now you need to understand that Anson was a sawed-off fence-post of a guy, maybe five-seven, a hundred and fifty pounds, but tough as a trunk full of rawhide dog chews."

Jay stared at him. Where was this going?

"So Anson and his date have dinner, and while they are working on dessert, a couple of big ole country boys two tables over start getting loud. Celebrating something, and washing it down with a lot of beer. One of the guys gets up to go to the head. He leers at Anson's date, gives her a 'Hey, baby!' and says something to the effect of,

'Why don't you drop this shrimp and join us, we'll show you a good time!'

"The woman smiles politely and tells him no. The guy, who is a real big bruiser, muscles on his muscles, shrugs and goes off to the can.

"So Anson and his date finish, pay their check, and head for their car. But in the parking lot are the two guys who were being raucous inside.

"Anson doesn't say anything, just goes to his vehicle and unlocks the passenger door to let his date in.

"One of the guys, the bigger one, calls out, 'Hey, Momma, it's not to late to join the party!'

"Anson straightens himself up to his five-seven, turns and looks at the guy, and says, 'She said she wasn't interested.'

"The bruiser gives Anson a go-to-hell look. 'Hey, Gramps, how would you like it if I came over there and stomped on you?'

"Anson just ignores him. He looks at his date and says, 'Let's go.'

"So the bruiser smiles, a nasty expression. He nods at the woman with Anson. 'Yeah, that's right old man. Run away.'

"Now Anson's getting pretty steamed himself by now, but he keeps his head.

"Bruiser starts heading toward them now, slowly. 'C'mon, babe,' he says to Anson's date. 'You can do better than this guy.'

"Well, Anson's had about enough of this. 'Look,' he says, 'you've had your fun, and you've had your chance. The lady doesn't want to go anywhere with you, and to tell you the truth, I'm getting pretty sick of looking at you myself, so why don't you just go away before you get hurt.'

"Now maybe Anson shouldn't have said that. Insulting a guy like this is about as effective as trying to put out a fire by throwing gasoline on it. But like I said, Anson was getting pretty mad by now himself.

" 'You're crazy, old man,' Bruiser says. 'You don't know who you're talking to, do you?'

" 'Doesn't matter, son. For the last time, turn around and go away while you still can.'

"Next to Anson, the woman is speechless, her eyes wide, and she's thinking that Anson is about to get himself a major whipping for goading this guy.

"Bruiser's buddy, who is almost as big as he is, catches Bruiser's arm as he starts for Anson. 'Don't do it, man. He's just another jerk, the world is full of 'em.'

"But Bruiser is ready to rumble, and you can almost hear what he is thinking: This little guy had just dissed him in front of a good-lookin' woman!

" 'I'm gonna make it one less full,' he says to his friend. 'Pal, you're about to get crap-stomped by Harley William Dahl. I don't care if you're some kind of karate or kung fu expert showing off for your lady, I'm a two-time winner of K-1, and the North American Heavyweight NHB champ. I break men twice your size in half just to warm up, and I am gonna pound you into the ground like a tent peg!'

"Harley takes a couple of steps, then pulls up short, as Anson comes out from under his jacket with a forty-five slabside, cocked-and-locked.

" 'Pleased to meet you, Harley. I'm not anybody special—just an old retired Marine who can shoot Expert with this here antique Colt. Now like I said, why don't you take a walk?'

" 'You can't do that!' Harley says. 'It would be murder.'

" 'You just told me what a champion fighter you are in front of a witness. I wouldn't have a prayer against you hand-to-hand—no jury in the world would convict me for shooting you.'

"Harley glowers. His buddy pulls at his arm again. 'Leave it, man!'

"Harley doesn't want to do that. He is mad. 'They'd fry the little coward!'

" 'The man has a *gun*, Harley! What do you care what a jury thinks? If it gets to that, you won't be around to see it!'

"Something filters through. Harley backs up a step. 'If you didn't have that gun—' he begins.

"Anson cuts him off. 'If the world had been flat, son, Columbus would have sailed off the edge, wouldn't he? I may be just a little coward, but I *do* have the gun, my ace beats your king. Go home and live. Come at me, and die. Your choice, it really don't much matter much to me.'

"And Harley looks into Anson's face and sees that the man *would* just as soon shoot him as not, and he lets his friend drag him away, cursing as he goes. Anson holsters the gun, opens the door for his lady friend, that's that."

Kent leaned against the wall. "Now, Anson is a modest man, not prone to bragging about how he does things. I heard the story from his date, who became his wife shortly thereafter. Nice lady, great cook."

Jay looked at Kent. "I must be missing the point."

"The point, son, is that no matter how big or strong or smart you might be, those don't offset everything. Here was Harley, a martial arts combat champion, and if he'd jumped Anson, he'd be pushing up daisies.

"You couldn't have beat the man who shot you—he had the superior weapon and the tactical advantage. You are an adept in your field, you could wipe up the floor with the guy in a computer duel, but it wasn't your arena.

"Were you armed?"

"No. I should have been."

"Maybe. But you weren't. And even if you'd had a pistol and knew how to use it, what if you come up against five or eight armed guys? You can't cover every base. There's no dishonor in being out-gunned. This was the attacker's game, not yours."

Jay blinked. The man was right. Intellectually, he knew there wasn't anything he could have done to stop it.

Emotionally, it was another matter. But still . . .

"Thanks, Colonel. I appreciate the ear and the advice."

"No problem. Next time my computer breaks down, I'll call you."

Jay managed a smile.

30

Thorn stripped away the VR gear and blew out a big sigh. This Natadze guy was getting to be a major pain. Thorn had expected to have found something else on him by now, but the man was just not there. He loved guitars and he shot people, that was pretty much it.

Clearly, Net Force would have to come up with some other approach. But what?

He looked at the clock. He'd been under for two hours, and he felt stiff and stale. Time to go to the gym for a little R&R.

As he got there, he saw Colonel Kent arriving at the same moment. In his left hand, he held his sheathed *katana*.

"Commander."

"Colonel. Going to work out?"

"I thought I might wave this old blade around a little, yes."

"Would you mind if I watched?"

"No, sir." A pause. "Tom."

Thorn grinned and followed Kent into the gym, which was empty save for them.

"If you had a sword, I could show you some of the basics," Kent said.

Thorn grinned again. "As it happens, I do have a Japanese sword in my locker."

Kent nodded, as if he wasn't particularly surprised.

Thorn went to fetch the weapon, a *katana* he had bought from the great-granddaughter of a man who had been a Japanese general in WWII. The blade was almost four hundred years old and still mirror-bright.

When he got back, Kent had stripped to his T-shirt and trousers, his feet also bare. He looked to be in good shape for a man his age. Or for a man Thorn's age. He knelt on the mat in that butt-on-heels position called *seiza*, his sheathed sword set next to him on the left.

"Can you get into this pose?"

Thorn nodded.

Kent pointed to his right. "Better sit over on that side. About six feet away."

Thorn kneeled, placing his own sword to his left on the mat.

"My grandfather knew all the Japanese terminology," Kent said, "but what it boils down to is essentially a very few actions you perform with the sword—everything else is built on those."

He bowed, touching his head to the mat, his palms down forming a triangle with his thumbs and forefingers on the surface. He came back upright, picked the sword up with his left hand, and turned it so the edge-curve faced outward. He pressed against the guard with his thumb.

"You loosen the blade in the sheath, like so."

Thorn leaned forward a little to see better.

"The first move is the draw—"

Kent pulled the sword's blade free in a single, fluid motion, whipped it outward to his left in a flat arc toward his right. At the same time, he came up on his right foot, his left knee still on the ground. As the sword passed in front of him, he circled the blade, twisting it from a horizontal slash from left to right into an overhead curve that came down straight in front of his body. During this, he set the sheath down, and brought his left hand to the sword's handle, well behind his right hand. The final part of the motion was much like a man with an axe splitting a log:

"The cut."

He opened his right hand, maintaining his grip with the left, and made his right hand into a fist. He hammered once lightly on the back ridge of the blade just ahead of the guard with the little-finger side of his right fist.

"The shaking of blood."

He opened his right fist, caught the handle in a reverse grip, let go with his left hand, swung the blade so that the point angled to his left, arced downward and then up, almost 270 degrees, to point at the back wall. Meanwhile, he used his left hand to catch the mouth of the scabbard, thumb on one side, forefinger on the other, as if about to pinch. He moved the sword backward, touched the sheath's mouth with the back edge of the blade, six inches above the guard. He drew the blade forward, right arm passing across his belly, sliding the spine along the sheath's opening. His thumb and forefinger looked as if they were wiping the steel. When the point reached the mouth, he moved his right hand forward, angled and inserted the tip into the sheath, then slid the blade slowly home. He used his forefinger to snug the weapon into place.

He did not look at the sword when he did any of this.

"And the re-sheath," he said.

Thorn grinned. Right out of *Seven Samurai*.

He put the sword back down, bowed again, then looked at Thorn.

"That's basically it. Four moves—pull it, cut, knock the blood off, and put it away. You can do it standing, squatting, kneeling, or even lying on your side. There are

a bunch of ways to cut, various angles and targets, other
ways to sling the blood and re-sheath, and you can use
the point to stick somebody, but that's pretty much the
core of *iai*. There are 'ways'—*do*, or fighting versions,
jutsus. Schools are a lot more formal—you wear *gi* and
hakama, get into the rituals, tie your sleeves up, start with
the sword in your sash, but my grandfather taught me that
the heart of the art was: draw, cut, shake, and re-sheath.
Kind of the Eastern version of the cowboy fast draw. The
iai gets the blade into play; after that, it is *kendo*."

"Fascinating," Thorn said.

"The idea is to cultivate a sense of awareness of everything, *zanshin*, they call it. You don't think, you just *do*.
After ten or twenty thousand draws, according to my
grandfather, you can just get to a place where you just . . .
manifest the sword. It just is *there*."

"Not much like western fencing," Thorn said.

"The Japanese have a different mind-set," Kent said.
"Kill or be killed—or both, it didn't much matter to the
warriors. 'The way of the samurai is found in death.' If
you were going to die, you wanted to be sure to take your
enemy with you if you could, but dying yourself was of
little consequence. Your life belonged to your lord, and
he could do whatever he wanted with it. Everybody knew
that. It makes for a different kind of match."

"I can see that."

"Want to try it?"

"Very much."

"Okay. Here's how you bow . . ."

The Dark Ages
Southern France

Jay Gridley rode the dragon. He was seated atop the
hundred-foot-long beast, just behind his ears, and what-

ever fear he had felt about going into VR was waaay gone. He was back and he was in control—well, at least here in VR, anyhow.

Though the setting was Europe, his dragon had a definite Chinese look to him, much more interesting than the standard European model. In China, dragons weren't just animals, they were wise, clever, could assume the shape of a man, and were often very sneaky. Sometimes that was what you needed from a dragon. But they could do brute force as well, when you needed that.

Jay watched as enemies fled, left, right, and center. Now and then, a bowman would loose an arrow, but his steed would blast the incoming missile with a *whuff!* of flame—said fire usually consuming not only the arrow, but the man who'd fired it, roasting him into a crispy critter on the spot.

It was not Jay's most peaceful construct, but it suited his mood. The arrows were queries, the archers firewalls, and the dragon Jay's best rascal-and-enter program. Against the fortified and nearly blast-proof walls of a first-class firewall, even the dragon's fiery breath would be useless, but here in the corporate realm, not everybody subscribed to the idea that such things were necessary. Some had what they thought was top-of-the-line software or hardware protecting their systems, but had been suckered. Some had what had been the best, but which had not been kept updated, and was no longer sufficient against the sharpest cutting-edge stuff. Jay's dragon was reborn regularly—he had access to the best, and he incorporated it into the eggs that hatched as needed.

Ahead, the French castle lay, surrounded by a moat, the drawbridge up.

The dragon stopped on the edge of the water.

"What say?" Jay said. "Can we do this?"

"We can," the dragon said. His voice was deep, almost a metallic rumble, a giant iron plate dragged across a sidewalk.

The dragon took a slow, full breath and blasted the moat with a terrific gout of fire. The flow of it went on and on—thirty seconds, a minute, two minutes.

The water began to bubble as it boiled. Giant green and scaled monsters, looking like crosses between alligators and sharks, floated to the surface, cooked, still thrashing in their death-throes.

"Cook 'em, Dan'l," Jay said.

A few moments later, the dragon dipped his taloned toe into the water, decided it was cool enough, then stepped into the moat.

The water came up only to his hips—the castle's defenders had not reckoned on such an assault. They reached the door, and the dragon thrust his fore-claws into the wood, the sound of it like a pile driver working. With a mighty effort, the dragon flexed his shoulder and ripped the thick door apart as if it were balsa. Splinters flew everywhere as the door shattered and fell away.

The dragon stalked through the opening.

Jay slid down the dragon's neck and side. "Thanks, I'll take it from here. If the King's Army shows up, give me a yell."

The dragon nodded. He blew a smoke ring the size of a tractor tire. The ring floated gently into the morning air.

Jay headed for the keep's library. He saw no one, the librarian had fled, and it was but a matter of moments before he found the lambskin scroll for which he had come. He looked it over, saw the information he needed, and nodded to himself. He left the scroll where he'd found it—it would do no good to take it, he couldn't show it to anybody in the real world. Possession of the information on it in the RW would make him guilty of a crime, and he couldn't use it as evidence in any event. But he wasn't looking for evidence, he was looking for knowledge. Different critter.

"I have you now!" he said, trying for Darth Vader's resonant voice.

"The King's Army approaches," called the dragon.

"End scenario," he said.

Jay sat, and without a word, touched a control on his flatscreen.

The holoproj appeared over the computer, and he turned the instrument around so that Thorn could get a view of the image from the front.

"Natadze," Thorn said.

"Yes. I used the three pictures we had and had the SC run a scan on images from television, newspapers, and magazines, and there he is. It's from *American Businessman*, six months ago."

Thorn looked at the picture. Natadze, in a dark gray business suit, stood among a group of other men dressed similarly.

"Watch this," Jay said. He tapped at the flatscreen and the image shifted so that Natadze and the others shrank and were relegated to the background. In the foreground, two men appeared. One of them was obviously presenting some kind of plaque to the other. They were smiling and shaking hands for the camera.

Thorn knew who one of the men was. "Samuel Walker Cox," he said. "The oilman."

Jay nodded. "Yep. The other one is Andre Arpree, of the International Chamber of Commerce, based in Paris. The award is for fostering business relations between Europe and the U.S."

"And what is our man Natadze doing there, watching such a thing, do you think?"

"He works for somebody connected to the event."

Thorn nodded. "Yes, that would be my guess, too."

Jay didn't say anything for a moment. He looked nervous.

Softly, Thorn said, "But you aren't guessing, are you, Jay?"

Jay sighed, then seemed to come to a decision. "I figured that Natadze worked for Cox or for Arpree. The thing is, neither of their corporate records are, um, accessible without a federal warrant."

"Uh huh." Thorn had an idea where this was going.

"And getting a warrant based on a picture of a guy standing in the background of an award ceremony is likely to be, um, difficult."

Thorn nodded. "Yes. If it was my company, I'd have a platoon of lawyers screaming bloody murder, trying to convince a judge that Net Force didn't have anything, they were just fishing and hoping."

"That's what I figured. We can't really make this guy into a terrorist, so the country isn't really at risk. Opening up the records of two major corporations, one of them French? Not likely."

Thorn's expertise was in computers, and he had been a hacker before he started selling the software that eventually made him rich. He knew where this was going.

"And even if you got it, we couldn't use it in court, Jay."

"I know."

"Legally, they'd fry us."

"Yeah."

Thorn took a deep breath, let half of it out. There was the law. And there was justice.

"So, okay. Who does he work for?"

Jay couldn't suppress a slight smile. "Cox. Our hitman Eduard Natadze is head of Special Security for Samuel Walker Cox."

Thorn stared at the holoproj. Wow. Wasn't *that* an ugly can of worms?

31

General John Howard was not surprised that Gridley had come up with the information; nor was he surprised that Thorn was being very circumspect about how such knowledge had come into their possession. Howard lived by a moral code based on the Ten Commandments, he was a religious man, and he knew that morality and Caesar's Law sometimes diverged. When in doubt, he followed God's laws—come Judgment Day, those would be the ones that counted the most. The wicked should be punished, and this man Natadze, and whoever set him upon his immoral chores, would certainly be among them.

On the other hand, if he and Net Force could be the instrument of that punishment in this world, he had no problem with that.

"The government will need a lot more evidence before this gets turned over to the AG for prosecution," Thorn said. "You don't kick in a billionaire's door and arrest him without a case as solid as a block of depleted uranium."

The others in the room—Jay, Abe, and Julio—nodded.

"So, here is the situation. We know who the shooter is, and we know—but can't prove—who holds his leash. We've done what we were supposed to do. What we should do now is turn it over to the FBI and let them run it down."

Every man in the room must have heard the unspoken but implied word.

Abe got to it first. "But?"

Thorn looked around. "This is tricky. For one thing, we have a personal stake in it—"

"Amen," Gridley said.

Thorn continued without speaking to that: "—and it would be nice if we could package it up neatly before handing it off to the FBI and the locals in whose jurisdiction these events took place. The fed gets first whack at it, but the city and county will have felony charges, too."

"And is our personal involvement enough reason *not* to turn it over?" Abe said.

Howard spoke up: "Well, I see where the Commander is going. It's not that we don't trust the feebs and the locals to do a good job, it's just that we don't trust them as much as we do our own people."

Abe didn't say anything, but it was obvious he had some problem with the idea.

Thorn said, "So, we can hand it off, or . . . gather a little more information ourselves first."

Howard smiled. Alex Michaels would have made the latter choice, and he'd have suited up and gone out into the field, too. Howard said, "You're the Commander, and it's your choice, but if my opinion counts, I'd say we collect a little more data on our own."

He saw Julio and Jay nod. Abe kept his face carefully neutral.

Thorn said, "There's more to it, as well. This guy, Natadze, came after Jay for a reason. What's more, the guy

he works for sicced him on Jay for a reason. That means
that they knew what Jay was working on, and that means
that somehow they have access to information they
shouldn't."

Again, heads around the room nodded.

"You guys have worked with the regular FBI more than
I have," Thorn went on, "but I haven't seen anything in
the files to indicate they could be the source of a leak."

"They've always been solid, if not quite as good as our
own people," Howard said.

"Still, once this goes over to them, there will be records. In short, people, once this gets out beyond us, it
becomes more likely that the guy we're after might just
learn that we're on to him. And if that happens, he'll
crawl into some deep dark hole and hide. We'll never get
him, then."

"So we keep it, then?" Howard asked.

Thorn nodded. "For now. We know the players. We
know where they live. The shooter isn't likely to go home
and just let us collect him, but if we can put the two men
together, that will give us something substantial. Why
don't we see if we can do that much?"

East Suffolk, Long Island

Their van was disguised as a plumbing truck, parked not
far from the front entrance to the rich man's estate. The
vehicle smelled like pizza, which is what the driver had
gotten for lunch on the way there. Not as luxurious as the
RV they'd used before, but a better fit for this area.

They had been on-site for an hour, in an upper-class
neighborhood on Long Island far enough away so Cox's
security patrol company wouldn't bump into them, but
close enough and in position to see what they needed to
see. The local police had been advised there was a federal

operation in place, but not told the details, and nobody ought to bother them. If the Georgian showed up, he would have to pass them to reach the front gate. If he came from any other direction, to the back or side entrances, for examples, other units were in place to pick him up before he reached them. Even if he arrived by helicopter, they should be able to track that with the radar the RV carried to the south of them. It was possible he could arrive on foot and sneak past, but not likely. It was a long way to town.

"What do you think, General?"

Howard looked at Abe Kent. "It's your show, Colonel. I'm just along for the ride."

"Bull," Colonel Kent replied. "Sir."

Howard smiled. "I think you've covered all your bases, Abe. Approach, fields-of-fire, good use of cover and concealment. Your strategy is good, tactics appropriate."

"Anything you would do differently?"

Howard looked through the mirrored windows of the van. "Offhand, I can't think of anything. The trap is set. All you can do now is wait."

Kent nodded. "Yes." He paused, seemed about to say something, but didn't.

"Go ahead," Howard said, "spit out the rest."

Kent gave him a tight smile. "I'm still not entirely comfortable with this procedure. We ought to be letting the FBI or the locals handle this. This doesn't fall within our purview."

"Technically, no. But you're covered, since I'm still officially running things. Buck stops with me—and Thorn, of course."

"That's not what I meant."

"I know. I'm just saying it." Howard thought about it for a second, then said, "Net Force runs on different rules than the Corps or the Regular Army, Abe. Sometimes, to get the job done, we have to . . . push the boundaries a little. Stretch the rules to cover the situation."

"I understand. I don't like it, but I hear you."

"Just like I understand that when the hot steel is flying and the bombs are going off, you do what you have to do and worry about defending your decisions later. The thing is, this bastard-unit of the National Guard kind of has to make it all up as we go along. Computer crime would seem pretty cut and dried, geeks in thick glasses pushing buttons and rearranging electrons and photons, but in my experience, that's just the tip of the iceberg. We've come across lots of guys who would just as soon shoot you as diddle a keyboard, and the problem with trusting the locals or even the regular feebs to handle them is just that, trust. There are local PDs that can knock a bad guy in the dirt faster than the Flash on speed, and some of the FBI field guys can run with the best, too, but when you're working with others you just don't know that you'll *get* the A-team. With your own people, you know what you have, and your troops are first-class. You have leeway to operate, given the Guard status, that you don't have in regular service units."

Howard paused, thinking about his words. "This guy Natadze is sharp," he said after a moment, "and from what little we know about him, he's skilled. His boss has more money than ten banks, and lawyers out the wazoo, so you have to be careful. If he shows up and gets spooked, he might be able to wade through the local police like an NBA star in a kiddie pool, so you don't want to take that chance."

"I understand the theory," Kent said.

"We're like Special Forces, SEALs, Gray Fox, Rangers—but our mission statement and defined responsibilities are, in practice, just general guidelines. There are times when we have to cross the border and thump the bad guys, and justify it afterward. It might not stick to the letter of the law, but it achieves justice, and that's what you have to keep in mind."

"I'm more comfortable following the rules," he said.

"Yeah, I hear you. Then again, I also remember hearing from a Ranger I knew about a certain major who, against the rules of engagement, took a volunteer squad and went deep into enemy sand to bring back one of his Marines who had been captured by a band of cutthroat fanatics. And when the bad guys resisted, they got handed a short cut to Paradise."

Kent shook his head. "Stupid, that major. Lucky, too."

Howard chuckled. "Davy Crockett's motto: 'Be sure you're right, then go ahead.' This guy we're after shot one of our people, killed at least one other person we know about, and has probably done worse. If we get him, the lawyers can sort it out."

"Yes, sir."

The com clicked on: "Big Bird, this is Baker Leader."

That was Julio, who was sitting on the estate's side entrance, using the command-only opchan.

Kent picked up the com mike. "Go ahead, Baker Leader."

"My people on the back gate tell me we have company. Cadillac limousine with New York vanity plate O-I-L-Y-2, approaching the gate. About a block away."

"Copy that, Baker. Can Baker Team give us a passenger status?"

"Negative, Big Bird. There is a driver reported in front, but the rear windows are opaqued. BT can't tell if there are passengers."

"Copy that."

Kent turned to Howard, raised an eyebrow. Howard nodded.

"Baker Leader, tell BT to detain the limo and ascertain if there are any passengers who might be federal fugitives inside."

"Roger that, Big Bird. Baker Team, you heard the man, stop 'em. I'm heading over there now. Sitrep as soon as we can. Discom."

"It's a risk," Kent said to Howard. "If he's not in the

car, we're screwed. If the Georgian is elsewhere, Cox will warn him off."

"True. But if he is in it, we have him. That's one of Cox's cars, and according to what we know, he and his wife and their company usually come and go via the front gate."

The next few minutes seemed to crawl by as slowly as a year.

Then: "Big Bird, this is Baker Leader. We have a negative on our target here. No passenger. Driver says he is here for a pick-up. We checked the trunk, too."

Kent frowned and keyed the mike. "Copy, Baker Leader. Cut him loose and back off—if he comes back out your gate, have your team stop him again."

"Copy."

"Return to your station, Baker Team Leader, in case somebody tries to leave that way."

"Yes, sir."

Howard and Kent looked at each other. "Maybe he's already inside," Kent said. "And this is his ride."

"It doesn't stand to reason that he's just going to get into the car and leave with a bunch of armed troops pulling limos over."

"You're right, it doesn't. If he's even in there."

Cox cradled the phone's receiver and said, "The limo driver just pulled through the back gate. He was stopped and searched by men in military uniforms."

Seated on the couch, Natadze nodded. "Net Force troops. They put it together. I am sorry."

"It was not your fault," Cox said. "Somehow, they figured out that you work for me."

Natadze said, "My presence here is a risk for you. I must leave."

"Won't they be watching all the exits?"

"I will wait until dark. I will create a diversion, and leave while they deal with it."

"A diversion," Cox said.

"Something bright and noisy," Natadze said. "It will draw their attention. I will take the cook's son's dirt bike and walk it across the fields to the north until I am well away from here."

"What will you do?"

"Go home. They don't know about my New York condo—it has not been under surveillance, I have made certain of that. I will release an electronic evidence packet I have to show that I have left for one of the Middle East countries with whom the United States does not have an extradition treaty. It will not be obvious, they will have to look for it, but they will come across the false trail soon enough. I will sit tight for a few days until they are gulled, then I will use a disguise and get back to dealing with the problem."

Cox shrugged. "I leave it to you, Eduard. This is your area of expertise."

"Yes."

The diversion was easy. Well after dark, the rear gate opened and a car rolled slowly out. A security cam at the gate was reset to watch this.

The military watchers moved in to halt it. The car did not stop, however, and it became apparent shortly there was nobody driving it as it coasted to a stop.

Thirty seconds later, the car burst into flames.

A simple timer and a small charge attached to the gasoline tank had been enough for that.

By this time, Natadze was gone from the house, at the fence on the north side of the estate, well away from any of the gates, crouching in a stand of tall, evergreen arbor vitae.

There would be much radio traffic concerning the fire, and while the confusion roiled, Natadze cut a hole in the chain-link fence, pushed the motorbike through the gap, and quickly crossed the road and into a field whose borders were also blurred by trees. They could have watchers on all the gates, but it was highly unlikely they would have had enough men to completely surround the huge estate, and they would not have worried about somebody leaving on foot—the estate was some distance from transportation.

Thermal vision he could do nothing about. He didn't have the equipment with him to deal with that. But even with night vision gear, it would have been difficult at best to see Natadze, who was dressed all in black, keeping a low profile, and moving as slowly as he could to avoid drawing attention.

Once he was well away from the road, he climbed onto the bike and started pedaling it, riding farther north until he came to a neighborhood street behind a water tower. There weren't that many roads here in this part of Suffolk, but there were a couple of small airports, and MTA stations to the south on the Ronkonkoma Branch Line, and it would be easy enough to loop around and leave that way. If he hurried before they cast a net to cover those.

He knew they would cast that net, and soon. The problem with his diversion was that it had pretty much told them for sure that he had been in there. A car blowing up like that was just too convenient for them to believe it was a coincidence.

They would know he had been there, and they would realize quickly that he was gone. Whatever he did would have to be soon.

Life was not always easy, but nobody had ever told him it would be. As long as you could stay a step ahead of the Reaper? That was as much as you needed, just one step.

Howard and Kent figured it out pretty quick. Kent got on the horn and called it in. "I want a full reconnoiter on the estate's perimeter, put spook-eyes on the scouts and tell them to look real hard."

Julio said, "Yes, sir."

"Discom."

Kent turned to Howard. "He's flown the coop."

"I expect so."

"He was there, John. We were right all along. And he got away."

"For now," Howard said. "Look, Abe, there was nothing you could have done about this. Even if we'd known—and I mean known absolutely for sure that he was in there—we would never have been able to get a warrant."

"Stopping that car going in gave us away, and you know it. It was my call, General, and I blew it."

"You don't have a working crystal ball, Colonel. I called it the same. You had to check."

"If he went over the fence and is on foot, we won't find him with the troops we have."

"We could call the local police in. Cover the roads."

"He'll steal a car, get to a ferry or airport pretty quick."

Howard nodded. "It would be best if we could get some indication he's out before we get the law rolling."

"I *will* catch this guy," Kent said. "No matter how long it takes."

"I believe you, Abe."

It was half an hour later when one of the teams covering the north side of the estate reported that there was a fresh cut in the ten-foot-high chain link fence there, big enough to let a man pass through. The team also reported what appeared to be bicycle tracks in the soft dirt next to the fence.

"He's gone," Abe said. "Again."

Howard nodded. "For the moment, Abe. For the moment."

32

New York City

Thorn sat at his table and sipped his drink—club soda over ice—watched the movers and shakers, and remembered what he had said to Michaels, when they'd met, in what was to be his office.

He smiled at the memory.

Here, the men wore tailored tuxedos—Armani, Sprach, Saville Row, or Hong Kong's best, with tasteful gold cuff links and custom-made Swiss watches. The women wore evening gowns that probably averaged eight or ten thousand dollars each. Some of the women were players, some showpieces—trophy wives or mistresses, movie starlets or models. There were a couple of boy toys escorting older women, too. There were enough diamonds, rubies, and emerald necklaces, earrings, and bracelets to fill a large bath tub, a king's ransom in cool ice. A typical high-end charity dinner and dance, wherein many, if not most, of the attendees could write checks for the cause in six figures and not miss it.

Thorn's own clothing was understated. He wore his

grandfather's opal ring and a basic Rolex stainless steel watch. His tux was well-cut, but didn't scream its maker's name out loud, and his shoes were soft Italian leather, spendy, but not ostentatious. He was new money, but knew that wearing it so that it showed was gauche.

He recalled how he had felt smug about Alex Michaels's cowboy hotdogging, going into the field himself. And how he—Thorn—would never do such a thing.

And yet, here he was. At a charity ball in New York, ostensibly to help orphans in the Middle East, but really here as a spy, plain and simple. Net Force's first efforts to catch Natadze and Cox together had been less than fruitful—but had only confirmed what they already knew.

He could understand the attraction of field work now, despite his good intentions when he'd taken this job. There was a bad guy out there, though not one who was apt to pull out a machinegun and start blasting. No, the quarry was rich and old, a man who had gotten a little head start by marrying well, but who had taken that advantage and used it to claw his way to the apex of a multibillion-dollar empire.

You had to have a little luck along the way, but you also had to be smart, ruthless, and willing to do whatever it took to get to the top of that hill, and then to stay there. If Thorn's modest fortune fell from Cox's pocket, he might not be bothered to stoop and pick it up.

Cox had been there for a lot of years. He'd been wheeling and dealing and making major fortunes when Thorn had been in high school. Cox was powerful, canny, and not above having his enemies squashed. A man like that was a worthy opponent, somebody who wasn't going to just roll over if you went "Boo!" at him, and something in Thorn wanted to beat the guy just to prove he could.

And part of that was getting a close look at the man, trying to get a feel for him, something you couldn't really do at a distance, or in VR. Good as it was, even the best virtual scenario wouldn't allow you to nail it all down.

So here he was.

"He's by the hearth," Marissa said. She had returned from the powder room and was pointing with her nose. "Talking to that BoTox'd blonde in black trying to look twenty-five but only managing thirty-something."

Thorn looked at Marissa. She wore a red dress, a deep, dark red sheath held up with thin spaghetti straps that set off her bare arms and shoulders. She had on a ruby necklace—borrowed and fake, she'd told him, but a good fake—four-inch pumps that matched the dress, and a small clutch handbag, and it all looked terrific on her. And she knew it, too.

She was one of three black women in the room, and one of them was a server.

"By the way," he said. "I don't think I ever thanked you for accompanying me tonight. It may be socially acceptable to go to one alone, but it looks odd, to say the least."

"All in the line of work," she said, but she smiled as she said it.

He saw that smile and found himself thinking that maybe someday soon they'd have to do this again, when they *weren't* working.

She turned and nodded toward Cox. "You going to go over and say hello?"

"Nope," he said. "The hostess is circulating. I made a polite request to her when I answered the invitation. She'll collect us eventually and introduce us to him."

Marissa raised an eyebrow. "That's how the rich folk do it? They wait for an audience?"

He smiled. "Yep. I'm a lightweight compared to a lot of these people, and nouveau riche, too, but I'm also a man who doesn't have to work, but who is dutifully serving his government. That's just enough to make me socially acceptable for a meeting with Cox at this kind of soiree. And having you as a date makes it easier—at this level, appearances count for a lot."

"You mean Cox might be a stone racist who calls his hired help names in private, but he has to be courteous to us in public?"

Thorn smiled. "Can't get anything past you, can I?"

She didn't smile back. "How long before the hostess comes looking for you?"

Thorn glanced at his watch. "I'm fairly low on the food chain. Maybe half an hour or so."

"Want to dance?"

"Sure."

They set their drinks on the table and moved to the dance floor.

It was not a young crowd at the charity dinner and ball—only a handful of people his age or younger—but old money learned the social graces early, and dancing was among them. Nobody was bumping into anybody else.

Strauss was not his favorite composer, but the music was being done well by the chamber orchestra, and he let it take him as he led Marissa into the number.

It was no surprise to him that she was a good dancer. He looked forward to moving a little closer to her when the orchestra played a slower number.

"I'm guessing they're probably not going to play any down and dirty blues, huh?" she said.

"They will if you want," he said. "Gigs like this, the band makes as much on tips as they do from the fee. The champagne is flowing—pay attention, you'll see waiters stopping by to whisper into the conductor's ear. There are people here who will drop a five hundred dollar tip to hear 'Stardust,' or 'Mood Indigo,' or even some old Beatles numbers. My guess is that somebody in that chamber orchestra knows just about anything you might want to hear, and the rest of them can fake it. I once heard the Seattle Chamber Orchestra at a charity ball play Otis Spann's 'My Home is in the Delta' and the first violinist made his fiddle howl like a train whistle."

"You are making that up."

He raised his hand. "I swear. If you have a favorite, I bet I can get them to play it for you."

"Yeah, right."

"Five hundred gets you a vocal to go with the music."

"No way."

"You want to see?"

"Why don't you just give me the money instead and I'll buy the CD? And a new deck to play it on."

He laughed.

The waltz ended, there was polite applause, and the dancers either headed back for their tables or waited for another tune to begin.

"I need to visit the men's room," he said.

He left her at the table, and found a waiter, out of her sight. He shook the man's hand, transferred the folded bills from his palm to the waiter's, and made his request.

He got back to the table. Marissa was sitting down, sipping at her iced tea.

The orchestra wound down another waltz.

"You're right," she said. "I saw a waiter go up and talk to the band leader a minute ago. You figure we're about to hear something from the big band swing era?"

He shrugged.

The conductor raised his baton. One of the cello players set his instrument down and stood. He was maybe thirty, with red hair and pale skin.

The violins cranked up. It took the crowd a few seconds to realize they weren't getting another waltz.

The cellist started singing "Big Car Blues," a pretty fair imitation of Lightnin' Hopkins's version of it, too. Never would have guessed he had it in him, to look at him.

When he started going on about that big black Cadillac with white-sidewall tires, some of the attendees laughed.

Marissa just grinned real big and shook her head. "Oh, Tommy. What am I going to do with you?" But she was tapping her foot to the music—as were at least a few others.

As the song wound down, Thorn looked up and saw Beatrice Theiron working her way through the crowd in their direction. She was seventy, but with enough knife-work and makeup that she looked to be in her late fifties. She caught his gaze and smiled.

Marissa looked to see what Thorn was staring at.

"Show time," he said.

He looks good for a man his age, Thorn thought. Fit, skin still mostly clear, lots of smile wrinkles. Very expensive caps on his teeth. His hair was gray and going white, the haircut probably a hundred bucks, and the tuxedo was immaculate, perfectly fitted. Italian leather shoes, too.

Beatrice Theiron spoke to Cox as an equal—her family's wealth, counted in the billions, came from munitions, and ran back to before the Revolutionary War. American money didn't get much older. The Theirons had been so rich for so long they didn't even think about it as anything but a force of nature, like the sun or the rain.

"Samuel, this is Tom Thorn, the young man about whom I spoke earlier. Tom, Samuel Cox."

"Ah, Tom, so nice to finally meet you."

He turned his full attention upon Thorn like a spotlight as they shook hands. A firm grip, enough to show he was a man, not enough to be a challenge.

Her duty done, Beatrice said, "Pardon me, if you would, I just saw Madame LeDoux, and I *must* run and ask her about her dress!"

She flitted away, spry for a woman well past retirement age.

Thorn watched her for a moment, then said, "Mr. Cox. This is Marissa Lowe."

"Please, call me Sam." Cox took Marissa's hand, flashed his high-wattage smile at her. "My deep pleasure, Ms. Lowe."

Marissa gave him a half smile and nod.

Cox released her hand and looked around. A waiter appeared as if by magic, bearing a tray with champagne flutes, still cold enough that the glasses were frosted. Cox took two stems, gave one each to Thorn and Marissa, took a third for himself. The waiter vanished.

"Nice trick," Marissa said, nodding at the glass.

He smiled at her. "One of the small perks."

He raised his glass slightly, and offered a toast: "To success," he said.

They clinked glasses. "Success," Thorn and Marissa echoed.

They sipped the wine. Thorn didn't think this was the same vintage everybody else was drinking—it was crisper, cleaner, with a hint of apple. Private stock? Probably.

"So, you are the Commander of Net Force," Cox said.

"Afraid so."

"Must be interesting, working for the government, after being in the private sector. It is just amazing what they can do with computers these days. I have no head for such things myself. Never quite trust them to give me what I need."

"It is a challenge at times."

"And you, Ms. Lowe, you are a federal employee, as well?"

"I am."

Cox grinned, and it was a sly look. "But not with Net Force. Let me guess: I'd say . . . the CIA?"

Her smile didn't falter a bit. "A good guess, Mr. Cox."

And Thorn thought, *"Guess"—yeah, right.*

"Please, Sam. We're past the formal stage, wouldn't you say? I feel as if I have known you two for a long time. Almost as if we have been doing business with one another."

It wasn't so much the words, but the look that attended them that struck Thorn. The comment about the CIA, coupled with a glint in the eyes and just a hint of a grin.

No question in Thorn's mind that the man knew he was being stalked, and exactly who it was on his tail.

Not that it would be hard to guess—after Natadze had snuck out of the estate, it would have been easy enough to put two and two together. Somebody stops his limo at the gate, and a couple days later, here is Thomas Thorn, Commander of Net Force, asking for an introduction?

No, it wouldn't take a bright bulb to illuminate that one, and Cox was certainly not dim. Thorn had known that going in. He was here to size up his opponent, see his moves, and it didn't matter if the man knew who he was and why he'd come.

Cox glanced at his watch. It was a plain-looking instrument, nothing the least bit ostentatious, but Thorn knew it was one of those handmade Swiss things that cost as much as a new Mercedes. Probably sat in a motorized box at home that would rotate every now and then to keep it wound when Cox wasn't wearing it.

"Oh, my, look at the time. I'd love to stay and chat, but I'm afraid I have to run—we have another of these things on tonight's schedule. Noblesse oblige and all that. A great pleasure to finally meet you both. I wish you good fortune in your endeavors, Tom and Marissa. And a parting piece of wisdom I learned from my track coach when I was in high school: Some days you get the bear and some days, the bear gets you." He gave them a slow, military bow, and left.

After he was gone, Marissa looked up at Thorn and said, "He's playing with us, Tommy."

He nodded. "Yeah. That last bit about the bear pretty much nailed it shut. He was *gloating*. He knows we know, but doesn't think we can touch him."

"I guess that much money and power buys a lot of confidence," she said.

"Even Achilles had his heel," he said.

"And if he'd worn a metal boot, he would have been invulnerable," she said.

"Whose side are you on?"

"Why, yours, Tommy. Your left side, as I make it." She batted her eyelids at him theatrically.

He grinned, despite his irritation at Cox. The die was cast. The man knew who they were, knew they were after him, and had the gall to stand there and spar with them about it.

We'll see who gets whom, Mr. Bear.

33

New York City

In the back of the limo on the way home from the charity dinner, Cox fixed himself a drink, bourbon over ice. He was not pleased. As soon as the Theiron woman had approached him, asking to introduce Thomas Thorn and his dark-skinned date, Cox had known. Net Force must have broken the coded file, despite what Eduard had done to prevent it. They knew he was a spy. They had come to take his measure for the coffin they hoped to build.

A quick phone call had given him some background information on Thorn, and on his paramour, who worked for the CIA. He had been armed a little better when finally they had spoken.

Cox sipped his drink. He had tweaked Thorn and the woman a bit, knowing a good offense was the best defense. Let them know he knew what they were about to keep them off balance, that was how he had fought his way to the top. Give back more than you receive, that was how you won.

Even so, he had to resist the urge to panic. Them *know-*

ing was not the same as them *proving*. He knew that. Unless they had ironclad evidence, something absolutely certain and incontrovertible, the feds would not move against him. The Russian was dead, the other copies of the file were either gone or about to be, and his name written in an old Soviet document? Any lawyer worth his salt could argue that such a listing could be nothing more than disinformation, designed to impeach a man's character, to sow distrust. It proved nothing in itself. Anybody could put a name into a file. For that matter, how do we now that the file in question wasn't simply fabricated altogether?

Yes, if they knew how much he did not wish such information to become public, they could hold that over him, but they did not know that. And any threats to smear him would result in legal and political troubles that would give a strong man pause. A politician would have to be very brave indeed to venture onto such a tricky path where a misstep could result in the end of a career. The most fiery federal prosecutor had bosses to whom he must answer, and his bosses had their bosses. The higher you went, the more political things got. Attorneys-General and Presidents did not blindly sail into uncharted waters.

A crafty politician knew that when you fought a giant, you had best be careful with your sling. If your first shot was wide, you might be crushed before you had a chance to reload.

And if you had but one stone? Then the risk was extreme indeed, and the payoff had better be worth it—and guaranteed.

Cox did not wish to come to blows with the feds, but at this juncture he felt certain that they would not be eager to start that war, either. They didn't have a walkover victory lined up. They couldn't.

He should have thought of this much sooner, of course, long before tonight, even. His first reaction to the threat of being unearthed after all these years, sending Eduard

after Jay Gridley, had been . . . less considered than it
should have been. He had, in retrospect, acted in more
haste than was wise. Then, even the hint of scandal about
such things had seemed insupportable. And there had been
several additional factors other than the Net Force file.

Now? Now, an accusation based on a single document,
without any supporting evidence? That could be laughed
off: *Me? A Communist spy? My God man, look at me!
I'm Samuel Walker Cox, I'm a billionaire! Are you out of
your mind?*

Even his enemies would smile at that one—unless there
was hefty proof to back it up.

If there had been a handler willing to testify, and supporting papers from official sources, that would have been
weightier, but a file allegedly given to Net Force by our
sometimes-friends, sometimes-not-friends, the Turks?
Where is their copy backing this? Lost, you say? What
about the Russians, surely they had supporting evidence?
Oops, can't find it?

My, my.

He was in a better position than before. Still not ideal,
but even so, if it got to that, he could afford the best spin
docs in the world.

If it got to that.

And, unless they came up with something else, Cox
was pretty sure it would never *get* to that. You didn't need
to be a weatherman to know which way the wind blew.
All was not lost.

He sipped the drink, finishing it. He needed to rein
Eduard in, he saw. If Net Force had broken the code, as
surely they had, or else they wouldn't have come to have
a look at him, then any further attempts against their people would be useless *and* dangerous. Eduard was loyal,
but suppose he was captured or killed? There might be
some way to link him to Cox, and that would give them
another bit of circumstantial evidence, however tenuous.
If they couldn't come up with anything else, he was safe.

Best not to give them a chance at anything else, no matter how remote it might be.

If your enemy's fire was burning low, giving him more fuel was unwise.

He dug into the seat pocket and came up with one of the throwaway phones. He thumbed in Eduard's number for the day.

Net Force might be a squall headed his way, but if he sat tight, hunkered down, and waited, it would pass. No point in risking the lightning by standing alone in a field.

"Yes?"

"Cancel the current contract," Cox said. "Clean up everything, neat and tidy, and don't leave any trash lying about. Nothing."

"Yes, sir," Eduard said.

And that was that.

34

University Park, Maryland

A week after his meeting with Cox, nothing new had developed on that front. The constant surveillance—which was costing a considerable amount of his budget—had not produced so much as a glimpse of Natadze and Cox together.

Thorn invited Marissa to dinner. He chose a small but sophisticated place where they could talk. He wanted to get to know her better, but he also wanted her take on some things that were bothering him, and he wanted them both without interruption.

After they had eaten and were lingering over coffee, he turned the conversation back to the party they'd attended. "You stood and listened to him taunt us," he said. "We know he is guilty, but we don't have the proof."

"What do we know that he's guilty of?" she said.

"He had at least one person we know of killed, albeit that one was a Russian agent and not a great loss to the world. And he had somebody shoot Jay Gridley—though he survived. The only thing that makes sense is that he was afraid of something Jay was working on, and my guess is that he's listed on that file of Soviet agents—that would explain him having the Russian taken out. It doesn't make *much* sense, a rich man spying for the Communists, but nothing else computes. The man was a spy. Maybe he still is."

He sighed. "I'm sure he did other things at least that bad along the way, but we don't have what we need to get him."

"That's how it works sometimes," Marissa said. She paused. "Let me tell you a story."

"Another story? You ought to have your own show on PBS," he said. " 'Marissa the Wise Woman Speaks.' "

"That's true, I should. Good of you to acknowledge it."

He laughed.

She said, "Where there's a will, there's usually a way. We're tropical creatures, our bodies are designed for warm climates, grasslands, trees. But we've come up with clothes that let us walk around at the South Pole, created machines that let us cover great distances at speed, allow us to cross land, the oceans—or to go deep under water, if we want. We've even been to the moon, through a cold vacuum where you'd die in seconds unprotected."

"Yeah, we're adaptable. So?"

"So, we don't always come up with the ultimate answer, but for every question, we usually come up with something. Consider the mata-you."

"What's a mata-you?"

"Nothing's the matter with me. What's a matter you?"

He laughed again.

"One born every minute. Okay, let's talk about snow runners."

He took a sip of his coffee. "Okay, I'll bite, what is a snow runner? Some kind of extreme sport?"

"Back in the hot summer days before refrigeration you usually drank your beer warm. If you wanted something to plop into your drink to cool it, you had three choices:

Wait for winter; collect and store a whole lot of ice in a cool dark place during the winter, like a cave or an ice house; or go to where there was natural ice and fetch it. In temperate or even tropical countries, you can usually find such places."

Thorn considered it for a moment. "Mountains," he said.

"Right," she said. "So while it might be ninety in the shade down in the flats, five or ten thousand feet up the local hills, there could be snow on the ground, frozen ponds, like that."

"Uh huh."

"The Romans, the Europeans, and even the South Americans had snow runners. Say you were the local king of the Incas down in Peru about the time Pizarro came to call, and you had a fondness for cold chocolate in the hot summer. What you did was, you sent your snow runners up to collect it for you. These were fleet-footed fellows who could run for marathon distances at a goodly clip—at least for the part where they got to the base of the mountain. They had to slow down some on the uphill leg, and coming down, they had these big, watertight baskets lined with leaves and wrapped in some kind of insulation, holding forty or fifty pounds of densely packed snow or ice chipped from a frozen stream, depending on the boss's tastes. The stuff would start to melt pretty quick once you were below the freezing level, of course, so you had to be fairly swift. By the time you got back to the temple, or wherever the king liked to hang out, much of it would be melted, so you'd be heading back up the mountain soon, and if the king was having a party, well, you'd be hustling."

"A busy life."

"Kind of like being a mail carrier," she said. "Lots of exercise outdoors, and the pay was relatively good. The snow runners would have eaten well, they needed to be in shape. But my point, Tommy, is that you might not be able to get at him directly, but it's like ice in your drink in the summer. You can find a way if you want it bad enough."

He sighed. "I suppose you're right."

"Of course I'm right. You just need to use that sharp brain of yours to come up with something that will do the job."

He nodded. She was right, of course. If only it were as easy as she made it sound.

35

Another week passed, and Net Force had nothing to show for it regarding Cox.

Yes, Jay Gridley had come across some information on the net indicating that Natadze had fled the country, but Jay had said it seemed hinky, and after Thorn examined it, he agreed. The data was too perfect—a little work had revealed flights, a name, and dates, but the passenger had never been photographed by any security cams, and the copy of his ID had somehow been garbled so that nothing remained of it but that it was on file as having been checked. Too easy, and both Jay and Thorn thought it was a red herring set to throw them off Natadze's trail.

What Thorn had hoped for hadn't materialized. Keeping teams in the field 24/7 cost a lot, and with nothing to show for it except suspicion, he couldn't keep justifying it.

Worse, he had spoken to an old friend who was working for the Attorney General, and just a few minutes earlier had had a long and hard discussion with the Director of the FBI. Neither set of comments had been encouraging.

Coming out of the Director's office had left him feeling stunned. He had thought he knew how politics worked, but she had given him a lesson in just how little he knew.

Reality was ugly.

And now, he had to pass that lesson along.

It wasn't going over well.

Jay said, "I'm sorry, I don't see the problem. This is a bad guy—he's probably a spy, certainly a murderer, and not to take it personal or anything, but he had his goon *shoot me in the head!*"

Kent nodded. "Gridley is right."

Fernandez said, "I third that."

Thorn sighed. "I don't disagree at all. Cox is definitely a bad man. But it has been pointed out to me that it's not that simple."

He looked at them, and knew that no matter how he tried, making them understand the total picture was going to be difficult. Especially since he didn't agree with it himself.

"Pointed out to you by whom?" Kent asked.

"A source in the AG's office. And my boss. Who got it from her boss, who, I shouldn't need to say, is the President of these United States and at whose pleasure we serve."

"Politics. That's just great," Kent said. His tone could have etched glass.

"It's not just that Cox is richer than Midas," Thorn said, "though he can afford to throw a brigade of lawyers at the government and probably keep from going to jail until he dies of old age—*if* we could even get a conviction—but that's not our worry."

"Then what is our worry?" Jay asked. "You're saying we don't have enough on him to arrest him."

"You know we don't. We don't even know for certain

why he did it. All we have is conjecture. Even if you cracked the code and found his name in the agent file, that wouldn't prove he *was* one."

"I'm working on it. I'll get it. What about his connection to Natadze? How would a hit man have enough on the ball to do all that corporate crap to hide his house? That had to come from Cox."

"*We* know that. But any lawyer with half a brain would get that laughed out of court—Cox didn't leave any fingerprints, and maybe Natadze read how to do that in a book."

"Bull," Jay said.

"I'm not arguing with that. Look, the point is, even if we had a mountain of evidence, it still might not go forward."

Fernandez, just promoted to captain, said, "Excuse me?"

Thorn shook his head. "I'll explain it to you the way it was explained to me. Remember the Enron scandal some ten years or so ago? Big company got caught doing some real creative wheeler-dealing, went bust?"

"Yes," Fernandez said. "So?"

"A lot of people lost their retirements, their jobs, their homes, and even their families, and they had nothing to do with the situation other than that their companies had invested in Enron."

Fernandez nodded. "I remember."

"Here's the biggest obstacle: Cox is the head of a multinational corporation worth more than some countries. There are tens of thousands of people directly working for him around the world, and millions of people indirectly connected to his businesses. Stock markets all over the globe trade shares in these companies."

"Like the Captain said," Colonel Kent said, "so what?"

"International concerns like Cox's carry a lot of weight. Given the nature of the world's economy, with everybody linked to everybody else, it's kind of like a house of cards.

Pull the wrong one out and the whole thing collapses."

Fernandez picked up on it first: "So, what, we're supposed to let this guy off because that *might* be a glitch in the finances of a bunch of rich folks?"

"It's not just rich folks. It's the proverbial widows and orphans who can't afford what you call a 'glitch.' "

"Are you saying that arresting Cox will cause a collapse of the entire planet's economy?" Jay said. "Come on!"

Thorn shook his head again. "I don't know. Maybe it wouldn't do anything at all. Or maybe having the head honcho revealed as a murdering Soviet spy might so rattle investors' confidence that they'd dump their stock en masse. Or maybe customers would be alarmed to the extent that they'd look to take their business elsewhere. We don't know."

He sighed. He did understand this himself. He was a part of that community, too. But he hated it, hated the very thought that Cox might be untouchable. "Look," he said, "once you start digging into the way the man operates—and that will have to be part of it—there's no telling what we are going to find. A guy who is willing to sell out his country, to have people killed, probably wasn't too scrupulous in his business dealings. I'd bet once the fed starts turning over rocks there, all kinds of ugly things are going to be revealed. There's no way to be sure."

"I don't give a flying fiddler's—" Jay began.

"Think of it like this," Thorn said, cutting him off. "Your sixty-four-year-old father is about to retire after working hard for forty years. The Cox empire shatters, the stock market goes into the toilet. The mutual fund where much of your father's retirement has been invested loses most of its value. That nest egg he's spent his whole life building just . . . goes away. He's probably going to have to keep working—assuming he can—and whatever assistance he can get from Social Security is, given how that program is teetering on the brink of a big abyss, going to be minimal."

"Yes, but—"

"Now multiply that by, say, a couple million late baby boomers who are going to retire in the next year or two. And it isn't just them, it's the shops they frequent, their children, their grandchildren's college funds. If a whole lot of people go on welfare, lose their homes, get sick, can't afford medicine or doctors, that ripple runs throughout society. It's the butterfly wings in Kansas causing a typhoon in China, Jay. It's not just a few rich folks who might have to skip buying a new yacht for a year."

None of the men around the table were stupid. He could see it working through their minds.

Finally, Jay said, "All right. So we can't just ride in with the troops and grab Cox. But we can't just do nothing, either. So what *do* we do?"

Thorn rubbed the side of his face. This was going to be the really ugly part. "I have been told that we can have the federal prosecutor work things out with the state and local authorities, and come up with an offer."

"An offer?"

"Yes. Quietly, behind the scenes. We agree not to go after him, and put forth some kind of deal that gets Cox to retire, to give up control of his empire, maybe a big fine."

"What?! The man is a killer!" That from Fernandez. "And the government wants to give him a *traffic* ticket?"

"Given what we have, proving felonies to a jury would be extremely difficult. He knows we're watching, and he isn't going to take a crooked step. There's nothing else we can find."

He paused, then went on, "If we had a confession, and video of him strangling a small child in front of a hundred witnesses, the process itself would still be full of pitfalls. He might be able to get to one of the jurors, offer enough money to buy their own small town if they want one. There are a hundred things that could go wrong in a trial, and we all know that Cox will have the biggest, meanest legal sharks in the world on his side hunting for these things. If he spent ten million, a hundred million dollars on his defense, it would just be pocket change to him. Maybe he gets off, scot-free, and meanwhile, maybe your father and a million other fathers like him wind up living in a shelter or on the street. Would you have that?"

Nobody said anything.

"A man like Cox lives for the game," Thorn said. "If we can take that away from him, that will be some kind of punishment." That was lame, and he knew it, but he had no other crumbs to offer, and he hated that.

"But he's still a billionaire living high on the hog," Fernandez said. "How much you figure he's going to suffer, when it gets right down to it?"

Thorn didn't have an answer for that.

"That's assuming he goes for the deal," Jay said. His voice was bitter. "We don't have enough leverage to do much. He might tell the feds to shove it, and dare them to take him to_court."

"That's possible."

"This sucks," Fernandez said. "Big time."

Thorn nodded. "Yes. It does. It's not right. But it's the way things are. I'm just telling you what I've been told. Our job was to catch him. We uncovered him. We're supposed to shut up and leave it alone from here on in."

That pretty much ended the meeting, with nobody happy—especially Thorn. As the men left, Thorn stopped Fernandez. "Julio, can I see you a minute?"

"Yeah. What's up?"

After the others were gone, Thorn told him. It surprised Fernandez, but it didn't take five seconds for him to nod his agreement. Thorn had been pretty sure he would go along. They thought alike about this particular subject. Thorn's grandfather had taught him that the law and justice were distant cousins; that when you were forced to make a choice between them, it was better to choose justice, even if it might put you at odds with the law. Laws changed, they shifted according to the whim of those who made them, and people sometimes made mistakes—just look at what the white man had done to the red man or the black man—genocide and slavery, and all of it perfectly legal at the time. There was the letter of the law, and then there was the spirit, his grandfather had taught him—it didn't take an eagle to see which was the right path.

So Marissa's story about the snow runners applied here. Maybe, just maybe, there might be another way.

36

Howard was cleaning out his temporary desk. The situation with Cox was effectively over, as far as Net Force was concerned. Jay was still doggedly trying to decode the file, and searching high and low for anything else that might swing the decision to back off in the other direction, but Howard knew a done deal when he heard one.

Sometimes you won, sometimes you lost. That was how it went. Losing this one, however—not only his last one with Net Force, but one with such a personal element, too—was going to be hard.

He looked up and saw Abe standing in the doorway.

"They are covering their tracks," Abe said.

Howard said, "Yeah?"

"Natadze's house just blew up. Pretty much leveled the sucker."

"Really?"

"Our surveillance people have been long gone, but the local police are investigating it. First reports say it was probably natural gas, but I wouldn't bet on it being an accident. Soon as the arson boys check it, I'm betting they find evidence of a trigger, even if it was a gas leak."

Howard shook his head. "I don't suppose Natadze was in the place when it went up?"

"No signs of a body. I'll keep you posted, if you want."

"I'd appreciate it, Abe."

"You looking forward to the new job?"

"Yes and no. It'll pay better. My wife will sleep easier. But it probably won't be as much fun."

"Anytime you want to come back and do a ride-along, let me know. You'll always be welcome"

"Thanks. I appreciate it."

Abe left, and Howard finished his packing. He was going to miss this, no question. But better-paid and safer had their appeal.

37

It had been dark for hours, and the neighborhood was quiet. Natadze's stomach churned and sent bile into his throat as he approached what was left of his house, slipping from shadow to shadow in the night, moving with great caution.

He had driven past once earlier in the rental car, and what he had seen had twisted his bowels and thrust a shard of icy fear into his soul. His house was gone.

He had one hope. The safe.

The gun safe—a Liberty Presidential model with Quad-fire protection—had been in the basement. If it had just been a fire, he wouldn't have worried as much. The salesman had shown him pictures of a safe like his that had been in a building that burned to the ground, and the contents, which included valuable documents, had not even been singed.

He'd had to hire a crew to take out part of the house's wall in order to install the safe, a massive, hollowed-out chunk of insulated steel that weighed fifteen hundred pounds. Natadze had the interior of the box redesigned so that he could squeeze five standard-size guitars into it, with room left over for his Korth revolvers. He always kept the Friedrich locked away when he was gone, as well as his Hauser; others, he rotated in and out. Currently, there was an Oribe, a Ruck, and a Byers in it. Less than a third of his collection.

The room in the basement in which the safe had stood was insulated and humidity controlled, with an automatic fire-retardant system that used carbon dioxide. The other guitars had been in their cases in that locked room, and, under normal circumstances, relatively protected. But when he finally arrived, having walked there from three streets over where he had parked his car, he knew there was no hope for anything outside the safe. The entire house was gone, save for part of the chimney, and the basement was hollowed-out and black. Even in the dark, he could see that.

Most of his collection of fine instruments—among them, an Elliott, a White, a Schramm, a Spross, and the new Bogdanovich, were *gone*. Blasted to splinters, burned to ashes.

It was like a hammer blow to his heart.

It was not the money. He could buy new ones, maybe even better than the ones he'd had, but there would never be others exactly like them. Those instruments had been unique, each with its own special voice, and those voices were now stilled forever. Murdered—because it had not been an accident. Somebody had blown up his house and the precious instruments in it. Somebody. And who knew it was his house? Who stood to profit if he were to be killed in an explosion?

This was not how the authorities did things in the United States. They would confiscate the house and what was in it, sell it all, make a profit. Not blow it up.

It made him want to cry.

Natadze stood in the shadows for half an hour, watching. It was late, there was yellow police tape strung, but no sign that anybody was there waiting for him. What would be the point in watching a burned-out house?

After he was sure he was alone, he moved stealthily, and climbed down into the rubble that had been his home.

The natural gas main had been in the basement. The force of the initial explosion had knocked the safe onto its side, hinge down. The paint had been burned off, but there was enough left of the steel dial to work. He used his tiny flashlight to look at the numbers as he input them.

The safe was designed to protect the contents against temperatures over fifteen hundred degrees Fahrenheit, according to the tests he had been shown, keeping the condition inside well below the flash point of paper for more than half an hour at extreme external temperatures. A normal house fire would never reach that. While it might get hot enough inside to damage the finishes, which was bad, there were partitions between each instrument so that falling over shouldn't bang them together. Only the Byers, which was up top and angled, was likely to move about much.

But—how much concussive force might have been transmitted into the safe? An explosion powerful enough to blow away most of a house and to knock a fifteen-hundred-pound safe onto its side was not a small matter.

His mouth dry with fear, he finished the combination and retracted the bolts. He nearly wrenched his shoulder lowering the door to the floor. He found he was holding his breath as he shined the light into the box. . . .

The Friedrich was in the middle, next to the Hauser. He took the Friedrich out first, and a great sense of relief washed over him. It was okay! The finish was smooth, unblemished. He carefully replaced it, removed the Hauser, and it, too, was undamaged!

The Ruck was whole! The Torres!

The Byers, topmost, had some damage. The side of the guitar nearest the safe's wall had been partially cooked.

The finish had bubbled up, and there were small cracks in it. They didn't seem to go into the wood of the bout itself, which meant that it could be repaired.

Thank you, God. And thank you, Liberty Safe and Security.

He put the Byers back into the safe, shut the door with some effort, and spun the dial. He would go and get his car, return, and collect his precious instruments. His condo in New York did not have a sufficient floor-strength rating to install a safe this large, but there were places where he could store the guitars until he could find a new house that could. A fireproof vault in a high-class storage company that specialized in rare valuables, antiques, furs, like that, would serve.

As he hurried to collect his automobile and return, the sense of fear and worry he'd had was replaced by one of rage.

Why had he done it? What had been the point? He would have known Natadze wasn't there. Why destroy the house?

And the only thing that came to mind was something Cox had said after his meeting with the head of Net Force at that party:

Clean up everything, neat and tidy, and don't leave any trash lying about. Nothing.

Trash? A man who would destroy a room full of fine guitars for no other reason than to be certain there was nothing incriminating in that room? Such a man deserved punishment beyond measure.

38

Cox, on his stair-stepper, with a few minutes left to go on the timer, smiled at the memory of the phone call he'd gotten an hour earlier.

He hadn't laughed when his lawyers told him about the government's tentative and careful approach, though he had felt like laughing. The government wanted to make him an offer, to spare the country the trauma of a trial. . . .

Cox had played high-stakes poker with some of the best. It had taken him all of two seconds to realize that they didn't have squat and were trying to bluff him. He hadn't thought they'd try this, frankly, and it was maybe not so surprising—if you couldn't get the whole loaf, or even half of it, you might settle for a few crumbs.

Not that he was going to give them even that much.

He had already put his spin docs into play, to scotch the rumors that would certainly show their faces eventually. The war on terrorism wasn't going as well as it should, the Middle East was still an unhealed wound, the country was on the edge of a recession, and in its desperation, the current administration was looking for high-profile targets it could attack. They needed a victory, anything they could flack into looking impressive, and the little people did love to see a rich and powerful man brought low. The spin docs would lay this out, and it would be the government who came off looking bad—not a man who had just given ten million dollars to various charities, and who employed so many people in so many good jobs.

The fed didn't have the weight, and Samuel Walker Cox was not a man to flinch if somebody yelled "Boo!"

"Tell them we are not the least bit interested," he'd told his lawyers. "Make it very clear to them that this is not a negotiating ploy, not an opening gambit. This is the end-game. Make sure that they know they have already lost."

That would piss them off, but—so what? They didn't have the cards, and if somebody called your bluff, you lost the pot.

The private scrambled line lit, and Cox picked it up. "Hello?"

"My house has been blown up," Eduard said.

"That's terrible." A beat: "We shouldn't speak of such things, even on a secure line." ·

"Who would do such a thing?"

"Why ask me? I don't know. An old enemy?"

"My old enemies are no longer among the living."

"It is just a house, my friend. We'll get you a new one."

There was silence. Then, "Yes, you are right. Forgive me for bothering you with this."

Somebody had destroyed Eduard's house? Who? Why? Perhaps it had been an accident?

He looked at the timer. Only a minute left. A house was nothing. He could buy Eduard fifty houses, he could sleep in a different one each week for a year, if he wanted.

Cox hit the stop button on the timer, letting his feet

slow to a stop. Someone had blown up Eduard's house? Who? Why? And more importantly, how?

Cox hadn't done it himself. He knew that. And he knew that Net Force would never be able to do such a thing. Which meant someone else knew about Eduard, and that just shouldn't be possible.

"This is serious," he said. "Go to ground. Give me time to look into this. Then we'll talk."

"Yes," Eduard said, and disconnected.

Cox resumed his exercise. There was only a minute left on the timer, but his thoughts were no longer on the stair-stepper, nor his total victory over Net Force. This was unexpected, and unexpected was always bad.

Natadze sat in the clean car, staring though the windshield at a bus that had stopped to disgorge passengers. Cox had reacted as though he knew nothing about the explosion, but Natadze was no longer fooled. There had been nothing in Natadze's house to link him to Cox, nothing. But a man that rich had different ideas about property, about the value of things. His only passion was in playing his business games. It was all about the deal for him. Money, possessions, they were just ways to keep score, to show that he was winning. Had Natadze mentioned his destroyed instrument collection, Cox would undoubtedly have offered to buy him news ones. A man like Cox would never understand that there were some things money couldn't buy. Perhaps it was time for him to learn that.

Natadze felt a great sadness underlying his anger. He remembered a fortune cookie he'd gotten at a Chinese restaurant, in England, of all places, years before. The fortune had said, "Minimize expectations to avoid being disappointed." That had been in line with his beliefs, and he had kept the slip of paper as a reminder. It was even now in his wallet. But he had come to trust Cox, to expect certain things from him. That had been his mistake. You could depend on no one in the world except for yourself. Sad, but true.

The bus pulled away from the curb, and Natadze followed it. There were things he had to do. Best he get to them.

39

Thorn sat at his desk, wondering if his decision to leave business and get into government service had been wise. His first major case had turned into a convoluted knot that Alexander the Great couldn't cut. Things were easier in the corporate world. Yes, there were political problems, but the bottom line was more important, and when you were the boss, you could solve a lot of situations by simply willing it so.

He sighed. He had known it would be a challenge, but not that it would be so frustrating.

His phone chirped. He picked it up. He would have to watch himself, he might take somebody's head off, the way he felt.

"Thorn," he said.

"Commander? This is Watkins, Main Gate Security."

Thorn looked at the guard's image on the intercom screen. "Yes?"

"We have a man out here asking for you, says it's a

personal matter. His name is, ah, Dennis McManus."

It took a second for the name to register. *McManus? Here?*

"The thing is, sir, he's carrying a big case full of weird stuff, and part of it is—"

"—a sword," Thorn finished.

"Yes, sir. Are you expecting him? He's not on the call list."

How silly was this? The guy just shows up at the gate? Carrying his fencing gear? Expecting Thorn to let him in and square off in some sort of duel of honor?

Thorn thought about it for a moment. Another day, a different time, he would have had the guard shoo the guy away. But the man had picked the wrong time to call. "Yes, I forgot to add him. Give him a visitor's tag, have somebody escort him to the waiting room outside my office."

After he shut the com off, Thorn realized that his heart was beating pretty fast. He knew why McManus was here: More than two decades, and he had come for a rematch! The guy must be missing a couple of screws.

Or maybe not. This business with the Russians and the rich man and even Marissa had shown Thorn he wasn't nearly as in control as he liked to be. That there were all kinds of things beyond his ability to make dance as he wanted them to dance. But, by God, he still knew how to wield a sword.

Maybe it wasn't crazy. Maybe this was exactly what he needed, too.

Thorn stood, and rolled his shoulders, loosening them. His own practice gear was in the gym down the hall. This guy wanted to play? Fine. Win, lose, or draw, this was something Thorn felt comfortable doing, and it would be one-on-one, nobody else to blame if he couldn't deal with it. And that was exactly how he liked it.

"Bring it on, buddy," he said softly, as he headed for the office door.

• • •

Thorn didn't smile as he met McManus. He dismissed the escort.

"Gym is this way," he said.

McManus didn't smile, either. Then again, he didn't seem surprised that Thorn would have his own gear here at work. A man might stop practicing, but once you were a serious fencer, you never completely put it away. On some level, it colored your thoughts forever. All the fencing buddies Thorn had kept in touch with who had competed in college still kept their blades, and while most of them didn't fence in tournaments anymore, all of them still trained. That Thorn still checked into the newsgroups on-line would be enough to tell McManus that he had kept up at least that much interest.

Once a swordsman, always a swordsman.

McManus followed him down the hall to the gym, and neither of them spoke. This time of the afternoon, the place was empty, which was fine by Thorn. Without a word, he went to get his gear, as McManus began unpacking his own.

When Thorn returned, he found McManus whipping his épée back and forth to loosen his arm and wrist. He had laid out his mask, plastron, and jacket, but had not put any of them on.

The button on the blade's tip was in place. At least the guy hadn't filed it sharp or anything, so he wasn't planning on it being a death match.

McManus caught the look. He extended the blade at chest-level toward Thorn. "You can check it, if you want. I don't want to hurt you, Thorn, just beat you. That director gave you the match I should have won. I could have been champion except for that."

Thorn shook his head. A true champion would have eaten the loss and worked harder to maintain his composure. A champion would have attacked his weakness and made them strengths. A champion would have kept training and practicing until he won. McManus wasn't in that class.

"You'll see," McManus said. He reached for his mask.

But that wasn't what Thorn wanted. More importantly, right at this moment, that wasn't what Thorn needed.

"Here's an idea," Thorn said. "Leave the jacket and mask on the bench. We fence as though this were a real duel—not to first blood, but to the death. The first *real* touch, one that would have been a serious or fatal injury if the swords were sharp, wins. No flicks, no whip-overs, no gamesmanship taps on the arm. We use the blades as if they were real."

McManus hesitated. He frowned.

"What's the matter, *Rapier?* Leave your guts at home?"

McManus gritted his teeth. His jaw muscles flexed and bulged.

"You challenged me, pal," Thorn said. "Would you rather just pack it up and leave?"

"No!"

Thorn offered the tip of his épée, to show the button was firmly affixed. McManus touched it, tested the tightness.

"You could cheat," the man said. "Pretend that a touch wasn't valid."

Thorn waved. "And so could you. But what's the point? There's no one else here. There are no hidden cameras watching us, no audience to cheer, and no director to fool. It's just you and me. One of us scores, we'll both know, and that's what this is all about, isn't it?"

Thorn stripped off his shirt, glad that he had kept in good enough shape so that wouldn't be embarrassing. He tossed the shirt onto the bench, turned his back, and walked to the middle of the mat. He turned around, his weapon pointed down.

"Fish or cut bait, Rapier. Your choice."

McManus practically tore his shirt off, and he hadn't gotten fat in his middle age, either. He strode onto the mat toward Thorn. They faced each other from six feet away. Thorn raised his blade in salute. McManus mirrored him.

"En garde!" Thorn said.

He expected McManus to be tentative. This was unfamiliar territory for both of them, fencing without protection, and while there was little chance of a fatal injury, it would be all too easy to lose an eye. McManus knew that as well as he did, and so he assumed they would both start slowly, each one trying to measure his opponent before the action got hot and heavy.

He was wrong.

McManus stomped his front foot, hard, trying to distract him, then threw himself into a lunge. His point started high, flicking toward Thorn's face, then dropping down into an attempt at binding Thorn's blade.

McManus had been practicing. Or at least he'd stayed in shape. He'd thrown that move tightly, and at speed. Good.

Thorn smiled and stepped back, out of range, declining the opportunity to go toe-to-toe with his opponent. As McManus came back to guard, Thorn threw him a brief salute.

"Nice try," he said.

McManus didn't reply. He merely dipped his point and advanced once more.

McManus liked to infight. Thorn knew that. He also liked to control his opponent's blade, beating and binding at every opportunity. Thorn knew that, too. The question was, what could he do with that knowledge?

As his opponent came forward, Thorn let his own point drift high, raising his guard as though he were going to press at McManus's face.

As he'd expected, McManus threw a quick beat at Thorn's blade, gauging, testing, probing. Thorn disen-

gaged, dropping below the blade and taking a small step
back, still pressing high.

McManus beat again, and again Thorn disengaged, setting up a rhythm, setting up an expectation, setting up his
opponent.

Beat, disengage, advance, retreat.

Again.

Thorn knew this wasn't VR. He didn't have an infinite
amount of room behind him, and couldn't keep retreating
forever. But then, he didn't think he'd have to. McManus
had never been patient.

He saw McManus's eyes narrow ever so slightly, something that would never have been visible had they been
wearing masks, and thought, *This is it.*

Beat.

Disengage.

Only this time, McManus anticipated his movement,
stepping forward more quickly to close the distance, his
own blade following Thorn's and trying to bind it. His
point came out of line, his hand lifting away from the
guard position as he tried to take Thorn's blade.

Anticipation, Thorn thought, *will get you killed.*

As McManus stepped forward, Thorn did, too, his own
point circling away from any contact with his opponent's
épée.

As they closed, their hips touched. In a tournament, the
director would have called halt, but this was not a tournament, and there was no director.

McManus reacted well, using the momentum of his at-
tempted bind to try and bring his point around, lifting his
hand, his arm, his shoulder even to try and strike at Thorn,
but Thorn was ahead of him.

Thorn's point had passed above McManus's shoulder.
He raised his own hand now, using his right elbow to
keep McManus's point away from him, and drove his
point solidly downward, striking McManus hard right at
the base of his spine.

Touch.

A killing blow.

Touché.

Both fencers froze, Thorn in victory, McManus in shock.

"E la," Thorn whispered, the traditional French phrase that literaly meant, "And there," but in reality meant, "In your face."

Then, still smiling, he turned his back and started to walk away.

Behind him, belatedly, McManus came back to life. There was a pause, then a gasp, and then Thorn heard him shout, *"No!"*

A moment later he heard another sound, one he had not expected. He heard a thud as McManus drove his own point into the floor, hard. He heard the stress of the metal as McManus continued to press. And then he heard the sudden snap as the tip broke off.

All that in an instant.

And then he heard the sound of McManus rushing toward him, broken blade in hand.

Thorn spun, his own blade flashing in front of him as he tried to come back to guard, but McManus was on top of him and there was no time for anything but pure reaction.

Thorn's blade was still pointed downward. He drew it sideways, intercepting McManus's broken tip, and executed a perfect clockwise bind, taking McManus's blade to the side. This took Thorn's own point away from the other man, but Thorn was no longer interested in scoring touches. He'd won. Now it was time to end this.

McManus stood before him, a look of unthinking rage on his face. His blade was off to Thorn's left, trapped— for the moment. Thorn's tip was pointed toward the floor, his blade locked tightly against McManus, his bell guard beside his own left ear.

Without thinking, Thorn drove his bell guard into

McManus's face, striking him hard at the bridge of his nose.

McManus cried out and fell down, blood flowing.

Thorn stepped forward one last time, standing over his fallen opponent, his left foot on McManus's broken blade, right foot resting lightly on his chest. He pressed the tip of his épée into McManus's throat.

"You're beaten," he said. "It's over."

He didn't wait for an answer. He didn't need to. He simply spun once more and walked away without looking back.

40

Natadze drove, Cox seated in the front passenger seat of the Cadillac. It was one of the sporty models, smaller and less conspicuous than a limo. They were on a long stretch of relatively empty road on the way to the city; not much traffic at this hour—mostly soccer moms and delivery trucks, and none of them close.

Which was the very reason he had chosen this road.

"We've won, Eduard. The government's offer makes that clear. They don't have enough to proceed, or they are afraid of upsetting the apple cart, whichever. It doesn't matter. They can bluster and threaten, but in the end, the victory is ours. They have nothing they can use to trace us."

Natadze nodded. He was remembering what was left of his guitar collection in the blasted-out basement of his house in Washington. All that carefully aged and worked spruce and cedar and rosewood, gone. He recalled the Spross with the unique pattern in its flame-maple back; the Hauser copy by Schramm, one of the early prototypes;

the new Bogdanovich with the natural-wood rosette—all of them and half a dozen others, completely destroyed. Yes, he had recovered the ones in the safe, but he had lost ten concert-quality instruments. For Natadze, it was as if somebody had destroyed a famous painting—even if you owned the picture, it would be a crime against humanity to desecrate it.

He saw the pothole in the road just ahead. Hidden in the trees and bushes a few hundred meters short of that was the little SUV wagon, chosen for its dark green color so as to blend in.

Cox said, "So we go on about our business as usual. Now that all traces of the file are gone except for the one Net Force has, there won't be any way they can corroborate it. We're home free, Eduard—whoa!"

Natadze hit the pothole with the right front tire, and the car jounced hard.

The hubcap he had loosened on the front wheel came off, exactly as he'd hoped. It rolled alongside the car for a moment, bounced, then fell over. He tracked it in the rearview mirror.

"Sorry," Natadze said. He made a show of looking into the rearview mirror. "Uh oh."

"What?"

"The wheel cover came off. It's lying in the road behind us."

He slowed the car, pulled onto the shoulder.

"What are you doing? It's just a hubcap. Leave it."

"It will only take a few seconds. Remember the milk truck?"

This had been key in Natadze's plan, a thing about which he and Cox had spoken recently. Apparently a milk truck had somehow dropped an empty plastic carrier that had not been properly stowed. The driver had noticed it at the time, but he had been in a hurry, and had left it in the road where it fell. It was just an empty crate, not worth stopping for. A motorist traveling the road shortly thereafter had either hit the crate, or swerved to avoid hitting it. The car's driver had lost control, slammed into a building, and had died. Cox had mentioned the incident to Natadze, railing at how the milk company's liability insurance would go up because of the lawsuit that was sure to follow, and how hard would it have been for the moronic driver to have pulled over and collected the fallen crate?

Cox remembered. "Ah, good point."

Natadze exited the car. He smiled at Cox and headed for the hubcap. When he was fifty meters away, he left the road and hurried to a large oak tree. Once he was behind it, he pulled the small radio transmitter from his pocket and flipped the switch covers up—there were two of them, for safety.

He leaned out, saw that Cox was still in the car, and ducked back behind the tree. He pressed the two buttons that sent the signal.

Cox turned to look at Eduard, and saw him leave the road. If the hubcap had rolled off the pavement, then it wasn't a danger, why was he bothering?

When Eduard ducked behind a big tree, a terrible premonition seized Cox. *No! Oh, no—!*

He reached for the door handle, jerked on it, screamed, *"Eduard, don't—!"*

The sound of Cox yelling his name was blotted out by the explosion, terribly loud in the sunny afternoon. A beat later, car shrapnel sleeted against the tree trunk, hitting hard enough to embed itself into the bark. The bulk of the explosive had been placed in front of the front passenger seat, in the air bag compartment, with another charge under the seat, and a third in the passenger door. The three together were sufficient to blast the car apart, and there was little chance that anybody inside would survive.

Natadze hurried to his hidden SUV, unlocked it, got in, cranked the engine, and pulled out onto the road. He pulled up next to the Cadillac, which was smoking, but not on fire, the vehicle wrenched and twisted as if attacked by an enraged giant. There was no need to get out and check—the man who had been Samuel Cox was certainly dead. One look at the smashed body confirmed that.

Cars were approaching from both directions, and Natadze accelerated and left the scene. It was time to leave the country for a while. South America, perhaps. Or one of the African countries where money could buy privacy. He had more than enough saved to live well for years. Maybe it was time to get serious about music, and to retire from his line of work.

But he didn't have to decide now. He would have plenty of time to think about it.

He looked into the rearview mirror at the destroyed car dwindling in the distance. "Say hello to the Devil when you see him, Mr. Cox. Ask him how he is enjoying my guitars."

41

Jay rushed into Thorn's office, breathing hard. "You hear the news?"

Thorn raised his eyebrows. "What?"

"Cox. He's dead! His car blew up!"

"Really?"

"According to CNN. A guy I know at CopNet confirmed it. Out on Long Island this afternoon."

"Huh. How about that."

"Maybe God decided to take a hand."

"Maybe."

"I gotta go tell Julio, and I need to call Toni and Alex."

After Jay was gone, Thorn leaned back in his chair and sighed. He had been feeling pretty good after the sword match with his troll stalker, but this news sobered him a bit.

Captain Julio Fernandez would act surprised when Jay found him, but he wouldn't really be surprised. They hadn't been able to nail Cox, for reasons beyond their control, but there was more than one way to see the scales balanced. Cox was guilty of much, and it was right that he should be punished. Like Marissa had said in her story about the snow runners: Maybe they couldn't come at him directly, but there were other, less orthodox paths. Back and twisty roads that arrived, eventually, at the same place. Not the first choice, but better than not getting there at all.

His private line cheeped. He looked down at the ID. Marissa.

He picked up the handset. "Hi."

"You heard about Cox?" she said.

"Yes, just now."

There was a short silence.

"We didn't actually do it," he said. "In case you were wondering."

"Good to know." She paused. "I'd like to drop by in the morning, sort of go over things and everything."

"I'd like that, Marissa," he said.

She was silent again and he smiled.

"Fine," she said after a moment. "Well, I'll see you then."

He agreed and they hung up.

But like Marissa had told him, there were other ways to approach a problem. Net Force hadn't killed Cox. There was no way that Thorn could have given those orders, and if any of his people would have carried orders like that, well, they wouldn't be his people for long. But *somebody* had blown up the hit man Natadze's house and his prized guitars, instruments for which he held great passion, even love. What would a man who was a killer do to somebody who did that to him?

Or somebody he *thought* had done it?

You run with killers, sometimes you paid for it.

Thorn thought his grandfather would be pleased.

Justice had been served.

EPILOGUE

"Boss," Jay said.

Thorn looked up and saw Gridley in the doorway.

"Not that it makes any difference to Cox, but I cracked the final piece of the Turkish file and got the list of names. There are some real eye-openers here, too, boss; I'm talking some names that you simply won't believe."

"Great work, Jay. I'm sure the FBI will appreciate that—he certainly wasn't the only spy the Soviets had here, and there have to be more we don't know about."

"Yeah," Jay said. "But here's the funny part: Cox might have been a spy, but *his name wasn't on the list*. He was all worried for nothing."

Thorn stared at him. "You mean if he had just sat tight, none of this would have ever happened?"

Jay nodded. "That's right. He could have lived happily ever after. How's that for irony?"

"Not bad," Thorn said, smiling. "Not bad at all."

Other Books by Steve Pieczenik

THE MIND PALACE
BLOOD HEAT
MAXIMUM VIGILANCE
PAX PACIFICA
STATE OF EMERGENCY

For more information on Steve Pieczenik,
please visit www.stevepieczenik.com and www.strategic-intl.com.

Tom Clancy

The Teeth of the Tiger

A Novel

PUTNAM

Tom Clancy's Power Plays

Created by Tom Clancy and Martin Greenberg
written by Jerome Preisler

TOM CLANCY'S POWER PLAYS: Politika
0-425-16278-8

TOM CLANCY'S POWER PLAYS: ruthless.com
0-425-16570-1

TOM CLANCY'S POWER PLAYS: Shadow Watch
0-425-17188-4

TOM CLANCY'S POWER PLAYS: Bio-Strike
0-425-17735-1

TOM CLANCY'S POWER PLAYS: Cold War
0-425-18214-2

TOM CLANCY'S POWER PLAYS: Cutting Edge
0-425-18705-5

TOM CLANCY'S POWER PLAYS: Zero Hour
0-425-19291-1

AVAILABLE WHEREVER BOOKS ARE SOLD
OR TO ORDER CALL:
1-800-788-6262

B677